Walking on Sunshine

GIOVANNA FLETCHER

PENGUIN BOOKS

PENGUIN BOOKS

UK | USA | Canada | Ireland | Australia
India | New Zealand | South Africa

Penguin Books is part of the Penguin Random House group of companies
whose addresses can be found at global.penguinrandomhouse.com

First published by Penguin Michael Joseph, 2021
Published in Penguin Books, 2022

001

Copyright © Giovanna Fletcher, 2021

The moral right of the author has been asserted

Typeset by Jouve (UK), Milton Keynes
Printed and bound in Great Britain by Clays Ltd, Elcograf S.p.A.

The authorized representative in the EEA is Penguin Random House Ireland,
Morrison Chambers, 32 Nassau Street, Dublin D02 YH68

A CIP catalogue record for this book is available from the British Library

ISBN: 978–1–405–92612–6

www.greenpenguin.co.uk

Penguin Random House is committed to a
sustainable future for our business, our readers
and our planet. This book is made from Forest
Stewardship Council® certified paper.

To anyone who has ever walked alongside, in front of or behind me – all in the name of boob-loving CoppaFeel! – Thank you.

I

Zaza

A smile is plastered on my face. It's a big smile – a toothy one, my huge mouth wide, my full lips stretched from ear to ear. I've been told on many occasions my smile lights up the room. Judging by the grins being fired back at me by our family and friends, I imagine my smile is doing the trick. Spreading joy. Spreading love. Playing its part.

By my side, Liam says something funny. The crowd cackle and cheer. He pulls me into his hip with one big swoop of his arm and kisses me on the cheek. Perhaps as an apology? Did he just crack a joke at my expense? Does his affection mean to reassure me? Appease me?

I wasn't listening.

I'd better listen.

I should be listening.

It's not enough to smile.

I have to be present.

'In all seriousness though, everyone in this room is in no doubt about who wears the trousers in this relation-ship,' he says into the mic, his voice booming around the back end of The Plough Inn – our favourite pub in West

London's leafy Ealing that's seen us in various states over the years: sober, tipsy, drunk, debauched, full of joy and love, tired, worried, scared, alone, heartbroken – utterly broken. Distraught.

Must.

Listen.

I look up at Liam's dark eyes as my mind scrambles to make sense of what he is talking about, wondering what on earth he could be saying that's keeping them all so entertained. That loving look. That softness. That kind expression that causes his eyes to crinkle as he looks back at me and gives the most loving of looks, taking in my face with such . . . pride. 'I'm so lucky you scrolled into my world and allowed me into your heart,' he says with alarming tenderness, as though he's forgotten that dozens of eyes are on us.

'And bed,' jeers some twat who's passing by, trying to be funny. I'm thankful for the interruption.

'And that,' Liam says nervously, his pale skin blushing as he turns back to our gathered loved ones. 'I met the love of my life, and have been trying to show her how cool I am ever since – and before I get interrupted again, I know. Not very.'

My heart aches for him. He has been so good to me these past few months, trying to be my absolute rock even when I've had no idea what it is I want and need. I'm fully aware I've not been my usual self with him, conscious of a familiar old feeling that's been creeping in no matter how much I've tried to push it away. But it's expected right now given the events we've been through. Surely. I'm meant to be questioning everything I have in my life, right?

'I might've held back from popping the question to retain a microscopic amount of control,' he continues, holding his hand in the air while pinching his fingers together. 'But I'm gladly handing it over knowing I'll be spending every day of my life standing next to the woman beside me.'

The room melts with an audible sigh.

It's romantic.

It's beautiful.

It's too much.

'I just like the fact you thought you had some of the control to start with,' I find myself quipping. They laugh. They erupt. It shakes my insides.

My eyes scan across the room, taking in the faces of people who seem so happy to be celebrating with us tonight. So many wonderful people we're so blessed to have in our lives still, yet they can't replace those missing.

My eyes fall on Vicky, my best mate, who I can see, even from this distance, is bleary eyed from the free-flowing prosecco and having to be supported by her husband Nick, who discreetly lets her lean on him. She's made an effort tonight too. Her makeup, although now smudged and less defined, is a far cry from her usual shattered-mother-of-two look. Likewise, I imagine her being graced five minutes to quickly put a tong through her shoulder-length brown hair to give it a bit of life.

Might've worked then but now it's lacklustre and sad. Like us. When I saw her earlier, looking so composed and normal, it was like a warm blanket of reassurance had been placed around me. I'm so glad she's here, despite me telling her not to put herself through it. But we'd both made a promise to Pia, and we had to do as she asked.

Vicky notices me looking at her and screws her face up into a grin, teeth on display. Her eyes shut as she juts out her chin – a gesture that makes her look the spitting image of her five-year-old-son Barnaby. She's already two steps ahead of me in this grown-up game of life. She had the wedding and has moved on to have two kids too.

Now I'm on the path to having the same . . .

A heaviness lands on my chest at the thought.

I gaze back at Liam and the feeling doesn't lift.

For the first five-and-a-half years of our relationship I wanted nothing more than this moment. I've wanted the commitment, craved that validation of our love – that declaration that I am the one he chooses over everyone else. And although I knew I never needed a ring to prove that to be the case – he is such a kind, loving and considerate soul, I realized in the end I did. Because that's the thing, right? That's where every failed relationship of my past should've been heading before it turned sour. The ring is how I know this is the real deal. That little piece of metal and that bling-bling diamond is what separates this love from the shit-shows and disappointments that came before. This is the path. This is what we all do. My friends all managed it – they've found the people who've declared their love despite the endless idiosyncrasies and flaws they stumbled across. My mates found the people who said, 'You know what, you're not perfect but I love you just the way you are,' or better still, 'You're my kind of imperfect,' and had worn the gowns or the suits to celebrate that match-up.

I saw them all doing it and wanted in on that narrative.

Liam is that storyline.

He was giving me all I've been hoping for. All I ever wanted.

Then Pia died.

One of my best mates exited the earth halfway through the narrative, married to another best mate Mike. It seems cruel and unfair that they weren't afforded the rest of their story, one that should've been completed with the comfort and boredom of old age, of them settling in around the fire at night to do puzzles and eat cake while talking about the good old days.

'To my future wife, Zaza!' Liam beams, stepping aside and giving me the floor. He leads them into a cheer – my brother Rich making more of a barking sound as he whoops in his own enthusiastic way, encouraging my cousins to do the same.

Liam holds the microphone out to me and, to his surprise, I wave it away.

Ordinarily I'd make a speech. I've never been one to fall into the role of 'submissive woman' and allow others to speak on my behalf. I've never been one to hesitate when grabbing for attention and having my voice heard.

But not now.

Now life seems so fragile. So short. So uncertain.

Who knows what might accidentally slip out if I were to take that mic to my lips.

Not now.

2

Vicky

'And they didn't wake up at all?' I ask again, following Rosie as she makes to leave. As usual our eighteen-year-old babysitter can't get out of the house quick enough. She must've heard us wandering up the street because she was already wearing her coat and pulling her Ugg boots on when we stumbled through the door.

'Erm . . .' she thinks, pausing while glancing up the stairs. 'Didn't hear them,' she shrugs.

'Right,' I mumble, handing her four ten-pound notes while not entirely sure whether to feel comforted by her vague reply or completely freaked out. Either my children have slept soundly not even realizing we've gone out, or they've woken up and she's been oblivious while binge-watching her favourite trashy TV shows. I'm praying it's the former as she's ridiculously reliable and never cancels on us – 'good' sitters are hard to find.

'See you then,' she grins, stuffing the cash into the back pocket of her jeans and flying out the door.

I twist the key in the lock and pull the chain across, before kicking off my heels and feeling my feet instantly ache and swell as I walk across the wooden floors. I groan, feeling more than my age as I make my way to my husband Nick who has gone off on the hunt for food, our usual way to round off a night out. I find him, jacket and tie off, sitting at the kitchen counter.

'Pizza?' he asks with a smug grin, swivelling the cardboard box in my direction to reveal the Pepperoni Special Rosie has barely touched but was very specific about us ordering.

'She didn't eat it?' I ask, sitting next to him.

'You ordered a large. She doesn't strike me as the sort to indulge . . .' His eyes are firmly on the pizza but they might as well be on Rosie's tight little butt.

I hate the wave of shame that washes over me at the thought. Shame for the bitchiness it drums up towards Rosie, and shame for how it makes me feel about my own wobbly and stretch-marked body. We're not meant to feel this way about our bodies any more. We're meant to embrace all our 'imperfections' and wear them with pride. That's what us women are meant to do now. It's hard to admit, but some days I don't feel like doing all the things I'm meant to.

'Her loss,' I mumble, tearing off a cold slice and cramming it into my mouth before my brain has a chance to tell me not to. Grease escapes down my chin as I start chewing. It's pure filth. My fuzzy head blocks out the remorse I know I'll experience in the morning when I get up and feel the bloat of my tummy. Sod it.

'For fuck's sake, she's not even washed up,' I tut, noticing the leftovers from the kids' dinners crusting up on stacked-up plates. 'Or tidied up!' I add, irked that the house still looks like it's been struck by a tornado – crayons, pencils, Play-Doh, Lego, Moana dolls, teddies, Anas and Elsas, a pile-up of cars and dozens of splayed books cover the floor and surfaces, nicely framed with crumbs, discarded Cheerios or lumps of dinner that have been lobbed across the room by Chloe, who was angry at the offering of fish pie – a meal she loved last week but tonight might as well have been canned dog food.

'Did you tell her to?' Nick asks, pushing his glasses up his nose while his eyes stay trained on his pizza. The state of the house is my domain and it seems I'm the only one who gets riled at the continuous cycle of mess that occurs around us.

'I pay her ten pounds an hour, Nick. I chuck in a free pizza and give her free rein of our wine cupboard . . . I didn't realize I had to specify that she wasn't just here to sit on the sofa and chat to her mates on Snapchat,' I grumble.

'Some people just need it spelt out. You can't be angry about something when you haven't expressed what you want,' he says, folding more pizza into his mouth.

'Yeah,' I bite, even though I know it's not his fault. 'I should've done it before I left,' I berate myself. 'Sod getting a pair of tongs through my flipping hair. Scraping dried salmon flakes off the wall would've been a better use of my time,' I say, while my thumbnail picks at the vandalized wall. Having grown up in a house where I felt scared to touch anything, I wanted my children to feel the opposite. The house is theirs as well as ours. It's the people in the home that are the most important thing. That said, I'd love the kids to have a little more respect for the walls we've worked hard to secure around them.

'Baby,' Nick says, pulling my attention away from the dried fish. 'You looked lovely tonight and that time was well spent.'

'Thank you,' I say, smiling at Nick's ability to still make me blush even after all these years.

'Worry about it tomorrow,' he shrugs, unknowingly deflating my heart before grabbing another slice of pizza.

I'm surprised he can't hear the expletives that are being thrown his way in my head. It's yet another thing for me to sort out tomorrow while he swans off to the office and gets to be an independent adult who can talk to other grown-ups and pee in peace. At home my coffee, if I have time to make one, will sit cold and untouched while I get on with the mounting 'to do' list that the fishy wall has now been added to. There's always something to be getting on with and doing, and that's around Chloe's constant whines and needs which mean it's difficult to do even the simplest of tasks.

If, right now, Nick were to throw down his pizza, pick up a sponge and go to work on the fishy splodge on the wall himself rather than waiting for me to do it, it would be the sexiest, most dashing thing he's ever done for me in his life. Sod buying me a dress and taking me to a fancy restaurant Richard Gere style, cleaning up discarded fish is where the pheromones are at.

I stop my stream of resentful moaning and tell myself I'm being unfair.

He's helped me through lots.

These last few weeks have been utterly awful. The worst. When Pia got diagnosed with breast cancer two years ago we all knew things were going to get difficult – even if she did make us promise to stay positive and upbeat, proceed with no sympathy or talk of her being brave or inspirational – but I don't think any of us really thought we'd be burying her. Not when she spent so much of the last two years travelling the globe with a smile plastered on her face. Our WhatsApp group is full of pictures of her on the edge of precarious-looking cliffs as she takes in the view, laughing under huge water-falls while completely starkers and dancing with locals she and Mike had befriended en route. She was a feisty little lady who worked to make sure every moment counted and that she got what she wanted out of life. Death wasn't that.

I swallow the emotion that builds in my throat. I keep saying I'm cried out, but I don't think that's true. Bless Zaza tonight. Standing up there like a mannequin at her own engagement party – a smile plastered on that I had to mirror back. I drank too much. I don't want the cloudy head I currently have but I couldn't help it. I had to keep sipping to get me through the questions and the tight smiles from Zaza's family and friends – people I've loved chatting to in the past but tonight felt too close for comfort. Happy, happy, happy. Truth is the fizzy grape juice has left me grumpy and emotional and I know I'm prone to nit-picking when I shouldn't on the occasions I've had one too many.

'Beer?' Nick asks, completely oblivious to my thoughts as he gets up and reaches towards the fridge.

'No th–'

'Fuuck!' he shouts, his arms shooting in the air as he just manages to stop himself from flying backwards. 'What the – ?' With one hand resting protectively on his chest, he reaches down and picks up the offending item with the other. He takes a moment before adjusting his black frames, looking like a jewellery dealer as he inspects one of Barnaby's trains with a frown. 'Nearly killed me.'

'Didn't though.'

'No.'

We both get lost in our thoughts, staring at the wooden toy.

'You'll miss the death traps when you're gone,' I say. 'There'll be no one to keep you on your toes while you're sunning it in LA in your swanky hotel overlooking The Hills.'

'Sounds boring,' he notes, opening the fridge and pulling out a bottle.

'Yep,' I nod, the weight of the alcohol I've consumed making my head hang heavily. 'Don't go.'

'Vic . . .'

'I mean it. No. No, I don't,' I shake my head. 'But I do. I really do.' I sound like Chloe when she's throwing around her stroppy demands and doesn't really know what she wants, yet I can't help but continue. 'Six days for one meeting, you can do that from here on Zoom or Skype. Or use House Party to spice it up a bit – save yourself the flight, save the planet. Stay.'

'It's a pitch, Vicky. You know they work best face to face. Don't make me feel bad.'

'I'm not,' I lie, aware that I've put him in a shit position and of the lecture he's about to give to win me over and tell me he's right to leave us yet again. I instantly wish I could gobble the words back up and unsay them. I've heard the spiel a million times and it never makes me feel better. It just hushes me up and eases his guilt as he goes.

'Advertising is all about being in the room and engaging someone, letting them feel your energy and get excited by you getting excited by them. You know that. You remember what it's like going into a room of creatives and giving over ideas you know they're going to love.'

'Remember it all well,' I say, feeling the sting of being reminded of my former life as a daytime TV producer. Something I chose to give up when we had the kids. Our kids, my sacrifice . . . lovingly and willingly done, of course, because there didn't seem to be another option I was comfortable with, but it feels like a different life. I'm a different person.

'You know what it's like when someone else pitches while you sit there thinking, "I could've sold that better." I don't want to send a junior over with this,' he sighs. 'And Vic, it's not one meeting. If it goes well then it'll be multiple meetings and mean big things for the company. For us. It's important. Huge.'

'Yeah . . .' I know he's right and I'm aware that I shouldn't be metaphorically grabbing on to his ankles to stop him from going, but the thought of doing this alone, of him not being in the same time zone as me to make exasperating calls to . . . It makes me feel flat.

I'm so tired already.

'I'm going to miss you,' I mumble, because what else can I say without him thinking I'm the worst mother in the world?

'Oh, mate,' he says with a soft chuckle, putting his unopened bottle back into the fridge before striding over, standing beside me and putting his arms around my waist, holding me close. 'I promise I won't be sitting around the pool doing nothing all day. You know I'm just going to be wishing I was back here with you guys.'

'Hardly,' I laugh.

'It'll fly by,' he insists, not denying it.

There's no point telling him he's talking utter bollocks and pointing out that I'm going to spend the whole time he's gone pulling my hair out, not without causing a fight. So I pout my lips in the way I've seen Chloe do a million times instead.

Nick studies my lips, the look in his blue eyes changing as he leans forward to kiss them. It's not the quick peck I've become accustomed to – the swift in and out, non-committal, functional hello or goodbye, good morning or goodnight. It carries intent.

His hand reaches up to my face, guiding my chin to one side as his mouth parts from mine and starts working towards my neck. His breath on my earlobe, the suction on my skin – it causes a groan to escape as my body melts with the action and begins to stir.

My head snaps me out of it, collecting my wanton body as it forces me to stop. I raise my shoulder, shrugging Nick off.

'You OK?' he asks, his eyes meeting mine. His voice is breathy, his lips plumper, his face full of sexual longing as he hangs over me.

'Not tonight,' I mutter.

'Why not?'

'I'm not in the mood.'

'You never are.' He manages to deliver his words without resentment or malice, more as an observation. A statement. It cuts deeper.

'We have two kids. The evidence suggests otherwise,' I say, unable to look him in the eye, knowing that he's staring at me.

'They're five and three,' he says, rising to his feet and taking a couple of steps back.

Wanting to break the atmosphere that's been created, feeling stupid and unhappy, I shift in my seat. My attention returning to the contents of the cardboard box, slowly tearing off another piece before taking a bite. Chew. Chew. Chew. Everything feels so laboured now I know I'm being watched.

Nick sighs. 'I'm going up.'

'OK. Won't be a minute,' I sing to my pizza.

His mouth opens to speak again but nothing comes out.

'Night,' he says, leaning towards me to give me a quick kiss on the head, one of the pecks I'm accustomed to.

'Night, night,' I reply through a mouthful of cheesy dough.

He leaves, shutting the door behind him.

I clench my jaw and screw my eyes shut.

I want to yell. I want to scream. I want to tell Nick that sometimes I look at my life and wonder what I'm doing it all for. Sometimes I think my kids hate me. Sometimes I don't think I'm very good at this mum thing. Sometimes I don't want to get out of bed. Sometimes sex just makes me feel shit. Sometimes I wonder why I'm living when she's not. Sometimes I don't want to mother. Sometimes. Occasionally. For a fleeting second. I want it to be over. Sometimes I want to disappear.

Snap.

That thought.

Frustration rips through me. I can't shout. Mustn't wake the babes. Instead I pick up the pizza remains, my whole body fuelled and loaded as I chuck it as hard as I can at the opposite wall.

It sticks for a second. Momentarily stunned into place before sliding into a heap of slop on the floor.

I am that heap.

3

Mike

I never realized how soothing it is to just sit and stroke velvet. To sit with your palm resting on the fabric while your thumb goes back and forth. Silky soft against your skin. It's therapeutic. Calming.

I never would've chosen velvet as a material to have on my sofa, especially not this green colour that covers our three-seater from sofa.com – it would've made me think of the teenagers who loiter at bus stops and parks in their matching tracksuits, but Pia loved it. She had an eye for putting a room together. She was the cool one. The one with effortless style and taste that could transform the blandest of rooms into something people would gush about when they came over.

It's more mint, actually. The sofa. Mint. She'd tell me off for saying green. Mint. Mint fresh. Probably sounds terrible but it's never felt too much. Everything in the room – the cushions, the prints, the vases, the side tables, the pouffes and armchairs – it's all just pulled together in such a way that it makes sense. Nothing stands out to pull focus, it's a team effort, building character and class. It's a calming space.

Up and down, up and down, my thumb goes.

I sit.

I've been sitting here for some time.

I've spent a lot of time sitting.

I don't want to be doing. Forgetting. Moving.

But then I do, because sometimes the emptiness is so vast that I fear falling into it if I stay still too long.

Thoughts come and go as I stroke. I don't hold on to any of them. I breathe them in and out like I've been learning to.

Outside the loose paving stone knocks to alert me of feet walking up the front path.

I jump up and pat at the pockets of my jeans as though I'm about to leave and trying to locate my wallet, keys and phone. The action confuses me for a second.

I rub my hand over the top of my head in an effort to generate some sense in there.

'Keep things light, yeah?' I hear Zaza warn from the other side of the window.

'I just hope I can keep myself together. The last thing he needs is me blubbing,' I hear Vicky reply.

'What he needs is us here. Be you . . . but be cool.'

'Right,' I hear Vicky say firmly, like she's taking an order. 'Fuck, I hope it's not always going to be this hard.'

They clearly haven't realised I just sit in silence these days, that I've stopped listening to music or watching the TV. None of it means anything. It's all just a distraction. It's all just noise. I don't need more noise. I need to find the peace in the chaos of my mind, not add to it.

I've seen them since, obviously. There was the good-bye, the funeral, and other days . . . I haven't just been sitting here stroking my furniture, developing a new fetish. But today is different and loaded because today is the day Pia pencilled in months ago. The one I start removing parts of her from my life. The day, she told me, I have to start taking action.

The shrill of the doorbell startles me as it rings through the ground-floor flat. Even though I've been expecting it my heart jumps. My feet move on autopilot to greet them, my hand shaking as it reaches up and fiddles with the lock, somehow magicking it open. The door swings on its hinges, the cold February air instantly filling my lungs.

There they are. Two of my dearest friends. Two women who've seen me at my lowest, and my very highest of heights. Zaza is a ball of colour in a jumpsuit that someone's chucked a rainbow at, her braided hair pulled into a bun on top of her head. Vicky looks like she left in a hurry – her top covered in various stains and her brown hair as wild as my own – yet she looks functional and determined, like she's ready to get some work done.

'Hi,' I manage.

'Hey,' Zaza replies, her eyes attempting to be wide and bright but appearing more shocked and alert.

'Hello . . .' adds Vicky, her voice strained.

I'm crushed by the awkwardness I feel watching them shuffling on the doorstep. They're inspecting me, seeing how I look, how I sound, how I'm dressed – but they're trying not to make it obvious. Two concerned friends tiptoeing around our collective grief in a bid to save us all from drowning in mine.

Is mine worse?

That really shouldn't even be a question.

Of course it is.

Maybe.

I was married to her.

I had declared my undying love . . .

'Should we just sack this all off and have a beer? We could get wasted and watch one of those pathetic girly films and cry for a few hours instead,' I find myself saying, my voice coming out as a squeak. 'I'll even let you watch a Hugh Grant one if you like. I'm feeling generous.'

'Nice try, champ,' Zaza says, a smile slowly stretching across her face as she pulls me in for a quick hug before squeezing through the doorway – as though I might change my mind and slam it shut, denying them access.

'You OK?' Vicky asks, before shaking her head. 'Stupid question. Sorry. It's a habit. As if you're fucking OK. This is fucking shit.'

'You can tell you're not with your kids,' I comment. 'Fuck this, fuck that. Or has Chloe started using the f-bomb as an adjective?'

'Shh you,' Vicky blushes, elbowing me in the ribs as I put an arm around her and bring her inside.

'Wine?'

'Oh God no. Tea, please,' she moans, walking ahead of me.

'Such good manners,' I laugh. 'Za?'

'Yes to tea.'

We shuffle through to the kitchen. As I pop on the kettle Zaza gathers mugs out of the cupboard and Vicky takes a bottle of milk from her bag, clearly having thought ahead to me and my empty fridge.

'What have you been up to, then?' she asks, reaching for the teabags and tossing one into each mug with a sigh. I'd have preferred a beer but it seems the decision's been taken from me.

'Just mourning my dead wife. What can I say . . . ? Let me guess, though,' I tease. 'You're never drinking again?'

'He's got you there,' Zaza laughs, jumping up onto the kitchen side and making herself comfortable – funny how we've always done this, no matter whose house we're at. Kitchen sides are always an inviting place for butts.

'Good party?' I ask.

'Beautiful,' Vicky says with a nod before releasing a grunt. 'I drank too much.'

'Really?' I gasp.

'She had that look in her eye,' Zaza shares, looking over at Vicky with admiration.

'I know the one.'

'Shut up you,' she laughs. 'It has been horrific though. Barnaby was practising his sodding recorder first thing. How the recorder hasn't been banned yet I don't know. If I was feeling more alive I'd have gone into his room and flung it out the window,' she says, her arms flinging forward in a throwing motion. 'Seriously, though. Kids and hangovers – I don't recommend it.'

'Noted,' I say, raising my eyebrows.

A look is passed between the two of them. It's a flicker, a waver, but I notice it. Kids. Children. Sprogs. I might not be afforded that luxury. Or rather, it's a part of life Pia and I missed out on experiencing together. We had tried. For a period of time we were at it like rabbits trying to make it work. After years trying not to get pregnant we were finally on a mission to do the opposite, but it was to no avail. We'd talked about looking into the situation further but her diagnosis arrived first, along with the understanding that hormones were feeding her cancer and that egg retrieval for some magical cancer-free time in the future was not an option for us. Had we wanted to we would have been looking at egg donation as well as surrogacy, or maybe giving a home to children already in the world who could benefit from our love. Cancer had shifted our focus and, in truth, I didn't care about what we could've had. To me it was a 'coulda, woulda, shoulda' that my mind didn't want to allow in. I just wanted to keep my wife alive.

The kettle switch clicks, allowing me the comfort of turning away to pour.

'Liam made a great speech,' Vicky says, opening the milk and waiting for me to finish.

'Surprised you remember it,' laughs Zaza, passing a spoon to stir.

'Oh ha ha,' Vicky replies, screwing up her face and passing my mug.

'Sorry I missed it,' I say, bringing the brew to my lips.

'Yeah well, bigger fish . . .' replies Zaza.

Another pause while we think about the bigger fish. It's a rather monumental fish.

'You know Mum offered to help me with this?' I say, diving in.

'Really?' scoffs Vicky.

'Yep. Told me she'd help me "get rid of it all". Said she'd come round and blitz the place. Get it done.'

'Very Brexit of her,' says Zaza, shaking her head.

'She didn't know about Pia's plans for today, I didn't tell her, but I think she just knows this is a hurdle. A job to work through. A part of the process, I guess,' I add, finding the words harsh as they leave my mouth. 'Something that has to happen at some point.'

'How'd she take you declining her offer?'

'You know Mum,' I grin. 'Ready to take a backseat and just leave me to it really.'

'Did she turn up at the door with some black bags and bottles of bleach?'

'Almost,' I laugh. 'She has turned up most days unannounced – usually to drop off some food or a card someone has sent her to pass on. You know, I think she'd find this easier if Pia had left me for someone else? I think Mum finds her dying on me a bit . . . inconsiderate.'

They chuckle, knowing my mum and how much she simply wants to help. You can't force a heart to heal when it's been shattered as much as mine.

'She means well,' Vicky smiles. Being the only mum of the group I imagine she sees my mum's input slightly differently to Zaza and me. Does she look at me and wonder how she'd feel if it were her Barnaby in this position? Probably. I bet I would if the tables were turned.

'Yeah. Thank you for joining me today,' I say, my lips forming one of the sad smiles they've become used to pulling. 'It means a lot.'

'Erm, we're not just here for you. She said she'd haunt us if we didn't, remember?' Zaza tries to lighten the mood while reminding us of the promises we'd made while sitting in Walpole Park last September. She hadn't set a date – there's no way she could've, but she had given us a timeframe, a certain number of weeks post death to sit before having to stand up and move. Zaza's engagement party was one of those must-happen events that Pia wouldn't hear of her cancelling, postponing or delaying – and that's where the whole idea of these little instructions, or the rules of her death, seemed to come from. I hadn't expected her to talk in this way, as though she were conceding to the inevitability of her death when we had avoided the reality in favour of travel and existing for so long, but there she was, facing it head on and making sure we did too. Pia knew life would continue and she wanted to make sure we were a part of it.

'Us being here is purely selfish,' nods Vicky into her mug.

'I was fine with the idea of her appearing at the window every now and then but when she said she'd disrupt my sleep for the rest of eternity I had to crack. I need my sleep. Damn her for knowing my weakness,' Zaza says with a shrug. 'Turns out her haunting us was a tad inconvenient.'

'Sometimes I wish she would though,' I admit.

'You all right?' Vicky asks, her voice full of concern. 'Fuck – there I go again.'

'Vicky, it's OK. I can answer the question,' I appease, hating the fact she's second guessing what she's saying to me when dialogue between us has always been so unfiltered, blunt and easy. 'No. I'm not all right. I don't know how to be or how to do. I've sat on the sofa for the past hour wondering how I go about starting to remove pieces of her from this place when I really don't want to.'

'Then you don't have to,' offers Zaza, as though that would actually be an option.

'You know I do,' I say.

'Fucking dead people. They always get their own way,' jokes Vicky.

It's enough to lighten the mood.

4

Vicky

'So today is scheduled for clothes,' I state, realizing that I have three ways of getting through this – swearing, sobbing, and utilizing my organizational skills. I've already showcased the earlier one thanks to my nerves, I've promised myself I wouldn't do the second, but now it's time to get serious and remember why we're here. It's the only way of controlling the lump that's continuously forming in my throat.

'Yes,' nods Mike, shifting on the spot like he suddenly doesn't know what to do with himself.

'Come on then,' Zaza says, jumping down from the kitchen side. 'Time to get cracking.'

Mike looks ashen but manages to start moving out of the kitchen and down the corridor to their bedroom. It's the last room you get to in their ground-floor flat, with huge double doors opening out to the garden. The sun is shining and I'm thankful for a little bit of light on this awful task.

'The boxes arrived then!' I say, taking in the dozens of boxes he's already assembled and lined up along the floor. Something about their emptiness chills me.

'Yeah, yeah,' Mike says, nodding his head. 'Thanks for that.'

'Pia would haunt you if you threw her clothes into plastic bin liners.'

'Think of the planet!' Zaza tuts, just as Pia would've said.

The side of Mike's mouth curls, but it's not really a smile. Just politeness getting the better of him, even in this situation.

'Anyone got any bright ideas on how to start this?' he asks, turning towards the wardrobe behind him, his hand reaching up to ruffle his hair roughly. I can't help but think he's trying to wake himself up, wishing for this all to be nothing more than a nightmare he has to endure before waking up to learn it's not real.

Mike takes a deep breath and steps towards the white built-in wardrobe, his hands hesitating before reaching out and pulling open the doors.

I'm aware of my lungs sucking up the air around me and feel it getting stuck in my chest as two rows of clothes are revealed, only a sliver of which belong to Mike. I'm awash with images before me of Pia wearing the items at various stages of her life – parties, christenings, pub quizzes and hangouts. Lots of denim in various shades of blue and grey – oversized shirts that used to swamp her tiny frame. A collection of colourful silk scarves hangs on the back of a door and on a shelf at the top are boxes and bags. The floor is lined with shoes. Nothing glitzy or showstopping like you'd find in Zaza's wardrobe, but stylish all the same.

Mike's hand reaches up, rubbing the fabric of a well-loved jumper between his fingers before bowing his head and letting it rest on the clothes before him.

I look over at Zaza and see her pained expression mirroring my own.

We give him time. There's no rush today, nowhere else we need to be, although there are a million places we wish we all were.

In time we hear Mike take a deep breath, and although it catches in his throat with a judder we hear the intent behind it. He's ready, therefore we are too.

'Do we go for one end and work our way across?' he asks.

'We could Marie Kondo it?' Zaza says, putting the ease back into her voice. 'Get it all out and on the bed before carefully deciding what to do with it all. That way we won't leave you with a half-finished job. You know, make sure we get it done.'

'Are you still pretending to be Boris?' Mike asks, making us laugh before we each look back to the wardrobe.

'Have you thought about where it's going to go?' I ask.

'Some stays with me – in case I ever fancy cross dressing, some goes to you two – whatever you want, and then the rest to the charity shop. Or dump.' The last word gets stuck in his throat but he carries on. I pretend not to notice.

'Right,' I nod, busying myself with finding a place on the bedside table to place my mug.

'We'll move it on to the bed,' says Zaza decisively, jumping into action.

'Can I just say,' I stop her, 'you're really channelling your inner Anneka Rice right now with that get-up.'

Zaza laughs while looking down at her clothes. 'She's my spirit animal today, for sure,' she grins, pulling on her jumpsuit and delivering a pout. 'Mike, you can stay by the bed and start looking through the different pieces once they're out. You can start by sorting it into piles.'

'Got it,' he nods, rubbing his hands together and getting himself ready for whatever garments we send his way.

We've slipped into functional. I can't be the only one who feels like the only way to get through this is to compartmentalize and separate the love for and loss of Pia with this action of packing her up and moving her out of her home.

I grab all the hangers I can manage and grunt as I carry them to the bed. If I were in my own bedroom I'd be chucking them down without a second thought, but Pia might as well be in my arms wearing every single garment – a vision that's aided by the smell that wafts up my nostrils. Pia. Washing powder, cooking and the hint of perfume lingering on items that have been returned to the wardrobe when not considered dirty enough to wash. It's like she's here and I know I'm not the only one to feel it. I'm aware of Mike's eyes watching me, taking in every garment and where my hands are touching them. I lay her down gently with great care.

We work slowly. None of us seems to be in a great

rush to actually get the job done. We savour the attack on the senses that continues with every piece being moved, trying to ignore the gaping hole being made in Mike's wardrobe.

'Mum got her this a few years ago,' Mike says with a grimace, holding up the most hideous jumper I've ever seen. Stripes of red, blue, yellow and grey run horizontally in dozens of different patterns. It's busy, and not very Pia.

'Mmm . . .' I nod.

'Bold look,' Zaza adds.

'I laughed when she put it on, which made her super defensive over Mum's choice – which apparently she got from a vintage shop especially, because she thought Pia would appreciate the gesture,' Mike shares. 'She did, and went on to wear it to as many of our trips to Mum's as she could without raising suspicions.'

We all titter at the thought.

'Keep it?' I ask.

'God no . . .' he frowns, placing it into the charity box. 'I'm sure someone else will love it.'

I turn back to the wardrobe and get ready to tackle the top shelf of boxes and bags. Right in the corner is a larger white box which I bring down with care – scared that everything else is going to fall on top of me. Thankfully it's pretty light. Once it's safely down on the ground I see Pia's handwriting scrawled across the top. In big bold black letters she's written 'HAPPIEST DAY OF MY LIFE!'.

'Oh,' I say, realizing what the box contains.

'Have you found gold?' asks Zaza, who's been perched on the floor folding clothes into various boxes – even the ones that are heading to the dump have been packed nicely.

Mike walks over, his lips pursing as he reads the words his deceased wife had written about their wedding day.

'Seems like a lifetime ago,' Mike coughs, visibly resisting the desire to reach out and touch the words that connect them. He hangs the dungarees he's holding over his shoulder and reaches for his tea, the third we've had since arriving. His eyebrows knit together as he takes a sip. His lips twitch.

'She looked ethereal, otherworldly in this,' I say, my fingers itching to get out the beautiful Stephanie Allin dress her mum, Zaza and I had all gone to help her pick. Needless to say she looked gorgeous in every single one, but as soon as she stepped out of the dressing room in this one – with its delicately plunging neckline, organza skirt and a stunning design of laced meadow flowers cascading down her arms and body, as though she were Mother Nature herself, we knew this was the one. Not only was it the most wonderful dress, but she lit up when she was in it. It heightened who she was. It drew out all of the goodness that my dear friend possessed.

My hand rests on the box, over her writing, wanting its contents to remain as perfectly placed as she's left it.

'Remember that the caterers cancelled the night before thanks to a double booking?' Mike asks behind me.

'Yes!' laughs Zaza. 'Pia made us stay up all night making endless curries, saag paneer, samosas and chutney.'

'You're forgetting the matzo brei, fried gefilte fish, challah, tahdig, kibbeh . . . There was so much food.' I chuckle with a sniff thanks to my now running nose, remembering being rushed to Tesco with a huge list of ingredients to source.

'I still say she planned the whole thing,' says Mike, an eyebrow raised as he drains his tea and puts down his mug. 'Pretty convenient that her mum had popped in to see us at the very moment we got the call – and once my mum got wind of what was going on it was as though all her dreams had come true. In she hustled, ready to use the coffee table as her creation station.'

'A real culture mash-up!' exclaims Zaza.

'Never known a feast like it,' I say, remembering the collection of flavours that had been passed down through the generations to help celebrate that special day. The fact it wasn't planned and rather had been done out of necessity made it even more perfect.

'What else do you expect from our mums?' laughs Mike. 'They'd been training their whole lives for a moment like that to occur.'

He looks back at the box beside me. No longer able to resist he picks it up and puts it back where I found it. The dress isn't going anywhere. He stays facing the cupboard and takes a breath before going back to the dungarees over his shoulder and deciding their fate.

He looks over with a slight smile as he goes by. I take in his watery eyes and return it.

Moving back to the collection of bags, my mind is

now on weddings – specifically my own which was six years ago. Crazy to think how much has changed in that time, and how different my life is now. Back then I was up at five each day to get into the studio to prep for the day ahead. Sometimes I'd be hectically getting ready for segments to be rolled out – chucking in some last-minute voiceovers before it aired, or heading out to location to meet someone new and film something either uplifting and engaging, thought-provoking and sombre or totally bizarre and wild. It was varied and fun, allowing me to swan into work each day with a spring in my step as I prepared to face the unexpected with passion and delight. It was fun when Nick and I first met. I spoke to different people every day, I had interesting things to talk about and a desire to listen to stories, understand and immerse myself in new experiences.

I think of myself walking into any room these days, invariably wrestling two children while looking totally shattered and exhausted with life, and I shudder. It's surprising he still tries it on with me at all.

It's not like I miss the woman I once was – that would mean regretting the kids and I'm not down with entertaining that thought in the slightest – I just miss feeling like me and having my own needs met once in a while.

'What's this bag?' I ask, pulling out a cotton bag from the bottom of the wardrobe.

Mike reaches out to take it, nodding with a smile on his face. 'Her let's-just-go bag,' he smiles, opening it up and pulling out a couple of thin cotton towels that had been rolled up. He places them up under his arm and then pulls another item from the bag, a black bikini. 'She treated herself to this before we went travelling around Brazil,' he recalls, holding it up. 'Most of the time she'd wear baggy slacks and vest tops, but as soon as we got near a beach this went on and she'd be in the sea within seconds, her arms sprawled out as she leaned back and allowed the sea to take hold of her – a pause in all the adventuring.'

I watch him, his eyes dancing as the memory hits him.

'A let's-just-go bag,' I repeat.

'No sense in waiting or being held back by packing.'

'So mundane,' I shrug.

'Exactly. Her travelling backpack is loaded and ready to go in the garage,' he laughs, pulling the bikini into his chest as he does so. 'This is the tamer "let's-get-out-of-London" version.'

'God, she kept this?' Zaza shrieks from the other side of the room, still rummaging around in the boxes we've pulled out. She holds up an outfit Pia wore to our one and only house party about eleven years ago when we all lived in Hackney. It was Zaza's birthday and she pretty much begged us to let her have 'a small gathering' to celebrate. It turned into a mammoth fancy dress party that saw us getting into trouble with the neighbours and being issued a warning from the landlord. We never did it again, and the Batman outfit Zaza is holding up never did get another viewing – not to our knowledge anyway.

'Whoa!' I laugh.

'She sat sewing these sequins on for hours,' she marvels, reminding me of how satisfied Pia was when she returned home one day, looking like she'd just raided an arts and crafts shop with bags of fabric, thread and millions of ideas on how she could turn it into something magical.

'She took it seriously,' Mike nods. 'Don't you remember what she made me wear?'

'I have it here!' sings Zaza, pulling a homemade Robin costume out of the box, her grin wider than ever.

'That bloody thing. It really chafed!' he laughs, grabbing hold of it and running it through his fingers. 'Knew I'd be her sidekick for life that night though.'

His words land with a punch.

We continue working away in silence.

I can't help the tears that stream down my face and on to her beaten leather Oliver Bonas satchel in my hands.

I hate that this is a reality for us.

'I brought some snacks. I'll get them,' Zaza mumbles, shuffling past.

I hear her sobs escape as soon as she exits the room.

'Alcohol might be a better idea,' mutters Mike.

5

Mike

That was never going to go down as one of life's more enjoyable days, but I have to admit I'm relieved as I shut the door on Vicky and Zaza at the end of the night, and begrudgingly grateful to Pia for making sure we came together to do it. Her funeral was a day of reminiscing with others, but today it felt like those memories were tangible and led by Pia because those clothes were ones she'd decided to see hanging in her wardrobe. They meant something to her.

Turns out nothing is quick and easy when you're saying goodbye to the love of your life. I guess the pain and heart-ache are the only exceptions to that – they both come flooding in and floor you before you have a chance to fathom what your life has become. Everything else is slow and agonizing. Creeping and lingering in the darkness.

I didn't realize how many clothes Pia had. Although in her defence, her bulging wardrobe wasn't because she was a big spender, rather she liked to keep hold of everything. Even clothes that were covered in moth holes or stains had still been afforded space. I felt bad placing them on the 'dump' pile when she'd clearly wanted to give them an extra bit of lifespan. If Vicky hadn't taken those boxes with her and offered to do the trip to the dump I don't think they'd have ever left the house.

Another thing I failed to predict was how hard it was going to be seeing other people handling her things and moving them around – even if those people were our best mates who loved her like I did. My heart ached at the sight. Every hand that touched her belongings seemed to be robbing me of parts of her, stealing her away, overwriting her being. Erasing her. Making this shit situation real while letting me know she's not about to wander back into the flat any time soon for a change of clothes . . . It was like I was taking her home away. Drawing the curtains and turning out the light.

I know Pia wanted me to do this today, she wanted to ensure I kept moving forward and didn't sit in my brokenness for too long, but maybe sitting in my grief is what I feel like doing. Maybe it's what I should be doing.

I grab a beer from the fridge. As I open it and hear the pressure disperse my body echoes with a sigh. I take a quick gulp and enjoy the cold liquid shocking my insides as it flows through my body. I rub at my face, enjoying the roughness of the stubble and the pull on my skin. When I stop my eyes fall on the full boxes out in the hallway. I'm meant to be taking them to the charity shop in the morning. 'My' collection went into two boxes and back into the wardrobe. A wardrobe that at the end of our sorting session looked back at me mockingly. A near-empty wardrobe to match my near-empty bed, house and heart.

Memories of Pia were attached to every single item unearthed today, with constant visions of her wearing them – her comfies when lounging on the sofa and binge watching *Breaking Bad*, her little black bikini when we were carefree, travelling around South America and taking in the world, and then her wedding dress on what I thought was the biggest day of our lives. She said it best though on that sodding box. The happiest. Not the biggest, but the giddiest, most joyous and pure. The biggest was her last. There's no denying that.

I make to go to the lounge but can't get past the ruddy boxes lined up in the hallway. My hand rests on one of them, my fingers curling to ease it open, uncovering the clothes we've decided should now be worn by someone else. I pick out the top item, a red jumper I remember her wearing the Christmas before last, and do what I have resisted doing with company around. I bring it to my face and I breathe her in. Deeply. Willing her to come alive to my senses. Willing her to be here with me. Willing her back. Desperately trying to grab hold of every last part of her that lingers in the fibres of the jumper.

'I'm so sorry,' I whisper, the heat of my breath hitting the fabric along with drops of tears and snot. 'I'm so sorry. So sorry. I'm so so so sorry.'

My knees go. I'm down on the ground now, cradling a box of my dead wife's belongings in my arms as I rock back and forth.

'I'm so sorry,' I repeat, unable to stop the words going around and around on a loop.

Sorry.

Sorry for not being able to protect her.

Sorry for not paying more attention to what I now know were symptoms.

Sorry for telling her the ache in her armpit was probably nothing.

Sorry for not making her go to the doctor's sooner.

Sorry for that one day last May when we both went to bed angry without declaring our love.

Sorry for finding her irritating when she kept talking during *Ozark*.

Sorry for not complimenting her more because she deserved to know she looked amazing every single day. Even when she rolled out of bed hungover, her face covered in smudged makeup from the night before.

Sorry for being a pain in the arse sometimes.

Sorry for not having sex with her more.

Sorry for being pathetic.

Sorry for the times we sat in silence when we could've been talking about everything and anything.

Sorry for no longer being able to see the beauty she saw in the world.

Sorry for not being able to stop death.

Sorry for having to be here without her.

Sorry for all the ways I've failed her.

Sorry.

I'm sorry for being so sorry.

I just miss her so much.

6

Zaza

I head home on autopilot, exhausted from experiencing such a mixture of emotions during the afternoon and having to hide so much from two of the people I love more than anything. Grief has brought us closer than ever as we try to comfort each other through this murky fog, but it's also made us more distant in many ways. We all know that to be the truth. We suppress some of the challenging words and thoughts we want to say in the hope of protecting those who will be receiving them. Not wanting our own darkness to encumber what little light they've so far been able to shield from pain.

There were moments when I was hit by several different (and conflicting) 'feels' all at once, which was confusing to my brain. It's no wonder it now feels fried. A nice bit of reminiscing about the funniest of nights could very quickly turn to us silently feeling the void of our new reality without Pia.

I felt good when I left. Lighter in some way, like you do when you've been at a dreaded funeral and celebrated the life of someone you've loved and realized how much they gave to the earth, but the closer I get to my house the heavier I've become.

It's struck me that, no matter how difficult the afternoon has been for me, I was allowed to walk out of that flat and back into a world I have built away from my old housemates. I can't imagine what it must be like for Mike.

Guilt descends on me with every step I take towards home.

When I arrive the front door closes behind me with a bang. I didn't intend for it to make such a racket, but it's as thunderous as my mood has become so seems fitting.

'You OK?' Liam calls out over the sound of the TV. I can tell he's sitting on the sofa – which is exactly where I left him playing FIFA several hours ago.

I huff, moodily removing my Chanel clutch bag and blue teddy coat before hanging them up in the hallway. I kick off my pristinely white Superga trainers and place a hand on the wall for balance before bending over to peel away my sweaty ballet socks.

'Babe?' Liam nudges.

I hang my head with a sigh. Without looking up I know he's closer now, peering around the doorframe to see what I'm up to.

'Yeah?' I reply gruffly at my trainers while picking them up and placing them against the wall. Purposefully taking my time.

'I asked if you're OK . . .' Liam's voice gets smaller.

'What do you think?' I ask, whipping my head up just as Liam's eyebrows shoot up.

'What?' I stand, shifting my weight to one hip.

'OK . . .' He backs away, looking as confused as I am about the hostility coming off me – but I've committed to it now and the fire in me doesn't seem to want to be extinguished just yet. 'I've got some work to do so I'll just . . .' He backs away, turning off his all-important FIFA game.

'Oh,' I nod, walking past him and taking in his jogging bottoms and sweater – he's literally been vegging out all day and now I'm here to play the dutiful wife role. 'I'll make dinner then, shall I?'

'I thought you'd have eaten?'

'When?' I bark.

'Za . . . babe,' he holds his hands up in the air, telling me he comes in peace. It angers me further.

'You're all right, Liam. You just do you,' I say, my arm gesticulating wildly between us. 'Don't worry about me.'

'Are you hungry?'

'What?' I choke.

'You get cranky when you're hungry,' he shrugs.

'I'm cranky 'coz life is shit sometimes and you don't seem to care.'

His jaw drops then closes in quick succession, his eyes narrow.

'What are you doing?' he asks, giving me some fire back.

'You've been sat there all day, and now you're going to go and do work?'

'I don't need to work,' he says, shaking his head.

'You just said you did.'

'You made it crystal clear you didn't want me around as soon as you walked in the door so I was going to give you some space,' he says.

'I don't need space!' I yell.

We stare at each other – me frowning, him totally taken aback.

'Zaza,' he says, his voice low and calm as both of his hands rest on his chest. 'You know this isn't about me or us. Be as angry as you like at the world, but this isn't about me, and you can't go throwing grenades into our relationship because life got shit. We're getting married. There's going to be a whole load of shit thrown our way in the decades to come and we need to be able to work it out together,' he says, his face full of sympathy and concern. 'We don't do this. This is rubbish!'

'I know,' I agree, matching his tone, feeling the steam ease off now some of it's been released. 'I'm sorry.'

'I know it's been a hard day. I'm trying to get vibes off you and go with what you're feeling. Not pushing or prodding, just letting you be with this . . .'

'Yeah . . .'

He sighs and cocks his head to the side, his eyes still studying me.

'Want to get a pizza and watch something?'

I nod.

He steps forward and wraps his arms around me. I succumb to the warmth and allow myself to feel comforted by his love.

For a moment.

'I'll go put my pjs on.'

'OK,' he says, kissing my forehead before releasing me – letting me know he doesn't consider me a complete twat.

His gesture fails to ease the itchiness in my head as I walk up the stairs to our bedroom. Instead of getting changed I sit on our bed and collapse backwards. With my arms draped over my face I become increasingly aware of the walls closing in on me.

An idiot would be able to point out that whatever Liam did when I walked through the door tonight would've resulted in me being a bitch and starting an argument. If he'd carried on with his game, argument. If he'd shot out of his seat and asked how it went, argument. I wonder at what point that became a thing. Since Pia's death? Or before? When did I go from wanting him to be the one person seeing the absolute best of me, to allowing him to be the only person who sees the worst of me? When did I start thinking it was acceptable for me to be so rude to him? I'm pretty sure he doesn't do the same to me. He shows nothing but love and understanding, yet he's become my punchbag. One day I might just hit too hard. One day the sparring might just be too unpleasant for him to stay.

Is this a response to recent loss? Or has communication actually failed us and been failing us for quite some time?

I wonder if other couples have moments like this. It's hardly something they'd share on Instagram or in witty Facebook posts. Is this the truth to all relationships? Did Mike and Pia have grouchy moments? Do Vicky and Nick unravel every so often and wonder if they'll ever feel connected in the same way again? Or is the underlying current of mine and Liam's relationship turning toxic? Or is it possible for one person in a relationship to feel entirely different to the other?

Am I happy? The question startles me. Partly because it makes me think about where I am in life and all the frogs I've kissed who turned out to actually be rats in disguise, all the first dates I've sat at cringing, all the guys who let me down without so much as a thought-through goodbye. All the tears I was glad to be rid of when Liam walked into my life and showed me how different things could be with his humour and caring ways . . .

Before Liam there were many frogs. Men who left me feeling broken and rejected. Yet, what about those flirtations that made my head go to dark and beautiful places, what about the times a connection was struck in the most unlikely of places, and what about the first kisses that left me gagging for more? I don't have that with Liam any more. I knew where I stood from the start with him. There were no mind games, no confusion, he was just real and that made me feel at ease.

Yes, I'm bewildered when I think about my happiness. Not because it makes me look to my past, but because it makes me look to the future and leads me to ask far bigger questions.

I am where I wanted to be in life. This is what I've wanted for so very long, yet now it's here I'm struck with the thought of never dating again, never having a proper flirt again, never having that tantalizing desire with someone new. No new firsts.

I wanted to be comfortable and remove the unpredictable, but now that seems like the scariest concept I've ever heard of.

One question loops continuously in my mind.

Is this it?

Unfulfilled, flat, lacklustre, distant. Is this PTSD? Am I acting out because I've been through such a massive, earth-shattering loss? Or have I actually stayed longer than I should've because of what was going on elsewhere in my life?

'Babe, pizza's here.' Liam's voice shouts up the stairs.

'Coming,' I shout, not moving an inch.

7

Vicky

'OK, can we use our fork please, Chloe?' I ask, trying my best to keep my tone nice and light, as if someone might be listening in and judging my parenting skills as we sit around the dinner table. She wouldn't nap today and from that moment on I knew the rest of the day was going to be a disaster. I got her into the pram to collect Barnaby from school – there's no way she would've walked there and back and I couldn't carry her the whole way so it seemed like the best option. After she refused her nap after lunch I knew we were at risk of her having a danger nap but, like an overly keen children's TV presenter, I was doing my best to keep her chatting and engaged the whole way to pick up. Once we got to the gate, though, Nihal's mum Neelam asked if Barnaby wanted to go over for a playdate. I must've only had my eye off the ball for a minute or so as I enjoyed my one bit of adult interaction for the day, but when I looked down she was sparko. I couldn't wake her up then (to be honest I was certain she'd lose her shit and I didn't want to feel that shame while at the school with other parents around), nor during the hour and a half that followed.

She woke up five minutes ago in a foul mood and screamed down the house. I've had to bribe her into her highchair with the promise of a Nobbly Bobbly for pudding, but even that has lost its appeal right now. She hasn't eaten a thing. Simply prodded or squished it with her fingers while wearing a face like a slapped arse.

'You know we don't eat the spaghetti or our meatballs with our hands, sweetie,' I sing, sounding utterly pathetic but choosing to focus on my own plate of spaghetti and the therapeutic action of twirling the pasta around my fork.

'I don't want it,' pouts Chloe, lifting her plastic Peppa Pig plate a few inches off the table and banging it down.

'Chloe! You asked for this!'

'No . . .' she shakes her head, a massive frown glaring back at me.

'You did. I gave you options when we were walking to school this morning – cottage pie, chicken nuggets or pasta. Remember?'

'I wanted green cheesy pasta,' whines Barnaby.

'Not now,' I say with more force than is necessary, throwing him a stern look which I instantly regret doing. His eyes widen at my angry face. His bottom lip wobbles. He doesn't cry like Chloe would though. Instead he does something that makes me feel a hundred times worse. He sucks it up. Stops himself. Does his little brave face. Why would I make my five-year-old use his brave face? I'm his mother! I'm meant to be the one stopping him having to use that sodding face!

'Sorry, baby,' I say, leaning over and rubbing the top of his hand.

'I want Daddy,' he declares, his eyes filling with tears, the brave face dropping.

'I know,' I nod, feeling his words hammer at my chest. 'We all miss him, but he'll be home before we know it. Three sleeps to go,' I say, making my face resemble something like a smile.

Barnaby nods, uses the back of his hand to wipe his eyes, then continues with his dinner. I hate that his life is disrupted so much and often wonder if things would've been simpler, easier and calmer had we not been blessed with such a driven and determined second child.

The problem is Barnaby listens far more than Chloe does. My words seem to carry more weight. I can be stricter, in a way, because he is older and has a few reasonable bones in his body. At least when I say something to him he seems to take it on board most of the time. I just never know what I'm going to get with Chloe.

'I want chicken nuggets,' she pouts.

'We don't have chicken nuggets. We're having pasta now . . .'

'I don't like it. It's spicy,' she declares, jutting her chin into her neck to get her mouth further away from the plate.

'You've not even tried it yet, Chloe,' I say, my tone ramping up ever so slightly into desperation.

She simply looks at me and blinks.

I blink back.

'Chloe?' I smile. Softly, softly . . . don't anger the beast. 'Think of the Nobbly Bobbly.'

The reminder of the after-dinner treat makes her cock her head to one side. With her eyes still firmly locked on me she reaches across the table, giving me a sense of hope that she's about to blooming listen and grab her fork and get eating. Instead she picks up her beaker cup, brings it to her lips, and then lets it topple out of her hands and on to the floor. The sodding thing opens and spills everywhere.

'No, Chloe! No!' I start, abandoning my own dinner to pick up the cup before running for the kitchen roll.

'Oh dear,' I hear her say. How she's mastered sarcasm so young is beyond me. Did she do it on purpose? It's highly likely. Can I prove my three-year-old is a conniving little mistress? No, she's too smart for that. Covers her tracks with her innocence.

'Don't worry. These things happen,' I say, knowing that if I scowl at her now there's definitely no chance she'll eat any of her dinner afterwards. 'Eat now, my love.'

She sighs and looks down at her plate.

I regularly wonder if I'm too soft on Chloe. Maybe I should be firmer in my approach and resist giving in when we're at loggerheads. But there's only so much tension I can take so yes, I absolutely do go for the easy way out when I have to. She's such a fiery little character, and I've learnt that you can't fight fire with fire. It just doesn't work. Not in our case anyway. Is this an age thing? A second child thing? Or simply a Chloe thing? I don't remember Barnaby being this difficult, but then I guess he had all of my attention. Perhaps second children all come out with their elbows at the ready, prepared to nudge their way through, whatever the costs.

Growing up, my mum only had to throw 'the look' in the direction of me and my two brothers for us to cease whatever it was we were doing she disapproved of. It was a look that said she was serious and that we'd gone too far. A look that let us know there'd be consequences if we continued with our 'testing' behaviour. I always assumed 'the look' was something you inherited as soon as you became a mum – like a superhero skill to defeat all the whinging and stop all the potential injuries.

I think my look might be broken though, because no one seems to take a blind bit of notice. Except Barnaby, I guess – but only when I've taken a frustration with Chloe out on him. Otherwise he's just as oblivious to my squinting glares of disapproval.

Perhaps I don't follow through with my words enough – like the time I said we wouldn't go on holiday if she continued to throw the toy cars at the radiator. She saw straight through that blatant lie and carried on chucking. As if I'd ever cancel our holiday – I took it too far and didn't stay within realistic parameters. Even tonight, we're playing a game. We both know that now the idea of an after-dinner treat has been introduced there's absolutely no way she's going to go without one, no matter what she does in the lead up to getting it. Not unless I want to spend two hours with a toddler scream-ing in my face while sitting in front of the freezer to stop her getting one out. So she will absolutely be joining her brother in the eating of a ridiculously named Nobbly Bobbly.

Chloe picks up one side of her plate and lifts it a centi-metre off the table before putting it back down, causing it to donk on the wood. She repeats the action with speed. Donk, donk, donk, donk, donk, donk.

I try to ignore it so that I can just get back to eating my dinner while it's still warm. If she doesn't want to eat that's her problem – I'm not going to let her ruin meat-balls for me too. I tell myself that, but I can feel the pressure starting to rise as a tightness grips my chest. It's the overwhelm. The overbearing feeling of being utterly out of my depth. I wish I was better at this. I wish I understood the techniques all those experts tell us to use to practise gentle parenting. I wish I was enough to keep her happy, content and able to do as I ask. I wish we could all smile and laugh more.

I chew my food miserably, trying to ignore the small but irritating sound she's creating, unsure if she genu-inely likes the sound or just wants to wind me up.

'Jacob did a trump in assembly today,' Barnaby says randomly, a giggle in his voice as he remembers.

The tapping stops.

'It was so loud,' he continues, really enjoying the tell-ing of events. 'Mrs France looked up to see what it was and everyone turned and stared. He went so red.'

'Was it smelly?' asks Chloe, instantly captivated.

'Yeah! Like dragon's poo!' nods Barnaby, shoving a whole meatball into his gob.

I resist telling him he should've halved it first.

Chloe chuckles at her big brother, picks up a fork, loads it with food and copies the action with a smile on her face. It's as though the last ten minutes of dramatic behaviour haven't happened at all. Even the way she looks has gone from angry gremlin to sweet and endearing.

Yes, OK – obviously I'm not utterly pleased with the topic of conversation but I'm thankful to Barnaby for helping us push forward with the mealtime and for us to actually be enjoying our food while it's still warm.

I take a breath, pick up my fork and shove in some pasta while I can. It's very rare I eat with the kids this early. I usually wait for Nick to get back from work and eat some more refined food later on with him but as he's away it would just be me sitting eating alone so I've opted to eat earlier. We haven't had the best mealtimes, there's always been some drama over what I've cooked or how I've sliced it, but this little moment of peace, where we're all just eating and content seems to erase all of that. I feel the heaviness on my chest ease a little. I'm sure it would ease completely if the thought of bedtime wasn't looming over us.

Thank heavens for the glass of wine I'll be holding by seven-thirty as I try and clean today's mess and get some washing on, all while catching up on some light and mind-numbing telly which doesn't require me to think.

The calm atmosphere across the table lasts for approximately a minute before my phone starts ringing with a FaceTime request. I totally forgot Nick was going to be calling to see the kids tonight. I was hoping they'd be fed, bathed and on the sofa watching *Room on the Broom* by then. Wanting them both to eat a little more before it all descends into chaos again I mute the call and move it under my leg to hide it, telepathically sending a message to Nick that I'll call him in five.

'Who was that?' asks Barnaby.

'No one,' I say, my eyes widening at him while I cock my head towards Chloe in a way that to any adult would mean 'Not now, let's eat while she's being reasonable,' but to my five-year-old brings about some confusion and a frown on his face.

'Was it Da—'

'Not now, Barna—'

'Daddy? Daddy, yeeeeeah!' screams Chloe over me. 'Where's Daddy?'

'I want to speak to Daddy!' shrieks Barnaby, his hands clapping together.

'Yes! Call Daddy! Now, now, now, now, now!' chimes in Chloe, her fist pounding on the table in front of her.

'In a minute, guys. First let's eat up our dinner and then we can give him a call after, when our tummies are nice and full.'

'NO! Daddy now!' Chloe shouts, flipping the entire

contents of her homemade dinner on the floor in protest. It lands with a splat and my heart sinks.

'Chloe . . .' I say quietly. This time I have no anger left to give, just deep-rooted sadness which causes my chest to sink as my eyes start to sting.

I grab the kitchen roll and go to the floor, saving whatever pasta tubes and meatballs I can on to the plate to return to her, before wrapping the rest in the towel and cleaning up. I'm so tired of this. Of continuously having to be the grown-up, of always having to be the one sorting things out. Of always being home. I'm fed up of having to be organized and patient as I hold up the fort.

Where have I disappeared to?

My phone starts ringing again. This time I'm not there to quickly mute it.

'Daddy, daddy, daddy, daddy,' chant both kids while bashing on the table.

I take a breath and leap in the air and pick up the call, taking care not to get pasta sauce over everything in the process.

'Hey!' I say, managing a smile.

'Babe!' Nick beams. He's sitting out in the sunshine. I can't see anything around him but I know his setting is very different to my own at this moment in time.

'Great timing,' I laugh. 'Chloe's just spilt her dinner all over the floor. I'll pop you here so you can talk to them while I tidy up.' I talk so fast Nick can't get a word in edgeways. His mouth opens to say something just as I plonk my phone on the table and rest it against the tub of wipes, positioning it so that both children can be seen.

I stand behind it and watch.

'Daddy!' sings Barnaby with a big grin on his face while Chloe looks at the phone bashfully, like butter wouldn't melt.

'There you are!' says Nick, his voice rising in pitch. 'Oh I've missed you so much. What did you have for dinner?'

'Meatballs!' grins Barnaby.

'Ooh, was it delicious?'

Chloe has the cheek to nod.

*

Bathtime and bed wasn't as chaotic as I feared it was going to be. Yes, speaking to Nick made them a bit giddy and overexcited, as did the Nobbly Bobblys they both ended up having, but they went upstairs when I asked, kept the majority of the water in the bathtub and listened when I said we only had time for two bedtime stories. In fact we had a rather wonderful time reading *Bumblebear* and *Zog* while Chloe lay in between my legs and Barnaby leaned his head against my shoulder. It was blissful, and definitely what I thought most of motherhood would look like.

When they asked if I'd stay in their room while they fell asleep I pushed the thought of the waiting wine to the back of my mind and drank them in instead, watching as they chatted nonsense to each other and wriggled around. When Chloe then turned to me, her eyes wide and imploring as she asked, 'Will you lay with me?' I practically jumped in her bed. I lay with her in my arms, sniffing her head, until she eventually gave in to the heaviness of sleep – which did take a little while longer thanks to the day's danger nap. Once I was sure she'd nodded off I kissed her soft lips and untangled myself, completely filled with gratitude and love. Those are the moments that keep you going when it all gets a bit haphazard and stressful – and they're the ones forcing mothers to declare motherhood (which I'd average as ninety per cent shit-show) to be utterly amazing and life-affirming – and they're the ones you have to cling on to and cherish when they do randomly happen.

Even though I'm later than usual to walk down the stairs and get on with putting the day to rest and getting started on the next, I realize with clarity that I needed that moment with the kids. I've been reset. I head straight to the kitchen to get on with the washing up and tidying the rest of the dinner things away, aware that my chest doesn't feel quite so heavy as I take in the mess.

I pop a podcast (an old Adam Buxton episode with Louis Theroux) on my phone before sliding it into my back pocket and zoning out while listening to their conversation about fathers and writing. While allowing my mind to run elsewhere, I get cracking.

An hour later, with a house that looks as it did when the day started and with bags and outfits prepped for tomorrow, I'm just pulling my Marigolds off when my phone starts vibrating in my pocket.

Nick.

'Hello?' I answer, chucking the pink rubber gloves back into the cleaning cupboard before reaching into the fridge for that long-awaited glass of wine.

When Barnaby was a baby I wouldn't dream of having a drink if it were just me at home, wondering what I'd do if something happened – like one of us got ill or a burglar broke in. I'm not sure when that changed but I decide to push away the mum-guilt that creeps up on me and enjoy the glug glug glug of the tangy white wine as it pours into the glass. Music to my ears.

'Are they both asleep?' Nick asks.

'Yes,' I smile into the phone, taking a sip of my wine. It's usually around this time, if not a little later, that Nick walks through the door from work. Ever since the kids entered our lives this has always been the first question he asks. The fact I'm usually downstairs in a tidy house and drinking something alcoholic should tell him all he needs to know, but I think he hangs on to the hope that one of them will be up and he can creep in to see them.

'Long day?' he asks.

'Hmmm . . . I think I've had better and worse,' I realize, heading to the comfort of the front room. 'You?'

'Not sure what to say without you hating me . . .' he replies, hesitantly.

'Are you at the pool?' I ask, rearranging the pillows

before falling on to the sofa – which is quite an ugly-looking thing but is surprisingly great to snuggle on. It's also quite magical as it manages to hide a number of stains and spillages the kids have covered it in over the years. I pull over the throw that I draped over the back and wrap it around me, feeling the cold now I've stopped. 'It's flipping hot there too, isn't it!'

'Possibly,' he laughs. 'I spent the morning up in my room before the meeting but have been here since getting back. The sun has been shining so . . .'

'You thought you'd make the most of it,' I sigh, full of envy. I know he should be making the most of being somewhere sunny, it's just I would really love to be in that sunshine with a pina colada right now. 'Ooh! How'd it go? Tell me, tell me! So sorry, I was distracted with the kids earlier!'

'Good. Back in tomorrow to meet the client.' I can imagine the grin on his face as he says it.

'That's amazing!' I squeak. The excitement of him being in Lala Land schmoozing with bigwigs is not lost on me, despite me having a wobble about him going and still being super jealous of the sunshine, his freedom, and being able to get on with his life without having to worry about school runs and bedtimes. 'Well done.'

'Thanks, baby. Also means I can't stay out here in the sun too long, though,' he says with a dramatic sigh. 'I definitely don't want to get sunburnt and end up going in there looking like a total Brit with a bright red nose and forehead.'

'What a shame,' I laugh, thankful that bedtime went well, otherwise I'd be snappy as hell right now at the thought of how chilled he's able to be while I've been so stressed here.

'Have you sorted the sitter for next week?' Nick asks, cutting in on my thoughts.

'Huh?' I ask, my mind flicking through what I have in my diary – a weather-based school project for Barnaby that's got to show all of the seasons and then a trampoline birthday party for his mate at the weekend; Chloe has ballet on Monday and then a softplay date on Tuesday, swimming on Wednesday, Bunny Hop on Thursday and Monkey Music on Friday. I'm pretty sure they're the bare bones of the following week. I don't think there are any 'me' plans that I need Rosie to sit for.

'You've not forgotten? And usually I'm the one put in the dog house for that.' Nick tuts, clearly pretending to be bemused.

'Stop being annoying and tell me.'

'It's Valentine's Day, of course.'

'Oh.'

I hadn't thought about it at all, which is strange as I've always loved the idea of being spoilt with romantic gestures and, at the very least, having a reason to get Rosie over and going out for some one-on-one adult interaction time with Nick. But Valentine's carries an extra messy emotion this year as it would've been Pia's thirty-third birthday.

My thoughts turn to Mike and how he might be

feeling about the day looming ahead. I'm sure he couldn't care less about the day full of hearts and cheesy poetry. I imagine that part of the Fourteenth has completely gone over his head. Instead the day will bring a very different heaviness.

Again.

'Have you actually planned anything yet?' I ask, knowing that he's usually phoning around all my favourite restaurants at the very last minute in the hope of blagging a table, or asking if I have time to do it. Nick is ever the romantic who likes to plan ahead and show he's making an effort. Not.

'Yes!' he says proudly.

'Right . . .'

My voice is full of uncertainty, regret and doubt. I know Nick hears it because he sighs in response.

'You don't even have to say anything. I know what you're going to say and yes. You're right,' he says, his low voice full of empathy. 'Give Zaza and Mike a call and make plans with them.'

'And you too? We can have Liam over and make a night of it.'

'Yeah . . . Sure.'

'Thank you, Nick.'

'It's only a day . . . and I'm sure La Trompette will have no trouble filling the table so hopefully I'll get my deposit back.'

'What?! You didn't!' I gasp, shocked that he's remembered the French restaurant I must've mentioned at the end of last year in the hope that we'd one day go, but never really believed he'd take up the hint and book it himself.

'No, I totally didn't,' he chuckles. 'I absolutely would've left you thinking I did if you hadn't asked, though. Think of the brownie points.'

'Ha-de-har,' I reply, unable to hide my disappointment about something I just said I was pulling out of anyway.

'We can do something proper another night. I'll sort it,' he says.

'Thank you.'

There's a muffle as Nick talks to someone else.

'You OK?'

'Yes! Food's arrived. Bucket of calamari, fries and salad.'

'Sounds deli–'

A thump from above stops me. I wait two seconds for the inevitable wailing to start. It does.

'Better go. I think Chloe's fallen out of bed,' I say, already getting up and putting down my glass, which I've barely managed to touch.

'Oh no. I lo–'

I hang up and make a dash up the stairs. Chloe is already stood on the landing with her arms reaching out to me. Her mouth is wide as she howls in despair. I scoop her up. She still screams.

I try taking her back to the room she shares with Barnaby; she still screams and sobs. I will never know how Barnaby manages to sleep through Chloe's wails and commotion, but he always does. My slumbersome son has never once been woken up regardless of my daughter's volume and hysteria. Oh to be so unaware.

I look over at my sleeping boy, splayed across his bed and dribbling all over his pillow. The important thing is that we all just get some sleep – it doesn't matter who is where.

'Want to sleep in my bed?' I whisper directly into her ear, hoping she can hear me over the noise she's making.

The sound is instantly turned off like it's a tap. She gives me a wide-eyed nod and nuzzles into me, her body bouncing as it attempts to regain control of her breath.

'Come on then,' I whisper, waddling into my room and wondering when she got so big. I pull back the duvet and place her on Nick's side of the bed, knowing full well she'll either be on my side all night, pressed against me, or across the pillows with her feet in my face. I wrap her up warm and stroke her hair away from her face. 'I love you, sausage.'

'Love you,' she says, looking a little shell-shocked at what's happened.

'It's OK. Mummy's here.'

At that her face crumples.

'I want Daddy.'

FML.

The next hour is spent explaining that he's away for work, that Mummy is just as good at hugs, and then being summoned back to the room any time I try to go back downstairs to one, lock up, two, phone Zaza, and three, finish my wine.

I give up and am in bed at a respectable quarter past nine.

8

Zaza

'You know, I just think it's only a day for us really – we can both celebrate with Liam and Nick another night and it will be no big deal, but for Mike it will be massive. Huge,' Vicky says into the phone.

'Yeah . . .' I say. I've been trying out a fancy new sheet face mask for work up in our bathroom, so I was crouched on the tiled floor catching up on *RuPaul's Drag Race* on my laptop (which is perched on the loo) when she called. I've warned her about only being able to move my mouth a bit with this on my face and as a result she's basically talked at me for the last five minutes.

'You think I'm mothering too much?' She jumps in.

'No, not at all. You're right.'

'Is it presumptuous to think he'd want to spend it with us, though?' she asks before getting distracted by one of the kids and starts hissing away from the phone – God knows why she decided to phone while she was cooking dinner – especially with Nick away. 'Sorry, sorry!' she says, returning her attention. 'Do you think it is?'

'I don't think so . . .'

I should've been the one suggesting this. I know more

than most what that shoddily commercial day of love can do to someone who's had their heart broken, or if they're just bored of spending the night alone. Valentine's Day and I have such a complicated history. I've spent so long hating it. I was single for years and it was incredibly depressing to see everyone coupling up and throwing around romantic gestures like their worth as a human depended on how OTT they could be. Don't get me wrong, I always had one or two offers floating around. Those were usually from an ex who didn't fancy being alone either and wondered if I'd keep their bed warm for the night. I never did. OK, only the one time but it ended up being good closure because the whole thing was so ridiculous. As if a Thai takeaway was going to win me over after confessing to playing around while we were together . . . I grabbed that pad Thai and left! Thankfully the following year I had Liam to spend it with.

Liam.

I was in quite an indifferent state by the time we met. I'd spent years chasing the wrong guys and getting hurt, or going for the good guys who turned out to be worse than the bad guys because they catfish the hell out of you before leaving you broken. I'd spent years watching my friends get married and moving on with the next stages of their lives and, after feeling the panic rise within me with each new announcement and each spanking new break-up, I had finally started to realize that it might just not happen. And I was fine pretending to be cool with that. I was busy with work anyway and I didn't really mind too much. Loneliness was better than heartbreak, I reasoned.

I didn't always feel that way, obviously. I wasn't totally hardened to the way society was making me feel like an unwanted spinster, but I had learnt to enjoy my own company the majority of the time, or just have a laugh with mates while not stressing about having someone to constantly check in with.

Then on my way home one night from a schmoozy work event I spotted an advert on the Tube for Find your Fish, a new dating app. I'd never been on one before, thinking they'd suck the romance out of that first meeting and that raw attraction that makes you adamant you need to go over and speak to the person who has grabbed your attention from afar, but something about the advert with its no-fuss design and happy-looking fish caught my attention – hook, line and sinker.

Following a rather painful attempt to put in my details and log into the system, Liam's was the first face that appeared. He asked what I was up to and we just got talking. We messaged on there for a week before we actually met up. I'll admit that when he said we were going to Wagamama I thought he was joking; of all the casual dineries on offer I didn't fancy sitting next to strangers while possibly having awkward date chat. I almost bowed out when he walked through the door in Covent Garden and started skipping down the steps, but then he turned to me with a grin on his face.

'You *are* joking!' I stated with a laugh, feeling relieved.

'Who doesn't like a chicken katzu curry?' he frowned.

'Huh?' was all I managed back before he started walking back towards me, trying to get out of the way of a group of mates who'd just walked in and would now be a space ahead of us in the queue for a table downstairs.

'Zaza,' he said, leaning on the wall next to me, his expression calmly amused, although not in a way I felt belittled by. He was far more attentive than that. 'Did you or did you not say that being hangry was your weak point and probably the thing you'd most like to change about yourself?'

'I did . . .' I nodded, feeling the right side of my mouth curl up in the glimpse of a smile at him referencing one of our many messages.

'Then why on earth would I put you in a position where we'd be waiting for hours for swanky food, only to find it was a minuscule amount that would do little to stop the hunger, let alone hanger?'

I looked at him quizzically.

'I promise this isn't me dipping in and out and being a twat with a quick exit,' he said, before screwing his face up bashfully.

'Nicely worded,' I quipped.

'Zaza, fancy eating some delicious food that'll be in front of us in minutes and then seeing where else the night takes us on happily full tummies?'

I looked up at him, at this man who'd made a simple

choice because he wanted me to be comfortable and my best self, and grabbed his hand so that we could join the queue downstairs.

Every first with Liam was so different to any that had come before, he'd simplified life and love for me. Yet now life has come along to make me doubt the indestructability of that.

I feel sad to push aside the idea of Valentine's but with my head the way it is right now it might be a good thing.

'Phone Mike,' I say, pulling at the face mask that's started to slip.

'You think?' she asks, shouting over the rising noise of Barnaby and Chloe in the background who are shrieking at one another like angry little banshees. 'You're right. We can't just turn up there. He might have plans.'

We both know he won't have plans with other people, not on the night nearly everyone seems to have things arranged, but he might've decided to spend the night watching old home videos or pretending it isn't happening at all – so it's good to give him the option of seeing our faces if he'd like to.

'I'll do that now,' she sings. 'And actually, I'll suggest meeting up here rather than going there again. Takes the pressure off. Phone you back.'

'OK,' I say, sighing as I put the phone down.

I peel off the mask and rub the left-over moisturizer into my skin before going downstairs to find Liam – he's having a self-confessed 'break from adulting' by playing on his game.

'All good?' he asks, giving me a quick glance.

'Can you pause it a sec?'

He gives a slow glance over, no doubt checking the expression on my face to see the level of serious that I'm interrupting him with and attempting to read the situation.

He pauses his game.

'Have you been crying?' He seems genuinely concerned.

'No! I just did a face mask.'

'Oh right,' he nods with relief. I see his fingers twitch towards the controls but he thinks better of it and rubs his hands together and puts the controller down instead. 'Shoot.'

'Just been chatting to Vicky and we think we should be with Mike next Thursday. For Pia's birthday, for Valentine's.'

'Oh,' he says, taken aback. 'But we have plans. I said I'd organized something.'

'Argh,' I say, having forgotten he'd told me he'd planned a surprise a few weeks ago. 'We can change them though, right?'

'Sure,' he shrugs.

'It's only a day,' I say, finding myself repeating the words I used to utter myself in the past when the day turned out to be less than romantic or special.

'And what'll I do instead?' It's a genuine question but instantly fills me with a guilt I resent him for.

'You're pretty good at doing this,' I offer, gesturing towards his favourite spot in the house.

'Thanks, babe,' he exhales, shuffling in his seat. 'The sofa doesn't give quite as much back. If you know what I mean.'

'You can come with us?' I offer, ignoring his comment. 'I think it'll be at Vic's, so Nick will be there too.'

'Hmm.'

'What?' I frown, wondering when he's gone off the people I love most in the world.

'I'm just wondering how long this is going to go on for,' he asks, looking at his hands. 'You pushing me away. We've had hardly any time together, just us.'

'I'm being a mate.'

'You're going to be my wife,' his eyes flick up to meet mine just as my eyebrows shoot up in surprise.

'And hopefully as my husband you'll be more concerned with my mental health than getting your leg over.'

'I'm not talking about sex, Za, and I am so invested in you and your health, you know that. This is about Mike, though. Not you,' Liam rolls his eyes. 'You're still here, and I'm still here.'

'Well, fucking hurray for that,' I grumble, turning on my heels and heading back up the stairs.

'So should I cancel everything then?' he calls behind me with a sigh.

I don't even bother replying, just stomp my feet a little louder and harder on each step.

When I pick up my phone in my bedroom there's a

voicemail from Vicky to say Mike's up for a night in with us, as long as Liam and Nick don't mind.

'Brilliant. I'm in.' I text her quickly, guessing they're all sitting down to eat at hers now and imagining the chaos.

I'm about to throw the phone back on the bed when a Facebook friend request alert pings up. I click through and see it's from Albie Montague, the new guy at work. We've spoken a handful of times as he's the new Picture Editor and he's wanted to discuss layouts, but nothing remotely personal. He's added me now though and it'll be too awkward if I don't accept him, so I do and then click through to his profile. His picture is something else. Some people go for the relaxed vibe with their mates where they're goofing around and having a laugh, but this is nothing short of Instagram/Tinder/anywhere-you-want-to-impress worthy. It's cropped from mid-chest up, so no one can accuse him of being too revealing, yet it gives just enough to let you know that the full package is probably impressive. Firstly, he doesn't appear to have any clothes on, so you can see the trimmed hairs on his chest which is also home to a curve of scrawling words tattooed in black. His dark eyes look straight at the camera, giving a seriously brooding expression. His beard is groomed to perfection, as is his swooping quiff of highlighted brown hair.

Hey!

Shit, he's inboxed me! I guess I have to reply.

Hey you!

Up to much?

God, he's starting a conversation now . . .

Testing out face masks. It's all going on.

He adds a picture of him with someone who, I assume, is his mum. Both wrapped up in coats with wellies on. A cute little dog running in front of them.

That's great. How have you been finding it at work?

Alright. Not too dissimilar to my last job. Just got to get to grips with the set-up and then get to know everyone now.

Yeah, that'll help you settle in and make you feel more in with the team. Everyone is super nice. There are usually drinks on Thursdays actually. Great time to mingle.

Do you go?

It's an innocent question, surely. Right?

Most of the time.

I'll tag along with you then.

My heart does that funny thing in my chest that I've not felt for years. A rush of adrenaline that's the result of someone else's attention. I really want him to click through to my profile and see I have a fiancé, just to make my situation clear. Although he's not asking me out so perhaps I'm the one being stupid.

Great.

It's a date.

Oh fuck . . . although, it's just an expression, right?

'I'm sorry,' Liam says nervously, poking his head around the door before walking in with two mugs of coffee and holding one out. 'I shouldn't have said any of that and didn't mean it in the slightest.'

'I know you didn't . . .' I say, aware of the guilt knotting in my tummy as I come out of Messenger and push my phone away.

'It's been tough for you and I can't say that's not put a strain on us. I worry.'

'About . . .'

Liam frowns. 'You being OK. We need to make time for each other and talk more.'

I nod in full agreement. Maybe now isn't the right time to tell him I've just agreed to a drink with someone from work. It's just innocent anyway . . . no point mentioning it.

9

Mike

One thing I've learnt about the women in my life, especially at this stage of it – you know, becoming widowed – is that they really don't take no for an answer. Their approach is vastly different to that of the men in my life, AJ and Reece who I've known since infant school, and who seem to be trusting that I'll get in touch when I'm ready to return for a pint and some 'bantz'. Not the women though, they are constantly checking in.

I could tell Vicky was full of purpose and determination when she called offering me their Valentine's evening, and therefore there was no point suggesting they stick to their original plans. They've tried to turn this into more of a 'group' gathering with Nick and Liam there too, but we all know that makes two couples and me. All hanging out on what is the most romantic day ever created to break broken hearts even further. My singledom, my non-plus-one life, my broken heart, is going to cause me to stick out like a sore thumb for quite some time.

I resisted telling her not to bother while insisting I would be fine, because going with it was the easiest option. Plus, what could I say I'd be doing? I have nothing planned and it might be time to actually leave the house for something. I currently have no purpose, whether I'm talking about every other normal day or my dead wife's birthday. Is now the time to create a tradition? Honour her in some way that I'll repeat year on year? I'm not sure. Should I just be getting through this year and kick-starting some big plans to celebrate her life next year? Or is next year too late?

I know the girls are doing this to make sure I'm not on my own, and to keep an eye on me and see how I've been doing. Well, I'm as they left me, I guess. I've not been back to work – my usual employers have told me to take as long as I need – and the visitors and callers have slowly stopped. I've come to realize that grief generates a morbid curiosity in others, creating a huge urge to get in touch and almost claim part of the loss from me. Part of me has enjoyed hearing the tales of Pia I'd not heard before or had perhaps forgotten, but alongside that is the endless list of offers. Offers we all know are empty.

'You will call if you need anything, right,' offers a 'friend' I've not seen since our wedding day.

'Of course,' I reply, knowing full well I won't.

Empty noise, but words that have to be said by them and me regardless. It's part of the act and the roles we must play, because just like every other part of life death comes with a guilt, and an expectation of how to behave. It's never enough to say you're sorry for the loss without feeling like you have to remove the pain or sorrow some-how. The truth is we all know we can't. That empty void of loss cannot be filled, no matter how many well-meaning gestures are thrown into it.

I don't know.

My mind runs through circles and thinks different things daily. All I know is that after the initial shock of death, the wanting to share the pain or 'fix the problem', things go silent. People are waiting for me to start 'moving on'. Whatever that means.

Because of the lull, it's mostly been me in the flat.

Our flat.

Isolation, which I guess is what this has become, has been a cathartic experience. I sit. Sometimes thinking, sometimes not. Then I'll get waves of having to do things.

I wish there was more of her stuff to sort. With her clothes gone I continued with Pia's Rules of Death (I do wish she'd come up with a softer name for it, but I guess it is what it says on the tin) and started tackling the book-shelves, her bills and receipts – transactions for silly things like coffee, salads or our weekly shop, but I devoured every single one. Willing them to trigger a memory and give me something more, bring me back some piece of her no matter how trivial.

Then there was the stationery cupboard, her sewing kit and bric-a-brac box. Stuff I know I'll need and use but that have so much of her pumped throughout them. Even the bright yellow tool kit is the one she brought with her when we first moved in together. It's all her. At some point I have to reclaim it as my own.

I sigh, my fingers forking through my growing hair and rubbing at my scalp.

God, I must look awful.

With my phone still in my hand I lift it up and click through to Instagram, heading straight to Pia's feed. As her smiling face pops up I'm hit with a fresh pang of longing. You wouldn't have known she was as ill as she was. I don't think I really did either. She had this ability to just go for it and push through, never wanting pity or for someone to say she couldn't do something. So she took on every adventure she possibly could. I'd hate to say it, but her diagnosis made her more fearless and headstrong. More adventurous. And not because she wanted to make the most of every second of her life and tick things off her metaphorical bucket list. I think it was actually because she couldn't bear to hear 'no' any more. If she was up and doing then people wouldn't treat her like she was sick and tell her she mustn't do something – because she was doing what even those doctors, specialists and nurses couldn't. She didn't look sick, and so we both just assumed she'd got the upper hand of her illness. But cancer isn't a game and it's not about winners and losers. There is just life or death. All or nothing.

I shake my heart of the hurt surrounding the final posts made to her account – one I had to post to report the news – and scroll down, heading to happier times, before cancer entered our lives and changed everything.

I enlarge a photo she posted on our seventh anniversary ten years ago. It's the two of us on the night we met at an under-eighteens' disco – which I remember being taken on a disposable camera at the end of the night. We were fifteen and had therefore spent the previous hour snogging each other's faces off, but not really talking. I'm not even sure I knew her name by this point – I just thought she was incredibly 'fit' and surprised she allowed me to spend time with her. I remember thinking she looked classy and cool in her glittery black dress that clung to her tiny frame. I was wearing my standard Ben Sherman chequered shirt and jeans. It was 'the look'. Under-eighteens' discos were essentially loads of kids pretending to be grown-ups – something I'm sure was helped along by the bottles of hooch we were all secretly swigging from when the adults weren't looking, or had 'downed' before getting in.

I remember her best mate at the time, Rachel I think her name was, capturing this photo of us just as we were about to say goodbye. The lights had been turned back on then, and even in those days, it felt like a sharp comeback to reality. I was just relieved she still talked to me when my spotty chin wasn't being disguised in the dim lighting.

She still reached up for a kiss goodbye, her slender arms draped over my shoulders and pulling me towards her.

'Can I have your number?' I asked between kisses, my voice doing that embarrassing thing where it bounces between octaves.

'You give me yours,' she insisted, pulling away. With that statement I thought I'd blown it, believing that by her having mine she could ghost me when she started seeing sense. Later on I realized it was so that I couldn't do the same to her.

We spent the next three years seeing each other on Saturdays or Sundays around our weekend jobs in Romford – I worked in HMV, which always sounded far cooler than it actually was, and she worked in Clinton Cards. We'd meet for lunch and share a bag of Dinky Donuts as we walked around the market, and then maybe met again for a cheeky snog after work before being picked up by our parents. Her Indian family never really seemed to mind that Pia was hanging around with a white Jewish boy, although it took my mum a while to get her head around the path my life was taking – and how it differed to what she'd hoped for me. She got there. I imagine they all thought it was going to be a short romance. A young crush that we'd quickly step away from broken-hearted before finding ourselves with partners who aligned with their dreamy visions for their offspring – an Indian guy for her, and a Jewish girl for me.

What actually happened was that we both applied for the same university in Brighton. Pia aced her exams and got on to her art course as planned. I didn't quite get the grades I needed and so after an anxious wait to see whether I'd get through in clearing I had the disappointing call to say the places had been taken and that I could try again the following year. That was never going to happen. Instead I upped my hours at HMV and started taking a distance-learning course in media studies while teaching myself how to edit my own content, only pausing for the odd kick-about with AJ, who'd decided to go straight into the family building company, and Reece, who'd decided to take a year out without any plans to actually do something with that time. He eventually went to Ibiza the following summer before his dad forced him into getting a job. He's now a postie in the area we grew up.

Learning away from a classroom wasn't quite how I wanted to pick up my skills, but it taught me to go off instinct rather than wait for a teacher to tell me I was 'right'. It was a move that eventually led to me becoming a freelance videographer, my employers mostly being big brands who want to create sponsored content with popular people online. On the whole they allow me to be as creative as I like with their chosen talent as long as it fits the brief, but the benefit in recent years was that it gave us the freedom to travel between jobs, and for me to press pause when needed.

Thinking back to Pia's uni days though, I'm reminded of the pang of jealousy I'd feel whenever I'd see her around all her student mates. They were living this whole other independent life away from their parents and could just do whatever they pleased, when they pleased. I still had to let Mum know what time I'd be home for dinner BUT I was still an outsider who drove in and out in his car, and was able to offer her mates discounts on all the new music releases when I was there.

Because we were only getting to see each other weekly before she left for uni it didn't seem like such a huge deal to be doing the same when she was there. We found a balance and made plans to move in together as soon as she was done with her studies, and figured moving closer into London would be fun. When we eventually started looking we quickly realized how expensive it was going to be, so looked into doing a flat share of some sort. That's when we stumbled across Vicky who had found a spacious three-bedroom flat in Hackney and needed people to fill it. Little did we know that flat would bring us two of our best friends: Vicky, who seems to have always had a maternal organized streak; and Zaza, who used to love a party. A year in and we knew we'd stick together for longer, although we did all decide to travel west to somewhere a bit greener, and cheaper. That's how we stumbled upon Ealing.

My attention moves back to the squares on my phone, each one triggering a new memory, a new thought. I flick past a few, looking at the images in detail before devouring the words she'd pieced together underneath. Somehow the love of my life seems closer and further from me than ever before.

My chest hurts and I find myself wondering if any of the old songs are true. Can you actually die of a broken heart? Is that a thing? A part of me definitely died with Pia, and I don't know what to do with what is left.

Who am I without her?

What do I want to do with my life if she's not in it? Because from the age of fifteen she has been in every single one of my future plans. I met and married the woman of my dreams and we agreed to spend the rest of our lives committed to each other, loving each other and bringing out the best in one another.

What am I meant to do now she's gone?

Is this who I am now? Have I lived all the joy my life had to offer me? Did it compact down into those seventeen years we shared? Am I meant to have already filled my boots?

Am I destined to long for her to be back here with me for the rest of my life? Will I forever be known as 'the widower'? Will this grief become who I am?

Is this my life now?

Is this it?

10

Vicky

'Right, come on then. In the car, both of you,' I say, with Chloe in my arms and the other hand holding the millions of things Barnaby apparently needs at school today. We're already late and I've no idea how when we were all woefully up at five-thirty this morning so have had ample time to get our shit together. I try to get to the car key so that I can unlock it but it's underneath all of the school crap. I try to wriggle my hand and unlock it using the button on the handle, but that's no use either. I dump Barnaby's stuff on the ground with a thump. 'No, Barnaby!' I shout a little too loudly as he absentmindedly walks towards the road. 'Stay by the wall or the fence. Come on,' I say, clicking the button and unlocking the car. 'Actually, you stay here, right next to me,' I say, swinging open the back door of the car and putting Chloe into her seat before strapping her in. She's used to the madness of the morning routine now so grabs her horses from the toy rack thingumijiggy that hangs off the back of the seat in front and starts playing.

'Right, you next,' I say to Barnaby, making a mental note not to forget all the things I've left on the pavement.

With my hand on his shoulder – I'm forever paranoid about my kids and roads – I walk a couple of paces to the back of the car only to notice the car behind, a flashy sports car, is practically touching my bumper. 'This way then,' I say, guiding him back to the front.

The car in front, a four-by-four, isn't as close, but it's close enough that I'd have to sidestep my way through and probably lean over my bonnet in a way teen films or music videos suggest is sexy – which is a pretty inappropriate thought to have stood next to my five-year-old at eight-fifty in the morning.

Who on earth would think it was OK to park this close to another car and just swan off without a care in the world? I'll tell you who. Commuters. Definitely not the locals. Just some posh city twats who have parked and walked to the station.

Now is not the time to get stressed about it, I tell myself.

'OK, you'll have to climb over Chloe,' I instruct, shoving him back the way we came and opening her door.

'My bag!' Barnaby calls.

'Shit, yes,' I mutter to myself, closing the door and scooping up the lot before getting into the driver's seat and parking everything on the passenger seat beside me. 'Is your seatbelt on, Barns?'

'Yeeeeeeeeeees,' he trills, just as I hear the click to confirm it.

'Great. Let's do this then.'

My sensors start kicking off as soon as I turn on the engine. I know there's no way I can go backwards first so hard steer and edge forwards. It feels like I've only moved a few centimetres before I get the flatline noise of the sensors telling me they're serious and to back up. I listen. Hard steer the other way, then reverse. Inches, flatline. I repeat the motions over and over, aware that I'm getting hotter.

'Bloody twats!' I mutter, hitting the steering wheel in defeat.

'We're still at home, Mummy!' shouts Chloe.

'I'm going to be late!' exclaims Barnaby, as though missing the register and having to go to reception to sign in instead is the worst thing in the world.

'It's OK,' I lie. 'And it's not your fault at all!'

I can only keep up the pretence for a couple of minutes longer before I switch off the engine.

'We'll walk!' I tell them with as much joy in my voice as I can muster. Thankfully Chloe's buggy and coat are both in the boot and I don't have to run into the house to get them. I press the button to release the boot and run out to grab it, only to hear it bang into the flashy sports car behind. It's not a massive bang – not big enough to cause a dent – but enough to anger the beast and set off its alarm.

Curtains around me twitch as neighbours peep out to see what's caused the early-morning commotion.

Taking a breath, I go back to the driver's seat and edge the car forward the few inches the four-by-four has afforded me. I then jump out, go back to the boot and grab the buggy, before swiftly putting it up with a one-handed flick like the bad-ass mother that I am (am trying my hardest to be) and then open Chloe's door to retrieve her.

'Not coming,' she insists, shaking her head, shrinking herself back into her seat.

'Come on,' I sing, quickly realizing that she won't be happy with this change of plan as I reach for the clasp of her seatbelt.

'NO!' she shouts, batting my hand away.

'Chloe, please don't do this,' I say quietly, willing the heavens to open up and shower me with patience. 'We need to get Barns to school, then we can go and have some fun.'

'Cold!' she barks.

'I've got your coat and a blanket. You'll be as snug as a bug.'

'Noooooooooooooooooooooooo!' she shouts at the top of her lungs, the sound just managing to cover up the shrill of the car alarm that's still blaring.

My mind goes to the twitching curtains and pictures my neighbours looking out and judging.

'It's time to get out of the car.'

She shakes her hand profusely.

'I'm going to be so late,' Barnaby mumbles, my heart aching as his bottom lip starts to wobble.

I watch Chloe as she turns her head and frowns at him.

'Come on,' I say, unfurling her stubborn little fingers and pushing the release button.

'Mummy, no!' she screams, but I have her now.

I pull her arms towards me and guide my surprisingly heavy toddler out of the car towards the awaiting buggy. As I start lowering her into it, it starts rolling backwards in a protest of its own.

I didn't put the sodding brakes on.

I place my foot behind the front wheel to wedge it in place. It still pivots so I have to clamp my knees around it at the same time, all while Chloe screams and tries to wriggle out of my arms.

I clamp her into the chair with my forearm while I quickly get her securely into the harness – not the easiest job when she pulls a limb back out as soon as I go to sort another. It's like something out of a comedy sketch, although not at all funny from where I'm standing having a full-on mum sweat.

When she's finally in I look up to see a young couple walking past with a look of horror on their faces.

'Something to look forward to,' I say to them, deciding, quite sensibly, to take my frustration out on them in a calm, passive-aggressive manner rather than on my banshee wailing child.

They scurry by in a hurry but I'm still snarling in their direction when I order Barnaby out of the car and get moving towards school, away from the prying eyes of judgemental neighbours and the car alarm that seems as persistent as my daughter.

It's a twenty-five minute walk. Chloe cries the whole way, despite me offering her snacks or, as a very last resort, my phone to take pictures on. I've ruined her morning/day/life and she wants the world to suffer as a result.

'Come on, Barnaby,' I hear myself snap when he can't keep up with my ridiculously charged pace. The guilt hits me instantly as I recognize, like with the strangers, I'm taking my frustrations out elsewhere. It's not his fault the twats blocked our car in, or that we're late, or that his sister is acting so irrationally. 'You're doing so well,' I cheer at his crestfallen face. 'You're so fast. Look at those legs.' As his face looks up at mine with pride my heart hurts.

We march into school, the gates abandoned and the playground completely empty, and head straight to reception to sign him in. Chloe has, thankfully, been distracted by her own shoe so the howling has momentarily subsided, but who knows when it might kick off again.

'Oh dear,' tuts the receptionist Miss Holmes with her arms folded across her chest and her head cocked to one side. 'Did we struggle to get out of bed today, Barnaby? Or was it Mummy who didn't want to get out from under her duvet?'

'Haha . . .' I smile tightly. 'I wish.'

'It wasn't my fault, Miss,' Barnaby pleads with wide-eyed innocence. 'It was the bloody twats.'

'Barnaby! We don't say things like that!' I gasp in shock and horror – at the fact he'd heard and remembered my own words, and then that he's repeated it at this unfortunate moment. 'I'm sorry,' I whisper to Miss Holmes, who is looking less than impressed. 'I don't usually swear around them. Not really . . . they do say kids have brains like sponges, though. I guess this proves it,' I say, chucking in something I hope sounds like a laugh.

'Right . . . just sign him in here,' she says, turning the register to face me so that I can sign where she's written a capital L in red.

'It's just, my husband's away on business so it's been quite full on and then we got blocked in so had to walk and –'

'Just sign and then I'll take Barnaby down to his class-room,' she says with a sickly sweet smile.

I do as she says and then turn to my son who, thank-fully, seems to have brushed off his faux pas with ease as he's now fidgeting and ready to get to class.

'Big kiss,' I say, leaning in for our usual squeeze and peck on the lips.

He smiles back at me then holds out his hand.

I look at it.

He shakes it and frowns.

'What?'

'Bag!' he laughs.

My heart drops. The sodding school stuff that I was so worried about leaving on the path has been left in the car – not only meaning I've let down my son again, but a clear indication to burglars that I'm a bit of a scatter-brain who might leave valuables alongside a PE kit and year 1 exercise books.

'I'm so sorry, Barnaby.'

His eyebrows shoot up in disbelief and disappointment as his mouth drops in horror.

'We'll sort you out, don't worry, Barnaby. I have a lovely notebook you can borrow for the day. I write all my spells in it,' Miss Holmes giggles in his direction, an air of something less pleasing coming towards me.

'You OK, Barns?' I ask softly, kissing his forehead and rubbing his deliciously soft cheeks.

He nods and shows me his powerful brave face, the one where his smile doesn't quite reach up to his eyes, as Miss Holmes drapes an arm over his shoulder and starts guiding him to class. 'Say bye bye Mummy,' she says without looking at me.

'Love you, Barney,' I say, my face still full of regret and guilt.

'Love you,' he mumbles loud enough for me just to catch it.

I stand rooted to the spot, watching him go, feeling like the world's worst mother. I know it's just a bag. I know I'm not neglecting him or mistreating him. I know I keep my kids fed, clothed, clean and safe – and that all they really need to feel is my love – but this seems like such a massive failure. I feel like I'm failing them constantly. Every day is a never-ending list of things to do and achieve, and that list is too long.

Getting the kids up (which is not too much of a hassle seeing as Chloe is up at five and desperate to wake up Barnaby), giving them both breakfast (while dodging the flying pieces of fruit, toast, and – if I'm really lucky – spoonfuls of Weetabix), getting them dressed (making sure both children will be warm enough, not too hot, or that they are in the right clothes), brushing teeth (whilst having a wrestle), putting on shoes and socks (whilst having a wrestle), leaving the house and getting into the car seat or pram (whilst having a wrestle), getting to school on time – and that's all before 8:55! Then there's the washing, the cooking, the after-school clubs and the mum politics, the homework, the tidying up, the guilt that I'm not talking to them enough, the guilt that they're not outside enough, or stimulated enough – or over-stimulated if I've let them play after dinner instead of enforcing some chilled reading time. Then there's witching hour, then more story time, followed by the toothbrush horror of overtired minors, all before finally wrestling them into bed and trying to ignore the continuous calls for me to go back in, yet failing miserably.

Some days it can feel like I'm failing before I've begun – while other days can make me think I'm doing amazingly and then bedtime will fall apart due to one of them being hyper, or refusing to get out of the bath, or brush their teeth, or sit still for a story, or just constantly bickering – all causing me to lose my shit and resulting in me weeping in the darkness on my child's floor while willing them to sleep.

If it was just Barnaby, I think I'd be a better mother. Should I admit that? Not out loud, obviously. It was my desire to have another child. Nick was happy with the one but I argued that it was barbaric. My little boy needed a home-grown friend to play with. I didn't realize I'd be giving birth to the devil's actual side-kick . . .

I look down at Chloe, who is calmly fiddling with the zip on her coat, and feel awful. She's not that bad . . . she's just a three-year-old who is learning.

To be truthful the real kick in the teeth comes at the end of the day, once I've juggled the kids and been pushed to my limits. Nick will come in the door wondering what's for dinner as he looks around our newly tidied house, clearly wondering what I've done all day as he relaxes and allows me to take care of him like the domesticated woman I am.

Mum, wife, mum, wife, mum, wife. It's relentless.

When did I lose myself in motherhood and wifedom? When did I stop just looking after my own basic needs? Did I ever look after them?

Life was varied and exciting once. Now it's about getting through the day in the most guilt-free way possible – which simply leads to more guilt being produced. My life has become a hamster wheel. I have to keep going or I'll tumble out in a rather unladylike fashion. There's no other option.

With Barnaby long gone, I steer Chloe out of the school and head towards the library – hoping we'll be able to catch their weekly story time slot.

I walk, with my head in a daze, wondering why this maternal side I was told I possessed doesn't always seem to come into play naturally, why sometimes motherhood feels like a list of things to get through rather than enjoy and savour. I thought I was going to be a fun mum, full of joy and spontaneity. Instead I just bark at my kids and ferry them around.

There's no thanks for the hours I put in, no gratitude for my unconditional love or understanding over how tough it can be. Just judgement, failure and guilt.

I can't help but feel broken over what my life has become. All because of one thought that loops in my brain continuously: Is this it?

I I

Zaza

I switch my alarm off and enjoy stretching out last night's dreams. I adore mornings. That heaviness that sits on your body following hours of sleepy nothingness, of being allowed to just be and rest. At the weekend I could laze in that dreamy state for hours – enjoying the sheets on my skin and the relaxing softness of a new day. Weekdays are a little different as I have work, but I like getting myself prepped and styled for the day and creating 'the look'. I have never been the sort to chuck something on without giving it great thought – the joy of getting creative is the only thing that ensures I leave the house clothed.

I roll over and am greeted with an empty spot next to me. Liam is usually snoring when I get up to start my morning routine so he must've snuck out of bed early without me realizing. A waft of something sweet and buttery cooking drifts up the stairs.

Of course, it's Valentine's Day. Ever since our big chat about having to make more time for each other Liam's been putting in a lot of effort. He's hardly picked up his game controller to play FIFA, not if I'm home, and instead he's been cooking, planning and proactive – he's been present and keen. Wanting to talk about my day, asking how I'm feeling and whether we should book a weekend away for the two of us.

He is all in.

Days like today are a reminder that it's nice to wake up loved and wanted. It's nice to have someone there to care for you.

I hear Liam on the stairs seconds before he pops his head around the door. He's already dressed. Completely ready in a suit – the fitted green one he knows is my favourite because it brings out the swirly brown of his eyes, with his dark hair swooped up to perfection.

'Breakfast,' he grins, walking in with a wooden tray – the smell of his familiar aftershave subtly drifting in with him. Funny how a smell can instantly give you an attack of the senses. Suddenly switching parts of you on that were fast asleep mere moments before.

'You've gone all out,' I grin, aware how much I fancy him in this moment and thankful that he's gone to the extra effort.

'I couldn't have you feeling we didn't celebrate,' Liam says, putting the tray down on my lap before his finger gently lifts up my chin for a kiss. Our lips cushion together in the familiar way they have for years.

His eyes glimmer and shine as they smile back at my own.

'Thank you,' I smile, looking down at his offering. 'Oh wow!' He really has gone all out. Come to think of it,

I've no idea where he's dug this wooden tray out from, but on top of one of the 'best' plates he's stacked six mini pancakes into a tower. He's then spooned coconut yoghurt and drizzled maple syrup over the top along with blueberries and delicate flowers that have been perfectly placed in the cascading liquid that drips down the tower's sides. A little jar has been filled with tiny vibrant flowers that add another pop of colour to the tray. It's the most stunning breakfast in bed I've ever had – not that I've been offered many. 'Did you have a Pinterest board to guide you?'

'Might've googled for a bit of inspiration,' he laughs. 'Coffee art needs a bit of work though,' he adds, his nose twitching at the turquoise mug that holds the results of his efforts. It's not exactly barista level, but I can clearly see where he's tried to create a heart shape.

'Better than I could do! I need to take a picture,' I giggle, grabbing my phone from my bedside and unplugging it before lifting it above his beautiful creation.

I quickly post it to Instagram with a hint of Lark filter, then pop a simple heart emoji and #valentinesday in the copy.

'Practice run,' Liam chuckles, sidling up next to me with his own tray that looks just as good as mine.

'Thank you,' I say, putting the phone away.

'Anything for you,' he beams, taking his phone out of his pocket and quickly pulling up some music – James Bay's 'Us' starts playing softly, another reminder. Another pull to my fiancé and intimate moments we've shared. I smile at the memory of two years ago. We'd met up for dinner after work and decided to walk along the South Bank towards Borough Market. Along the way there was a busker standing, guitar in hand, eyes closed, completely lost in the music he was playing. Hand in hand we stood and listened, then, with a gentle bend of the wrist, Liam guided me into his arms and we danced in the twinkly lights of the river, lost and found all at once. We searched for the original song on the way home, and even though nothing would ever quite beat the magic of the mystery player we stumbled across, I'm still aware of my heart softening as soon as I hear it.

'All good?' he asks, sitting close enough for our shoulders to touch.

'Absolutely,' I say, holding out my fork to his so we can chink them together – a gesture that's become our tradition whenever there's an absence of alcohol at a mealtime. I can't even remember when that became a thing or even the first time we did it. A first I can't remember . . .

We sit and eat. It's delicious so I make groans of delight with every bite which makes Liam laugh. He looks so pleased with himself. He really is so very sweet. This is all very romantic and everything my single self from years ago would've longed for.

As soon as the cutlery returns to the plate after the last bite has been eaten, Liam takes the tray and plate away from me and puts it to one side.

He swivels on the spot, undoing the buttons of his suit jacket slowly, his eyes on me. One shoulder free, then the other, then the jacket is removed. The tie is pulled free in one practised move – but I'm with him before he gets to the top button of his shirt, taking over the undressing, longing for his body to be as naked as my own. Hoping for this to feel exciting and full of surprises, desperate for it to erase the doubt that's been lingering. Wanting to crush its power and anchor me where I'm meant to be – because surely this is exactly what Liam has tried to do this morning – remind me.

It seems both of us are clinging on, trying to pull me back. I run my fingers through his hair and tug at it. I don't want this to be nice. I need to feel the passion and know this can make me feel alive. I need to want him.

*

When I was single it seemed that everything on 14 February was geared towards making me feel pathetically alone. Today, I don't feel that. I don't feel that crushing ache of longing to have someone else validate my existence, but I'm aware there is something tingling away at my emotions. I thought a life-partner would leave me feeling completely fulfilled, but this year the lonely hearts day has turned my thoughts to the things I might be giving up.

Earlier was good. It was the best sex Liam and I have had in ages and made me realize an oxytocin hit was hugely needed. I definitely still fancy him and am so grateful that he knows what he's doing in the bedroom and I'm not having to retell a guy what I like, or go along with it out of politeness (I never did – I always gently nudged them in the right direction and if they weren't interested in getting that right then I wasn't willing to compromise). Those are the major perks of being with someone I totally know and love – and who gets how my body works. So what is it that's causing me to doubt what I have, or make me wonder if a happily ever after is actually what I want?

Regardless of what my head is doing I float into work – which could be because of the good shag and the explosion of endorphins, but heavily helped along by the gorgeous burnt orange Ganni maxi dress I've teamed up with white pumps and a little leather jacket. A wave of satisfaction washes over me when I swoosh passed Albie's desk and see him double-take in my direction. I smile back, reprimanding myself as I continue walking. The messages have continued since the weekend. All just light and polite with the occasional flirty line thrown in, but it's only harmless. Truth is I've been enjoying the back and forth and dipping a toe into the unknown – it's nothing, just banter.

Liam and I don't really do banter any more. We're beyond the stage where we message each other throughout the day about the banal and ridiculous. We let each other get on with our jobs knowing we'll catch up in the evening over dinner and wine. In fact, if it were Liam contacting me this much it would be irritating when he's aware of how busy I am and how much I have to get done each day.

A hefty stack of parcels awaits me as I arrive at my

desk, causing my stomach to perform an excited flip. Valentine's Day means a lot to beauty brands and they do all they can to spread the love (and secure some extra coverage in the mag) when there's a clear celebration to get behind. Valentine's Day is obviously a big one, but so is the whole of December where each day feels like someone's raided Selfridges and dumped the loot on my desk – for we all know people love to spruce themselves up and add to the glamour at the endless festive parties and for New Year shenanigans. Alongside those and Mother's Day (oh yes, I still get flowers, lipsticks and facial offers even though I don't have my own children), Easter and Festival season (not exactly a day but people love playing with their looks over the summer months), I've also in the past had deliveries for National Hat Day, Pizza Day, Random Acts of Kindness Day, and Just Because Day – and that's as well as the steady stream of PR gifts that arrive daily to alert me to a new shade, formulation or product in a line. It's endless but I never complain. Yes, I know there are only so many creams a girl can use, but walking in and seeing a Bobbi Brown, Charlotte Tilbury or Jo Malone bag perched prettily on my desk does fill me with joy. I like things, and I don't think that necessarily makes me a bad person. I appreciate them and devour them. It's part of my job.

Today, though, we're having a beauty sale at lunch because my storage cupboard is beginning to look more like disorganized chaos rather than the beautifully functioning beauty showroom I need it to be. I've cleared out the excess lipsticks, eye shadows, foundations, mascaras, nail varnishes and every lotion and potion you can think of and they'll all be laid out for the rest of the office to forage through and donate money for whatever they take. I've chosen Smalls for All to raise for this year, an organization which collects and distributes underwear to help women and children in Africa. I quite liked the idea of raising money on this day that's so heavily associated with new underwear being for fruity time in the bedroom, and giving that essential item to those in need instead.

Before I can tackle the deliveries I start up my computer and click through to an article I've been piecing together for the next issue, a feature on the ageless cat flick along with reviews of different eyeliners available to perfect the look. I sent out little packs around the office for people to try, and funnily enough the cheapest option outperformed the designer brand, something I know our readers will love.

Happy with the wording I then forward it to be edited and puzzled together with the correct images, which really bring the pieces I write and curate to life. This bit of my job is fiddly, but with so many different products constantly flying around, thankfully I'm always super organized. It doesn't take long to gather what's needed.

'I've got some pages for you to approve,' Albie says, breaking my flow while slowly sliding papers across the desk in front of me.

'Oh,' I startle.

He lingers.

'Thank you,' I mutter, feeling my cheeks blush as his thigh brushes against my arm. I shuffle in my seat and rearrange the fabric of my dress.

'A group of us are going out later if you want to join us?' he suggests.

I look up to see him staring at me hopefully.

'Oh, I have a thing. With my mates,' I start, not wanting to go in-depth about Pia and suddenly not so pleased with this situation. Chatting over Messenger feels different to whatever this is in the flesh.

'You mean he forgot?' Albie asks, looking at me incredulously. 'That's a lazy sackable offence, surely? He's getting too comfortable now he's put a ring on it,' he states, finding himself hilarious even though he knows nothing about our situation. I don't really want to tell him that Liam is also coming with me, even if he is being slightly dragged along for the night.

A frown is all I manage before my phone starts buzzing next to me, with Vicky's name flashing on the screen along with a silly photo of her wearing the biggest grin.

'Sorry, got to get this. Enjoy your night,' I say with a smile, then grab my phone and swivel away from him on my chair, aware of him pausing before walking away.

'One night. I just wanted one fucking night put in his diary,' Vicky says, her voice full of hurt and exasperation. 'I wanted him back early, but now he's going to be back late – super late, so I'm going to have to put the kids to bed first. I just wanted him to be here to ease the pressure and help out.'

'We can help out.'

'It's not that. I do it on my own every night. I just wanted things to be calm and make things easier.'

'I don't know what you're talking about, your house is always calm.'

'Oh very funny!'

'OK, OK. Look, he's going to be home a little later. That's fine,' I reason. 'We'll be downstairs waiting for you with a big glass of wine. It's only us. It doesn't matter.'

'But it does.'

'Vic, it's one night,' I press. 'All that matters is that we're together for it.'

In the pause from the other end of the line I hear Vicky's breathing start to slow down.

'Do you promise to make the glass of wine a large one?' she asks.

'Exceptionally so.'

'Perfect.'

Once she's off the phone I quickly text Liam with the update.

> Bad news, Nick has to work late.

It doesn't take long for him to reply.

> Bummer. I'll leave the three of you to it then. ;-)

> You don't need to do that!

I'm wondering whether his hesitancy is down to him simply not knowing how to be around the three of us right now and the relief of being 'let off the hook' or really thinking us mates need to work out what our new normal is without him hopping around in the background.

I absolutely do. Say hi to them both. Love you. xx

You too. Xx

12

Mike

I expected to feel reluctant walking towards Vicky's door. This is the first significant 'day of note' without Pia. After lunch with my parents and in-laws, where I couldn't eat much due to the intensity of the day, I thought I would be shattered and wondering if I could duck out of the whole thing and sit in the darkness of the flat instead – succumbing to the emptiness. Yet I feel buoyed along by the bag in my hand. As a result of more clearing, and Pia's parents doing their own rummage at theirs, I'm in possession of more Pia. A pile of photos showing her doing the things she loved – from the daft to the inspiring. I think it'll be a nice talking point and I'd hate Pia to become the elephant in the room. Maybe it'll break off any awkwardness with Liam and Nick, who probably aren't too enthusiastic about me trudging through their plans, and let them know it's OK to talk about her.

I hear the noise before I even set foot on Vicky's doorstep. She's screeching, as is Chloe. It sounds like total carnage in there. I hear the sound of the doorbell alerting them to the fact I've arrived. Silence follows from inside, then the thumping of feet running down the stairs.

'Mike! Come in, love,' Vicky beams, throwing open the door with the biggest forced grin on her face I've ever seen. Her hair has formed a nest on top of her head and her face is flushed – but that smile is cemented on.

'All good?' I ask, glancing past her towards the eerily quiet stairs, surprised the kids haven't come down yet, seeing as they're clearly awake.

'Absolutely,' she beams in reply, grabbing my arm and pulling me into the house. 'Nick's not back yet. He's had to work late. Drink?'

I take my shoes off and follow her into the kitchen, noticing the white wine she's already tucking into.

'Long day?'

'Same old,' she almost cackles. 'Wine or beer?'

'Beer, please!'

'No prob–' She's stopped in her tracks by the sound of Chloe screaming from upstairs, which despite hearing the commotion before coming in, makes me leap out of my skin.

'Muuuuuuuuuuuuuuuuummy! Mummy! Muuuuu-ummy!!' she wails.

Vicky's smile wavers. Her eyes close as she visibly steels herself. 'Sorry, help yourself. I've just got to –'

'Go! No worries,' I say.

'Thanks,' she smiles, reaching for one last mouthful of wine before shuffling out of the room and up the stairs where I hear her trying to hiss instructions over Chloe's protests.

I grab a beer and neck half of the bottle. Crazy to

think our lives are so different when we spent years living together, living the same life.

My thoughts are interrupted by the doorbell.

'I'll get it,' I call up the stairs, not entirely sure if Vicky can even hear me over the noise being made.

'I love them but . . .' Zaza is stood with her hands over her ears, a grimace on her screwed-up face.

'Happy Valentine's!' I laugh, throwing open my arms to welcome her in.

'Put like that I have to say I've had worse,' she declares, dropping her act and happily strutting in.

'Just you?' I ask.

'Yes. Liam had a . . . thing,' she shrugs. 'Come on.' I watch as she starts making her way up the stairs.

'No! I don't think we should interfere,' I whisper, pleading.

Zaza stops halfway up, swivelling in my direction. 'The only people that say that are the ones who think they could do a better job while they sit there judging, so get your arse up here now.'

'I just . . .'

'You get Barns, I'll sort Chloe.'

'Deal,' I concede, putting my beer on the side before taking the stairs two at a time.

'How are my favourite little humans?' Zaza asks with a huge smile on her face, leaping into their room like everyone's favourite children's entertainer.

Both kids have their arms around her waist by the time I'm through the door. It's a sweet sight, although you wouldn't think so by the look on Vic's face. Still kneeling by Chloe's bed, she looks bereft, broken and on the brink of tears. She busies herself by clearing the books and toys that clutter up the floor.

'Are you having a sleepover?' asks Chloe, her blotchy face looking up at Zaza.

'Not tonight.'

'Oh!' she moans.

'But, Mike and I thought we'd read you both bedtime stories tonight. You have to promise to get into bed and pretend you're super good children who listen to big children though.'

Barnaby and Chloe steal a look at each other before running to their adjacent beds and getting under their duvets – one covered in unicorns, the other intergalactically inspired.

'You, in the shower,' she orders Vicky. 'We've got this.'

'You don't have to,' says Vicky, holding on to the bed frame as she gets off the ground.

'We want to,' I say.

Vicky glances from us to her kids who are now looking more than angelic.

'Thanks, guys,' she says before turning to the kids with a whisper. 'You two listen to Aunty Zaza and Uncle Mike. I'll be back in a bit.'

'Of course they will – we're the novelty act,' Zaza says with a gentle laugh.

'Yeah,' Vicky sighs. 'I won't be long.'

'OK, Barnaby. I'm thinking space!' I say, heading to

his side of the room that's full of planets, stars and rockets.

'Yes! This one!' he sings, holding a book above his head and shuffling over on the bed.

'Are you reading or am I?'

He considers the question before replying with a smile. 'I'll read. You chillax.'

He bashes the space on the pillow beside his head, gesturing for me to join him.

'Fair enough,' I laugh, doing as he says and getting comfy. 'Chillaxing it is, but I do snore, so you're going to have to make this interesting.'

'Some good voices?'

'Yes, please!' I say, hearing Zaza and Chloe get started on their own book about a pooping dinosaur.

No wonder Barnaby didn't want me to read, he's a better reader than I am. He didn't hesitate once, even over the nerdy space words that I definitely would've pronounced wrong. I sit beside him with a grin on my face. Astounded by the brilliance of this little boy who was actually grown by one of my mates. He's a walking miracle.

By the time he's done Zaza has joined us to listen, continuously throwing proud aunty looks my way. Chloe fell asleep on the last word of her book, even though she'd been giggling a few pages before, and I hadn't realized that being older Barnaby would be on chapter books. This particular chapter seems to be the longest any author has thought into existence, but luckily, for tonight at least, he has a captive audience hanging on his every word.

When he finishes he grabs his bookmark, carefully popping it in the book before placing it on his bedside table.

'Thank you, Barns,' smiles Zaza, giving him a squeeze while wearing a look full of admiration. She stands up and checks once more on Chloe, who has already wriggled free of her covers.

'You really are one smart kid,' I declare to Barnaby.

'I'll read to you any time, Uncle Mike,' he offers, looking incredibly pleased with himself.

'Night, Barnaby,' I say, leaning in to give him a kiss on the head.

He rolls over and turns off his lamp. As Zaza and I make to go his voice speaks quietly in the darkness.

'Do you think she's having cake today?'

I stop in my tracks as a lump of emotion forms in my throat, a pang of elation suddenly hitting that she's been remembered by him. 'The biggest cake you can imagine,' I manage to whisper.

'And balloons!' adds Zaza.

'That's nice . . .' the duvet rustles as he turns and cosies into his bed, happy with our answers.

Zaza and I take an audible breath at the same time before leaving the room, bumping into Vicky on the landing, looking refreshed.

'No! Already?' she says. 'Can you come back every night?'

'God no,' Zaza jokes, leading us down the stairs. 'I owe you a large wine.'

'I'm already on it,' Vicky laughs, heading into the kitchen where she gets a glass out for Zaza. 'You can be in charge of the music instead. Nothing soppy. Let's go for some classic anthems. Do you need another, Mike?'

'Yes, please!' I say, just as the doorbell rings again. 'Nick back?'

'Not likely. He's been busier than ever since coming back from LA,' tuts Vicky.

'Oh. Just us then?' I realize.

'Lucky us,' she winks. 'I ordered us some food.'

'I'll go!' I say, walking out of the room and wondering if it being the three of us was the plan all along or really has happened by chance. I'm not fussed either way but hope Liam and Nick aren't pissed off at me for pinching their other halves. They've each sent the odd text now and again to check in. More so than some of my other mates, actually, but I imagine they can't step away from the situation like the others can when they're living with women so linked to my grief.

When I get to the front door it is indeed a delivery guy instead of Nick, and the waft of curry coming from the brown paper bags as he passes them over makes my mouth water. Carrying them through the house my stomach gives an almighty growl at the idea of being fed imminently – something that's not been happening much recently.

'I hope you guys have got the plates ready, because

otherwise I'm going to gnaw through the bags!' I say, carrying them through.

'Sit!' Vicky orders, gesturing to the table she's magically laid in the twenty seconds I was gone.

We don't bother with any small talk, instead we focus on getting the food out, plated up and in our gobs. The sound of Virgin Radio fills the room. Only when we're groaning from excess do we chat.

'God, I remember in the early days of meeting Nick – I'd literally eat like a sparrow.'

'Why?' I ask.

'I thought it would impress him, or that it made me look good in some way. Nice girls don't stuff their faces . . .'

'And look at you now,' laughs Zaza.

'This is what comfy looks like . . . and it might just be the most I've ever eaten on Valentine's since we first got together. I really hope Nick isn't after some later, because I feel like a happy bloated seal right now, not a . . .' She stops, allowing laughter to spill out. 'God, what's sexier than a seal?'

'Lost your metaphor?' I guffaw. 'Gosh, a sexy animal. Hmmm . . . I'm not really into that but at a stretch maybe a penguin?' I jest.

'I guess it really depends what Nick's into,' chimes in Zaza, attempting to keep a straight face but losing herself in giggles too.

'Is he more of a safari-type man or are sea creatures actually his thing?' I add.

We laugh. The sound of laughter making us giggle, cackle and snort some more. I laugh so hard my stomach hurts from the sudden use, breathing is difficult and tears stream down my face.

'Aaah . . .' we sigh in unison, the laughter slowly petering out before rising once more and then falling.

'Oh laughter, how I've missed you!' I smile into my beer, taking a happy swig – perhaps tipsier than I thought. 'I have some things to show you before we get hammered and can't see them properly.'

I jump to the kitchen side and grab my bag, bringing it back to the girls.

'It's not a seal outfit, is it?' laughs Za.

'I have a feeling we're going to be searching for sexy seal outfits by the end of the night,' Vicky says, shaking her head into her hands.

'OK, you know when bands release unseen photos from their time together and everyone loses their shit? Well, this is our version. Photos of us that I hadn't seen until today. I don't even remember them being taken.'

'Photos of us younger, drunker and stupider? Bring it!' says Vicky eagerly.

I pull the packages out of the bag and on to the table, open one up and pull out the pile of photographs, splaying them across the table for them to see.

'Shit!' Zaza shouts at one – a picture of all four of us sprawling across our one and only sofa in Hackney. 'That's the night you guys moved in!'

'What on earth am I doing in this one?' Vicky yelps,

picking up an image which seems to show her trying to get into our fridge, the entire contents of it removed to the floor to help her in her attempt.

'No idea, but look at this one!' Zaza laughs, turning the paper in her hand towards me. 'You, in the bath unconscious – Pia giving you a cold shower to bring you back round.'

'Eeesh!' I laugh. 'Judging by the grin on her face she's enjoying that a bit too much.'

'Guys! Our first group holiday!'

'Was that the Ibiza one when we discovered that foam parties weren't for us?' Zaza asks.

'I nearly drowned!' declared Vicky.

'Here's when we went to Amsterdam!' I say, picking up a much more civilized photo of us on a bridge together – all straddling bikes.

'Didn't Vicky almost crash on that bike?'

'You guys insisted on taking us to a café! And not just any café – you know the sort. The smoking kind. The ones where –'

'We get it!' laughs Zaza. 'You have a spliff.'

'God, remember when I was fun?' Vicky sighs.

'Are we calling you driving into a stationary tram "fun"?' I ask.

'Spontaneous, adventurous – void of any actual responsibility! Remember when everything was just simple?' Vicky adds.

'We didn't know it was, that was the problem,' I say.

'We laughed, a lot,' nods Zaza.

'Laughed and planned! Remember when Pia decided we should all give up our jobs and work on a cruise ship for a year? Just for the experience?' says Vicky.

'Can you imagine if we did?' laughs Zaza.

'She was always trying to get us to jack in our jobs!' I smile. 'She'd make us watch anything by David Attenborough just so we could plan our hypothetical excursions around the world.'

'She certainly wasn't boring,' says Vicky, picking up her wine glass. 'Do you remember that time she made us all chuck out anything we owned that was yellow because she was sure it brought her bad luck?'

'She was more impulsive than I've ever been!' says Zaza. 'Even after she was diagnosed. She did more in that time than I've done in my whole life.'

'She was determined to enjoy it,' I nod, thinking back to the fun we had zooming across Italy in a rented convertible, gazing at the Northern Lights in Norway and then the time we spent visiting every festive market Germany had to offer. There was always something new to explore and discover with Pia. 'I doubt I'll do anything quite like that any time soon. This is the furthest I've been out since.'

'But you will!' encourages Zaza.

'I dunno . . .' I shrug.

'Why not?' asks Zaza, a serious look on her face.

'She's not. I'm not . . .' I stammer.

'What's this?' Vicky asks, pulling out a piece of paper that looks like it's been quickly torn from a notebook and shoved into the pile of photos I found earlier. I recognize the writing on it instantly.

Rule of Death – Non-negotiable. Let's-just-go. Have an adventure.

I wince at the note, trying to imagine when Pia might've written it and how much pain she would've been in trying to get the words down. It's short and to the point, making me think it was towards the end. At any other time her hand would've danced across the page, her sentences turning to paragraphs, her paragraphs turning to pages of thoughts and wishes.

'Well, how's that for timing,' mutters Zaza.

'Yeah,' I sigh, wondering how I'm going to successfully drum up the drive to go anywhere, despite Pia's orders.

'*We* should do something!' Vicky blurts, her hands wildly gesticulating around the table and back to Pia's note. 'Us. Us three should do something.'

'An adventure! A trek to somewhere amazing,' chimes in Zaza, clapping her hands together as she says it.

13

Zaza

The thought hangs in the air for a moment or two as we look at each other, sizing up our reactions. Vicky looks set to burst at the idea, Mike looks confused and I feel like this could turn into the thing I didn't know I needed. I have to do something to help me process all the big emotions I've been feeling lately. I need time to breathe and work out what it is that I want so that I don't risk ruining something that might just be the best thing that's ever happened to me. A shift in my focus might just save me from myself.

'We . . .' Mike starts, his finger waving between us in a slightly more controlled manner than Vicky just did, hesitating as he formulates his words, and opinion. '. . . could.'

'We can,' nods Vicky.

'It's a nice idea but let's slow down a minute. It's not that easy to just get up and go,' says Mike, his eyebrows meeting in a frown as he stares at the paper in his hands.

'Defeats the purpose of the Rules and the let's-just-go side of things if we all sit and don't do as she's said,' I suggest with a shrug.

'You have a wedding to plan,' he says, his voice rising

a notch. Pointing at me before turning to Vicky and repeating the gesture. 'And you have a very busy husband and two kids!'

'You're making factual points,' nods Vicky thoughtfully. 'I've never left them for any period of time but that doesn't mean that I shouldn't. It might be good for me – and them!'

'I've just agreed to my first job back. I've got work,' he continues to explain, his mouth twisting.

'Big job?' asks Vicky.

'Not massive but it'll start the ball rolling and get my feet back in the door so I can see whether it feels right,' he explains, talking as though we might think it's too soon for him to be doing it.

Having watched him over the last few months I think we both feel far from that. Normality is needed, a sense of forward motion. He needs a focus, and this added nugget is a part of that. I know it is.

'All right, we don't have to go right this second then, we can take our time and plan it before we all scoot off to the airport,' I reason. 'And it's not like any of us can go for a year-long hiking around the world trip anyway. Let's be sensible here –'

Vicky interrupts with a dramatic sigh. 'If this were a film we'd be halfway to the airport right now having snatched up a swimsuit and a toothbrush. I'd be standing up through the taxi's sunroof and laughing my head off while looking young and free.'

'Welcome to real life where stepping away from your

responsibilities requires lots more preparation and for-ward thinking,' says Mike.

'But we should do it,' I say, loving Vicky's enthusiasm even if it might be fuelled by alcohol consumption, and the fact that Mike looks like he's warming to the idea. 'Let's adopt the let's-just-go motto and go somewhere. There will always be excuses for us not to do something, but a million reasons why we should. Ten days must be doable for us all . . . or two weeks? I should have no trouble getting time off work,' I say, aware that, all being well, I'll need a chunk of time off next year for the wed-ding and honeymoon, but they shouldn't fall within the same work year. 'I can ask first thing.'

'I'm sure my mum and dad or Nick's mum would love an excuse to spoil the kids for a bit . . .' reasons Vicky, beaming at the possibility.

Vicky and I both turn to Mike expectantly.

His eyes travel back down to the paper. 'Fuck it,' he whispers, his mouth unable to resist the deliciousness of a smile.

Vicky bangs on the table defiantly. 'That's the spirit.'

'Let's raise a glass to it before any of us can back out,' I say, holding my wine out in front of me.

'To let's-just-go in a sensible fashion!' Vicky sings, banging her glass into mine.

'Hear, hear,' smiles Mike, holding out his beer bottle for us to toast against.

'Should we have a little look at where we could go?' Vicky asks.

She's up on her feet before we can even give her an answer, retrieving her laptop from across the room and running back over with it. She dives back into her seat with a wobble before flipping open the screen and bringing up Safari.

'The Sahara is meant to be stunning,' suggests Mike, having taken a deep breath.

'That's a lot of sand and I'm afraid, when it comes to sand, I'm only interested in the beach variety and enjoying it with a cocktail in hand,' I state unapologetically before taking a huge gulp of my wine.

'The Himalayas is meant to be enlightening and spiritual,' says Vicky as she types, images of trekkers surrounded by snowy mountains appearing on her screen. 'Cold . . .' she observes, her nose crinkling.

'Are you hoping to join Za on her beach?' Mike laughs. 'Are you two sure you're up for roughing it and trekking? It's not glamorous, you know.'

'Erm, excuse me. No need to talk to me about roughing it, my life is made up of events involving poo, wee, sick and tears. My standards are pretty low to start with.'

'Mine not so much,' I admit. 'But I think I'll cope without a fresh towel for a week.'

'Towel? Try without a shower!' Mike laughs, a proper belly laugh that makes him keel over in his chair.

I can't even pretend to be offended by his reaction, because seeing his face light up with an explosion of joy is such a beautiful sight.

'Ooh, I know! We once covered something at work – remember when I had an actual job and used to be exciting?' asks Vicky before ploughing on. 'We once followed a bunch of celebrities who were about to take on the Inca Trail in Peru. I ended up doing a research chat with one of them and it sounded incredible. They ended up in . . . God, what was the name? Mum-brain!'

'Machu Picchu?' helps Mike.

'That's the one. Stunning. All these structures on top of this huge mountain . . .'

'I know it,' I say, then correcting myself. ' "Know" is a loose term, I mean I've definitely stalked a few travel Instagram accounts where they've been there and raved about it.'

'It does look incredible!' comments Vicky, before laughing at a picture of a llama pulling a funny face.

'Pia always wanted to go back to South America, but type in Lares Trek,' Mike says to Vicky, interrupting her llama joy. 'We met loads of people who were going on to do the Inca Trail, so many in fact that it was hard to believe it wasn't just one steady stream of tourists and travellers making their way along it.'

'Well, that would be shit,' mumbles Vicky.

'It would definitely take the shine and magic out if it's as busy as a Sunday morning in Ikea,' I pout.

'As if you're ever in Ikea on a Sunday morning,' laughs Vicky.

'No, but your posts about the Sunday breakfasts have

regularly left me feeling it's somewhere I don't want to frequent,' I admit, pulling a silly face at her.

'Ha-de-har,' she says, rolling her eyes at me as she focuses back on the screen.

'Wow!' I find myself saying as Vicky types in the key words and pictures of mountains, valleys and breathtaking lakes appear on the screen.

'The Lares Trek still ends up at Machu Picchu but it's not as heavily footed,' says Mike knowingly. 'We bumped into a family once who'd just completed it, said it was just them and their Sherpas the whole time and that the only other people they bumped into were people from the local communities. You still have the busyness of Machu Picchu to contend with, but that's the same with most places like that nowadays. Click on that link – they're a good company,' he instructs, pointing at Vicky's screen.

Our heads come together as we take in the information.

'There's a train ride, a shower and a bed!' I yelp.

'Ha! After days of intense trekking,' Mike adds. 'I like how you skimmed over that part.'

'Just look at that view,' I tell them, taking in the image of someone in front of the most stunning backdrop of rippling mountains.

'It's somewhere we never got to go,' says Mike.

'Let's do it,' exclaims Vicky, clicking through to see when that particular company has dates available. 'What are you both doing in May . . . that's three months away.'

'I'll have to check with work but, yeah. I could be free,' I nod.

'And the kids?' I ask Vic, who hasn't taken her eyes off the screen since the dates popped up. 'Will they be OK with you going?'

She thinks for a moment. 'They'll be absolutely fine. Quite frankly, if I don't go on this trip I'll be heading for a nervous breakdown and no good to anyone by the time the year is out.'

'I hear you!' says Mike.

'What about your wedding plans?' Vicky asks, turning to me.

'There's nothing that a bit of time away will mess up,' I laugh, thinking more in financial terms and how to juggle the cost of a wedding and a long-haul trip, but knowing I can make it work. 'What about you, Mike?'

'Sounds fucking ace. Gives me time to get this job done and then head off.'

'Are you ready to leave your flat and Pia yet?'

'Pia isn't here,' Mike shrugs, shuffling in his seat and straightening out his legs. 'I thought I'd say a few words to her earlier and wish her a happy birthday. You know, talk to her ashes. The words simply wouldn't come out. It's not that I didn't have anything to say, there are so many things I wish I could say to her, things I want her to know or ask for her help on. But I don't feel like she's here, around me. Today confirmed for me that although her body is gone, everything that made her great and wonderful – her spirit, her soul, her zest – isn't. Instead she's out there. Free of any kind of weight that pinned her down.'

'Then let's join her and be free of it all for a bit too. Maybe you aren't supposed to be inside talking to her ashes, but getting rid of your own shackles and remembering her with life and living.'

'I'll drink to that!' I declare, holding out my wine glass for them to chink. 'I'm in!'

'In!' chimes Vicky.

'In,' croaks Mike.

I don't know who cries first, but before I know it we descend into a mixture of tears and laughter. We're doing this!

14

Vicky

'Oooow,' I groan into my pillow, unable to open my eyes, my head feeling like it's either about to explode or cave in on itself from the pressure it's enduring. How much did I drink last night? No point measuring by the glass, I feel like I was guzzling by the bucket load. I must've been. How on earth did I manage to go on such massive benders when we were younger and then bounce into uni or work the next day? Well, I was probably still drunk, plus I definitely used to make the most of the all-you-can-eat Pizza Hut deals at lunch the following day to take the edge off.

Maybe I'll treat Chloe later. She'll love being let loose on the ice-cream machine!

A piercing scream fills the air causing me to scrunch up my face and pull the pillow over my head in an effort to block out the torturous sound of my daughter having what, I imagine, is her first tantrum of the day. They must already be downstairs, meaning I must've slept through them coming in to me, or maybe Nick went in to them. Oh fuck, it's not even the weekend, I realize. Nick has to go to work and I actually have to mother today.

I slowly peer from behind the pillow to glance at my alarm clock. It's five past eight!

'Shit!' I hiss as I jump out of bed, my head aching and pounding beyond belief as I chuck on the nearest pile of clothes (all elasticated and black), smooth down my hair and head downstairs.

'I DON'T WANT THAT!' I hear Barnaby cry hysterically before I even get into the room.

'But it's mango, your favourite,' Nick says rationally.

'No,' I croak, walking in. 'That was before. Now it's watermelon.'

'Do we have any?' Nick asks, giving me a quick kiss, managing not to look too aghast at the state of me – which I imagine is quite something and hugely contrasting to the sight of my handsome husband who is already in his suit, ready for work. He also smells amazing, and judging from the sour taste in my mouth, I do not.

I nod.

'Sorry, Barns,' he says, grabbing the offending bowl back to make the switch.

'This is yucky!' shouts Chloe, who has been studying the toast on her plate since I entered the room.

'It's toast,' shrugs Nick.

'It's black!' she shouts, hurling the toast across the room at him as though it's a frisbee. She narrowly avoids his suit, yet he laughs.

'There's no getting past you!' he pops another slice into the toaster and chucks her the unwanted mango to eat in the meantime. She's a mango guzzler so is instantly appeased. 'Nice work,' I state, thankful that he has it all under control.

'How's the head?'

'I can't even answer that right now.'

'You were sprawled across the bed, fully clothed and sparko by the time I got back.'

'No! Was I?' I ask, realizing he must've got home really late in that case.

'Absolutely. Knew it must've been a good one so thought you'd appreciate some extra sleep.'

'Thank you!' I say. 'It really was great.'

A gasp escapes as I remember the hours we spent trawling the internet, with Zaza and Mike having to stop me from using my credit card to book the whole trip before we'd had a chance to plan properly. Instead, I sent a polite email to the company requesting a hold on the dates before going on Amazon and ordering a she-wee. I've no idea why that was the item I decided to impulse buy, and I doubt I'd have the guts to use it, but there we go, first trek item bought. This is a thing. We're going.

'What?'

'I'm . . . erm . . . and there's no need to panic because we can call in the grandparents for help and all that – I'll call them today to make sure they're fine with it, but I think I'm going on a trek to Peru with Za and Mike,' I cover my mouth once the words are out, waiting for his reaction.

'Peru! Peru! Peru!' shouts Chloe. 'Like Paddington!'

'Yeeeeah,' I nod slowly, surprised I didn't make that

connection when she's currently obsessed with the little brown bear. 'I'm so sorry, I should've talked to you about it and made sure it was OK,' I say to Nick.

'You haven't booked it, have you?' he asks in surprise.

'Before talking to you? Of course not . . . I came very close to it, though,' I admit, aware of his eyebrows raising as I say it. 'I know you're busy and this isn't a great time for me to be swanning off like this. Not when you've just won a pitch and have a million things on your plate, but is there ever really a good time for me to do something like this? I don't think so. I think something else will always pop up and I just need to bite the bullet and do it. Plus there was a note and we knew we had to. It's one of her Rules –' I stop the verbal diarrhoea that's coming from my mouth as a flashback to my teenage self, begging my parents to let me go to a club, springs to mind. 'I just really want to go,' I say simply.

'Wow,' he laughs, as though he finds my behaviour amusing. We both know that had it been the other way around and he'd been the drunken one provisionally booking time away with mates then I'd have a little more to say about the matter. That said, our roles within the house are so different. He's always away anyway.

'I think it'll be good for me to . . . have some time,' I say, wanting to confide in him properly about how I've been feeling lately, yet knowing now might not be the right time with the kids around and when we're in the middle of the morning mayhem.

'And it will be,' he says, flashing me a smile before

grabbing the toast out of the toaster just as it's the perfect shade of brown. He butters it, adds a smidge of Marmite and hands it to Chloe before giving her a kiss on the head. 'Be good for Mummy today, she has a sore head.'

'Did she bash it?' she asks, eyeing me suspiciously.

'Something like that,' I nod, grimacing at Nick.

'Bye, sausage,' he says, pulling Barnaby in for a squeeze before heading to me and grabbing both of my arms. 'I honestly think it's a wonderful idea.'

He gives me a quick kiss on the lips, so quick it hardly even counts as a kiss, and he's in the hallway grabbing his bag and coat, ready to make a swift exit.

As the door closes behind him I find myself feeling overwhelmingly sad at his reaction. Maybe it's the hangover, but I just would've liked him to wonder how he's going to manage without me for ten whole days, even with the help of our parents. Or am I so undervalued and unseen here that he has no idea what I undertake on a day-to-day basis?

Before I can stew on the feelings further, I catch sight of the time and start whizzing around to locate coats, shoes and Barnaby's lunchbox – firmly deciding that I will be treating Chloe to an all-you-can-eat Pizza Hut lunch.

Mike

On waking up, before I even open my eyes, a glimmer of excitement flutters within me.

There is something ahead of me. Not the future I wanted or hoped for, but plans. For the first time in months, instead of the dread that has embedded itself into every fibre of my being, there is something else. Optimism. Hope. Chance.

Zaza

I wake to an empty bed, but unlike yesterday morning I'm not greeted with the smell of pancakes wafting up the stairs. Instead I can hear the sound of Liam joining in with a Peloton session downstairs, the teacher barking out encouragement and Liam grunting back.

My memory of getting back last night is a little hazy, but I do remember coming in and being very excited while spilling the news about our Peru trip. Liam wasn't best pleased and told me so before huffing off to bed, leaving me to feel pretty miffed.

Now that I'm not drunk and giddy the guilt has started to creep in. Maybe I should've consulted him before saying I was in, especially as I'll have to dip into our savings to do it. I don't think we even got on to that part of the conversation last night.

I definitely could've handled the situation better, but I don't regret our plan and I'm glad we were with Mike when he found the note. Not only did us seeing it mean he has to see the Rule through, but it's also given Vicky and me something I think we both need, too. I just wish

Liam saw it the same way. It's like he's annoyed that I'm doing something without him, as though my engagement ring has suddenly morphed into chains. Or maybe that's a feeling that's on me and nothing to do with him and his actions at all. It's another reminder that one moment you're footloose and fancy free and the next you've signed your life away in a relationship and having to consult another person about every single aspect of it. It's draining. Where's the fun and spontaneity?

Pulling back the bedsheets I head downstairs for a coffee and some bircher before I have to start getting ready for work. Liam wanders in just as I'm grating an apple into my cold bowl of oats. He's puffing away in that post-workout way and streams of sweat drip down his red face.

'Did you even look at your diary?' he asks after snatching a breath, leaping straight into it.

'Gosh, mop yourself up,' I say, chucking a tea towel at him while screwing up my face. I know some women find the sight of a man dripping in perspiration a turn-on, but I'm not one of them. Instead, it actually makes me feel quite uncomfortable. A little queasy.

'Za!' he says, doing what I've asked with an exasperated look on his face.

'Yes . . .'

'It's my brother's wedding!' he says, pursing his lips.

'That's – that's –' I think for a moment, knowing that I saw it when I looked in my diary very hastily last night. 'That's the day after I get back.'

'But we're travelling up early the day before.'

'Oh ... crap! I forgot that changed,' I whine, my hands covering my eyes at the error of not only my time management but for reading his reaction so wrong. It's not that he doesn't want me going somewhere without him, it's that we'd already made plans to be somewhere together. 'I'm sorry. The dates are only pencilled in at the moment but I would land in the morning on the Friday anyway. So I could make it up to Liverpool in good time,' I say, feeling stupid.

'You know there are welcome drinks planned that first day,' he tuts grumpily. 'You didn't even run it by me.'

'I've said sorry for that and I really am,' I frown. It takes a lot for me to say sorry, I'm stubborn like that, so I don't appreciate having to repeat the sentiment. Especially when it was a genuine oversight and I've already offered a solution if he wants me there that badly.

'It's a big day for my family,' he continues, piling on the guilt.

'I know.'

'Seeing as you're going to be a part of it you'd think you'd want to be there.'

'Liam, it's not our wedding, is it?' I snap, starting to feel less reasonable. 'So what if I get there late to the drinks when people are already a little tipsy? It's not the main event and no one will be waiting for me to arrive to get the party started! You can go up ahead of me if you're really concerned about missing out on a beer or two.'

'Don't be petty,' he says, leaning back on the kitchen side with a pained expression on his face, as though I've just told him I hate his whole family. I don't. 'Honestly, I don't know what's got into you lately, but this is what adults in a committed relationship do – they consult each other before making plans that might impact the other. I'm allowed to be upset. I just wanted you properly for a few days.'

'You get me all the sodding time,' I whine, reluctant to repeat my apology for a third time.

'Like this?' he scoffs before shaking his head, gesturing at the space between us. 'Well, lucky me.'

His shoulders are slumped as he exits the room and marches up the stairs, leaving me feeling guilty and tense. This is totally my fault and an innocent mistake on my part, but I'm not sure what else I could've offered beyond what I already have. Admitting my faults doesn't come easily to me so holding my hands up was huge. His rebuff of that, his need to hammer home his point and make sure I understood it – which I did – makes me want to revoke the 's' word altogether along with any notion of moving the trip dates.

It's stupid.

I know he's allowed to be upset, just as I am, but I don't know why I feel the need to sweep his feelings away as though he's overreacting when I act in certain ways that push him away and spark a tension between us. We both know that if it were the other way round I'd be fuming and telling him to change the dates of the trip straight away. I'd certainly let it be known how pissed off I was. I wouldn't let it lie.

Fifteen minutes later I'm sitting at the kitchen table, my bowl still untouched due to my loss of appetite, when I hear Liam rush down the stairs and head straight out the front door. He doesn't even shout out goodbye.

Three Months Later

15

Mike

'Do you mind if I grab the aisle seat?' calls Vicky as we're walking towards our allocated seats on the crowded plane, squeezing past other passengers who have reached their spots and are now faffing about retrieving bits and bobs from their hand luggage rather than moving in a bit to let others through. No matter how much I've travelled this has always been and will always be a continuous bugbear of mine.

'I have longer legs!' I say, remembering how relieved I was at having a little space to stretch out when I was allocated the aisle seat.

'But I'm a nervous flyer. I'll be needing the loo every five minutes. I'm worse now I've had kids,' she rambles, completely oblivious to people looking over and listening to her overshare. 'Honestly, I was meant to go and see someone about it but you know how it is, I always end up at the bottom of the priority list. I've had to start wearing pads.'

'Stop, stop, stop!' I say, laughing as I place my hand on her shoulder. 'It's all yours, but thanks for sharing.'

'Sweet friend,' she says, patting my hand before

stepping aside to let me into my new seat, which is sandwiched between her and Zaza who has already made herself comfy by the window. I place my rucksack in the overhead luggage compartment and squeeze in next to her. Taking a deep breath I wiggle my body into a satisfying position I think I can bear for the next few hours until I need to get up and stretch.

I can't believe we're here. In many ways it feels like we booked this trip only last night, and in others it feels like a lifetime ago. Everything and nothing has happened since. Vicky has quietly taken on the role of project manager, her first email landing at nine-thirty in the morning the day after we'd concocted this plan, or were told we had to do it by Pia's note. A note that is still in my pocket now. Vicky was chomping at the bit to get everything firmly booked in before any of us changed our minds. You'd think once everything was booked she'd leave us all to it, but no. Every day that's followed I've had a message or call about some fact she's found out about Peru (like three-quarters of the world's alpaca population resides there), or an update on what she is and isn't bringing with her (she settled on a pair of knickers and socks for each day, but only two bras). Vicky has thrown herself into this trip full of gusto like she's about to become the new Bear Grylls, whereas Zaza's approach has been to make everything that makes trekking and camping wonderful, like immersing yourself in nature and roughing it for a bit, less so. Having popped her bag on the luggage scales at check-in she has more luxury items than any trekker has ever dared to travel with. She has reassured me she's spent her evenings decanting her must-have toiletries into smaller bottles, so at least that's something.

I haven't had the time to do anything other than grab my let's-just-go bag and pack my day sack for the plane. After taking on the one commission in February it turned into a bigger job than I'd planned for, with many hours at my desk trying to build them the content asked for at the spec they required. The brand were pernickety with every single frame, a challenge I admired them for. There was definitely no room for slacking. They demanded my full attention while on the job.

I'm not entirely sure if I was ready for such a huge amount of pressure but the reality is that it's transferred me somehow from there to here. Nothing within me has changed, I still feel as broken inside, but outwardly I'm back at work so people have stopped checking in, seemingly assuming I'm 'moving on'. I've even been for that pint with AJ and Reece, which was as normal as normal can be when someone's wife has died. Other than the obligatory and non-committal 'You been all right?' at the start I wasn't asked again, and Pia wasn't mentioned for the full two hours we were together. It was an act that was purely for their benefit because not talking about the woman whose absence makes me feel fractured and incomplete seems more awkward than doing so. Hopefully they'll be able to talk about her in time, realizing that every time she's mentioned a little piece of my insides vibrates back to life.

'You good?' Vicky asks, having only just stopped fiddling with her bag and sat down with a sigh.

I'm about to answer when the air stewardess comes over offering complimentary bubbles. Three hands go flying in her direction, snatching up the plastic cups in haste.

'Anyone else nervous?' asks Vicky.

'Don't know what you're talking about,' I laugh, supremely aware of a fluttering in my stomach. I might not have had much time to focus on this excursion of ours but familiar feelings of anticipation and excitement have been building within me since sending over the final edits last night. I'm surprised I managed to sleep.

'Shall we toast?' asks Zaza, holding out her cup to mine. Vic does the same.

'To . . . ?' I ask.

'God, this could be a heavy and emotional one,' says Zaza, her hand placed over her chest as she takes a slight pause. 'To Pia for being persuasive, even in death. May she guide us on this trip and make sure we don't get flipping lost or stranded up a mountain,' Zaza says seriously.

'Couldn't agree more,' Vicky nods. 'To our Pia getting us home safely.'

'You do realize she had an awful sense of direction?' I laugh, while trying my best to make some sort of clink with their plastic cups.

We each take a mouthful and then sigh collectively.

'Lovely,' I smile, instantly feeling my body relax.

'How are you feeling, Vicky?' asks Zaza, taking another graceful sip of her drink while Vicky necks the rest of hers.

'I've been an emotional wreck if I'm honest,' she states, as though we'd be surprised by her admission. 'I've never been away from the kids for this long. Or this far away . . . I was crying putting my spare laces in the bag the other day. It's not taken much to set me off.'

'Are you worried about how Nick will cope?' I ask.

'A little bit, I guess. But he seemed totally unfazed when I first told him about this and his stance on it hasn't changed a bit,' she frowns. 'Literally, it's like he thinks having the kids on his own for a week is going to be a complete doddle.'

'Maybe this is what he needs,' suggests Zaza.

'He might even enjoy it,' I shrug.

'Oh, he'll love it in so many ways and he's always so playful and fun with them, you know. When you have one-on-one time with your kids there are moments when it's absolutely amazing and wholesome – where everyone is laughing and they look at you with this magic in their eyes, but then there are also the meltdowns and the tantrums you struggle to navigate through. It's just not that easy. Kids aren't easy! You can't give them one hundred per cent of your attention all the time,' she protests, peering into her cup as though willing more alcohol to appear. 'Anyway, I've popped some homemade dinners in the fridge and the freezer along with details of how to heat them scribbled on top, and Post-it notes on anything electrical and useful that he hasn't touched before – like the washing machine.'

'He doesn't know how to wash his own clothes?' gasps Zaza.

'Well, he probably does,' Vicky backtracks. 'I dunno, he must've done it before we met. I'm not sure how we fell into such stereotypical roles within the house when we both believe in equality, but we have.' She looks perplexed at the discovery, as if it hadn't really occurred to her before.

'Are you happy?' I find myself asking.

'I will be if we can find some more bubbles,' Vicky smiles, shaking her empty glass at me, her lips pressing into a smile.

Although I can sense there's more going on than she's saying, I don't push the matter and instead peer over the seats in front to see if any might be on its way. Sadly the airline staff have their life jackets on and seatbelts in hand, ready to give us the standard safety briefing.

'We'll get some later,' I whisper.

'Plenty of time,' she agrees.

'I've got an idea,' announces Zaza. 'Let's all watch the same film. We have to press play at the same time. It'll be just like a silent disco version of going to the cinema only with crappy screens.'

'Ooh! Let's have a look what's on!' Vicky giggles, snatching up the magazine from the seat in front of her and flicking through its pages, tilting it towards us so that we can see too.

'What kind of film were you thinking?' I ask. 'One

that's going to make me want to be a superhero and save the world or one that's going to turn me into a blubbering mess?'

They both look up at me, Zaza has an eyebrow raised, and Vicky is pulling her best 'cute' face that makes her look exactly like Barnaby.

'Smut it is then,' I agree.

'Fantastic!' Vicky smiles. 'Oooh! Look, the new Billy Buskin one. Yes!'

Her excitement stops me from moaning in protest. It's clear Vicky has zero time that's hers, so if she wants to watch her favourite crush (not a secret, she had posters of Billy up in our flat years ago), then who am I to stop her. Plus, after living with three women for years, I've actually grown to love him myself. Not only is he a pretty face but, ever since he's moved away from the teen drama side of things he's proved himself to be super talented too.

'Did I tell you I saw him on my way home from work a few months ago?' asks Zaza.

'Excuse me, what?' asks Vic, her hand pushing me back into my seat to get a better view of the gossip. 'What was he doing? Who was he with? Oh, gosh! Was he with Sophie? And their new puppy?'

'Wow . . . you know your stuff,' I note.

'We all have our strengths, Mike. Mine are clearly pushing babies out of my vagina and knowing all there is to know about Mr Buskin.'

'My strengths pale in comparison,' I reply.

'Or does the mention of her strengths make you go pale?' Zaza laughs.

'Hard to say.'

'Tell me everything!' Vicky demands.

'I was walking down Shaftesbury Avenue on the way to the Tube and he was coming in the other direction.'

'And . . . ?'

'And I don't remember anything else. I was chatting to someone from work so I was distracted . . .'

'Who?'

'Albie. You know, that guy who started a few months back,' Zaza shrugs.

'Right . . . and he stopped you making any actual observations on, arguably, the most stunningly beautiful man of our generation?'

'I guess . . . ?'

'You're useless.'

'Shall we start the film?' I say, interrupting them mid crush talk.

Ten minutes later, once the plane's in the air and after Zaza and Vicky have finished fidgeting in their seats and are finally settled with snacks, the entertainment system is up and running and we're settled in watching *Reaching*. We laugh in the opening credits, then again in the opening scene, turning to each other with tears in our eyes. The ninety minutes fly by, and although, like most good love stories, there's a tinge of sadness and heartache in the film, there's also a feeling of optimism and hope, which leaves us all exhaling with joy at the end. I forgot how much I love a soppy film. Since being on my own I've purpose-fully steered away, thinking they might be too much for me emotionally – but that was brilliant. Cathartic even.

We take it in turns to climb out of our seats and go to the loo, and on my way back I grab a bag of Kinder Schoko-Bons from my bag to share. I check on the rest of my bag while I'm there, on the Tupperware box that I decided to bring with me.

My hand rests on top of it for a moment. I take a breath.

'Are you getting chocolate then?' Vicky asks, breaking into my thoughts.

'Yes!' I say, grabbing them before zipping my bag shut.

16

Zaza

By the time we're off the second flight, through passport control, have collected our luggage and been driven by minibus from Cusco airport to Hotel Prisma, I'm shattered and ready for my final night of luxury before roughing it in a tent for a few nights. I have never camped or had any desire to do so before. I'll be honest, whenever Liam and I go away it's with the freedom of two people who work hard for their money and therefore want to spend their time off in comfort and glamour. Not Beyoncé-level glamour, don't get me wrong, but fancy kaftans around the pool, champers by the shore and the biggest straw hat I can get in my suitcase – you get the drift. When I'm away I like to live my best life.

Liam has been finding my attempts at becoming 'trek ready' hysterical. He's hardly a regular camper either, but somehow the adventures he went on as a kid when he was in the Scouts left him far more experienced than me as an adult. I'm looking forward to that changing when I get back and can regale him with our tales – all while enjoying the great big hotel bed I'll be slipping into for Liam's brother's wedding.

The wedding.

We had an uncomfortable few days following my trip announcement with me feeling guilty, stubborn and indignant and Liam being weird and tense about the whole thing. Eventually I decided to bite the bullet and call Liam's mum, and then his brother. I know Liam and the thing that would've been upsetting him was the thought that they'd be irritated with him for my actions, or even feel negatively towards me about it.

Neither of them was particularly bothered so I came off the calls feeling like I'd made a mountain out of a molehill. It was a gesture, though, and for Liam it symbolized me waving a big white flag over the whole thing.

I'd love to say everything has been good between us ever since but that's not entirely true. I'm no longer outwardly showing my frustrations to him, yet there's still a feeling of unease within me, making me feel off balance.

Prepping for this adventure has been a welcome distraction.

I know this trip is going to take me out of my comfort zone, and that's something I've been set to embrace (with the help of all the luxury aids I could find, like individual shower sheets to wipe myself down with each night seeing as we won't have water to wash in, travel-sized versions of my normal creams and potions, and a blow-up travel pillow with a silk case – although that is a necessity in my book). Yes, I've prepped myself to be surprised, but after so many hours of travelling I simply long for one night of comfort to recuperate and gather myself before heading into Peru's wilderness.

The moment I look out of the minibus window and take in the sight of our yellow hotel I have hopes that inside is going to be a snug little sanctuary. Prisma Hotel might look a little rough around the edges with its patchy paintwork, but the various potted plants lining up outside on the pavement and beneath the windows give me hope. The lady at the front desk is incredibly welcoming and cheerful as she checks us in and gives us mugs of the local tea, however her smile can't hide the basicness of the building around her that isn't quite the spa I'd longed for. I mean, there isn't anything wrong with it necessarily, but I guess I was expecting more and maybe, just maybe, I'm more attached to being at home than I've realized. Plus, the tea is revolting.

Mike and Vicky seem happy enough when we arrive so I keep my feelings of disappointment to myself. Whereas I remain pretty quiet, they let out pleasing noises, lots of 'oohs' and 'aahs', as we make our way through the foyer and see the way the building opens up in its centre to expose its four floors and an atrium with a glass roof letting in floods of light. More plants and foliage are potted and left to drape over banisters and cascade down the walls.

Sunshine, glass, plants – it all sounds heavenly – but something about the place just doesn't capture me like it has the others. That feeling has quadrupled since walking into my double room. Standing here, taking in the sight of its bareness, the heater on wheels that's been moved in, the firmness of the hardest bed I've ever sat on, and the steadily loud noise from the street outside, I can admit to myself that I'm underwhelmed.

Or maybe overwhelmed.

I can't decide.

Either way, though, it's not the best feeling to have at the beginning of a journey that's meant to challenge me into finding out who I am and reveal parts of myself I didn't even know existed. If a hotel, one that other people look at positively and are able to enjoy – even marvel at – makes me feel on edge and uncomfortable, then how am I going to feel living in a tent?! A bed is far better than a sleeping bag on the ground, even if I have brought a thin blow-up mattress with me. There's heating here, there's privacy, there's a bathroom. I'm not going to have any of that in a couple of days.

I stop and take a breath.

I have to get a grip.

In less than fifteen minutes I'm meant to be meeting the others for a chat with our trek leader to talk through what's going to be happening over the next few days. Hopefully a little more knowledge will help settle me in. Lesson one of the trip, I don't do well not knowing what's ahead and not being part of the planning. I'll feel better with a map in my hands and some sort of itinerary.

First up I need to get out of these clothes that I feel like I've been stewing in since I left home almost twenty-four hours ago. I slide my suitcase on to its side and open it on the floor, pulling out some fresh clothes to get changed into – a simple cerise pink maxi dress and a pair of gladiator sandals, which I'm hoping will be breezy and light as it's quite muggy out.

I peel myself out of my travel clothes and head into the bathroom. It might make me slightly late, but my skin is so sticky from the journey that I need to shower before leaving this room. I turn the valve to heat up the shower and go to get my towel.

That's when I see it sitting on the toilet. A curl of black mocking me from the seat, and for a moment I am rooted to the spot in horror.

The tears that have been threatening to fall now leap from my eyes. I force myself to take a breath, make myself get under the water so I can wash my sweaty body. The tears coming thick and fast as I try to ignore 'it'.

My shower is a quick and functional in and out. I step into my knickers straight away, hastily rub in some body lotion and pull my dress over my head. The tears are still streaming down my face as I step out of the bathroom, just as someone knocks at my door.

I wipe my face to remove the tears and try to look happier as I swing the door open.

Mike's face falls at the sight of me.

'What's wrong?' he asks, coming straight into the room in a panic.

'It's nothing,' I sniff, wiping my face with a towel and putting on some face cream. 'I'm being silly. I'm tired, that's all. You know what I'm like when I don't get enough sleep. I shouldn't have watched films the whole flight. My bad . . .'

'You can tell me,' he encourages gently, placing a hand on my arm.

I exhale, covering my face with my hands.

'I just found a hair on the toilet seat,' I squeak. 'Pubic.'

Laughter escapes from Mike as he pulls me into his arms. 'Gosh, you doughnut. I thought something had happened.'

'Were you not listening?' I frown, peering up at him. 'It's like a bad episode of *Four in a Bed*.'

He smiles back. 'You've never been travelling, have you?'

'Nope,' I say, curling back into his chest.

'I can't tell you the amount of hostels I've stayed in where I wish it were only a pubic hair I'd found on the toilet seat, in the shower, or even on my supposedly fresh bedsheets.'

'What . . . !' I respond in horror, leaping out of his arms and around to the bed. 'I haven't even checked the sheets yet!'

Mike's laugh blasts across the room, as his body bends over double, his elbows resting on his knees.

'It's not funny,' I say, picking up a pillow and chucking it in his direction. He pretends it's hit him far harder than it has and rolls to the ground.

'I said it's not funny,' I repeat, unable to stop myself from laughing with him. 'And get off that floor – who knows what else might be down there.'

He takes his time standing up, and his face is glowing with amusement when he looks back up at me. 'Za, this isn't a hostel, it's a hotel – and a decent one at that.'

'Hmmm . . .' I say, sounding unconvinced.

'You'll get through this,' he says, with what appears to be sympathy, sincerity and kindness.

'You think?' I whimper.

'You're already doing it . . . sort of,' he smiles. 'You'll breeze through this – and by this I mean the whole trip, not just this one night in a warm and safe hotel room. More than that, you'll enjoy it. And I'll be here to help if you need me.'

'Really?'

'That's what friends do!'

'In that case, oh great friend of mine . . . will you help by removing the pube?'

'Are you joking?'

'Does my face look like it is?' I ask, my eyes wide and imploring. 'Because if so I'm really not surprised Liam is finding it difficult to read.'

'He is?'

'I think it's more me than him,' I admit. 'I've not been the easiest person to live with lately.'

'He's marrying you so you must be doing something right,' he offers.

I screw up my face in reply. 'Maybe not the conversation to have on jetlag.'

'One for the mountains.' Mike nods, his palm rubbing

over his face before he snaps into action. 'Come on then, let's go get the offending item.'

'My saviour! You won't miss it,' I say, pointing towards the bathroom door.

He rolls his eyes and strides through, like a superhero about to take on the world and save the day.

'For future reference, Za,' he calls out, making me peer in behind him. 'Just one sheet of loo roll, two if it's an exceptionally big pube, fold it over in your hand and then simply brush,' he says, guiding me through the action as the hair falls straight into the loo. He drops the toilet roll in before flushing.

'Has it gone?' I ask.

'It's gone for a swim . . .' he says, sizing up the loo as the water still swirls around. 'Erm, yep. You're free. Well done,' he says, pulling me in for another hug and rubbing my back – like you might when a child's fallen over and hurt themselves. 'Feeling better?'

'Much,' I say, enjoying the hug. 'Don't get me wrong, this place is still not my idea of luxury, but the removal of said pube has improved matters considerably.'

'Glad to hear it,' he says with a nod of the head as he steps back, clapping his hands together. 'Right, I was actually knocking to see if you were ready for this meeting. It's not just us three – we're in with others who are doing the Inca Trail too.'

'Yeah,' I nod, looking around the room to locate my handbag and key, remembering that we have the first day with the others. 'We're not going to have to mingle with them though, are we? They aren't going to be trekking with us anyway so there's no real point.'

'Wow, it's a good thing you didn't go travelling.'

'And it's a wonderful thing the rest of them are buggering off so the three of us can have some proper time together.'

'You're such a delight.'

'And you know it!' I laugh, passing him my handbag before grabbing a red scarf from my suitcase and looping it from the nape of my neck to the top of my head into a bow. 'I'm ready. Let's mingle jingle with our temporary mates.'

Mike shakes his head at me as we walk out of my room.

17

Vicky

'Hey!' I sing into my phone as soon as it's picked up.

'Hello, my backpacking wife,' Nick croakily says back, leading me to imagine him tucked up in our comfy bed, wrapped up in our creased sheets.

'Oh no! I forgot you'd be asleep!' I whisper, remembering that not only do we have thousands of miles between us, but six hours too. 'I'll phone back tomorrow. I just wanted to check in . . . are the kids OK?'

'Sound asleep.'

'Good, good,' I say, feeling a sudden longing to go in and see them sprawled across their beds, no doubt with their duvets thrown off them and their mouths wide open. They both sleep like me. 'I'm sorry I woke you.'

'It's OK,' he replies softly. 'Glad you're safe.'

'You sleep. Love you.'

'Love you too.'

The call cuts off, I imagine him dropping his phone sleepily next to him and the panic he'll have in the morning when he can't find it. Or maybe it'll get lost in the covers and he won't hear the alarm meaning they'll all be late. Sod's law states the kids will start sleeping in while

I'm away, an anomaly that'll quickly disappear when I'm back.

I shouldn't worry, Nick's mum should've arrived earlier and she's usually up before the kids anyway. She'll run the ship better than I do, I'm sure.

I put my phone down next to me, aware that it's highly unlikely anyone will call me when everyone back home is asleep, and look around the room.

It's surprising how uncomfortable not having anything to stress over has become. It's as though I've dropped the ball somehow, stopped spinning the plates or slackened the rope – and although there should be a joy in that, it feels like I've forgotten my responsibilities rather than travelled thousands of miles from them. I feel like Kevin McAllister's mum in *Home Alone*, sipping champagne in first class while her kids sit back in economy (I couldn't do it myself but it sounds like a great start to a holiday), with an uneasy feeling that something is amiss.

I thought my body would melt into relaxation once I was away from the tension I've been carrying with the motherload, but instead there's an uneasy weight lingering across my chest. My absent children pinning me down, reminding me of what I signed up for with parenthood and where I should be . . .

My hand rubs over my heart while I take a deep breath, shifting in my seat.

I was relieved to be here and checking in after so much travelling; it feels like weeks ago that I said goodbye to

Nick and the kids. As soon as I closed the hotel door and turned to my room, I realized that this must be the first time since Barnaby came along that I've felt singular, that I've felt left to my own devices and not constantly needed, that I've felt still. It was eerily quiet, and it's not as though the room was silent because I could hear scooters beeping and people shouting out on the street below, but they're not my people or my concern, so they didn't cause the same adrenaline to pump through my body as my own children do when they scream, holler and wail for my attention. I am able to zone them out with no fear of neglect or unbearable consequences, like someone getting seriously hurt.

I am briefly unwanted, unneeded, and have nothing to do other than focus on me and what I want to do. So I can't help but wonder what it is I actually want to do now that I have been released of my maternal responsibilities. Moments like this are what I've dreamt of during meltdowns, tantrums and challenging moments from the kids. I've literally wanted to scream, 'I'm fucking done, I want to stop now.' Yet now that I'm away from those moments and alone I don't want to run a bath, drink wine, play music that I like loudly and swear like a trooper like I did before kids. Instead, I realize that all I really want to do is sit. Just sit. Simple, hassle free, and in no way world-stoppingly inspiring, but it's needed.

Are you happy?

That's what Mike asked.

Am I happy?

I guess it depends what time of day the question is asked and what's going on. When Nick is home at the weekend and we're out in the park and the kids are running around with massive grins on their faces? Completely and utterly. There are snatches of time that I look at Nick and our smiling kids and just feel an overwhelming sense of this being every single thing that I've ever wanted. When I'm verging on burnout, trying to be everything to everyone and do all of the little tasks around the house that make our lives run as smoothly as possible? Maybe not, although organization does give me joy so that is a tricky one. In the middle of one of Chloe's meltdowns? No, absolutely not. I am painfully unhappy and out of my depth in those moments because I know I have failed in my approach and abilities to be what she needs. I am not the mother I thought I would be. I am not the woman I thought I once was. That is what scares me, because sometimes I don't know who I am any more. How can something that completes me also make me feel so broken? It doesn't make sense to me.

My happiness is so linked to my children's. I once heard 'you're only as happy as your unhappiest child' — well, what if that child seems mostly unhappy when she's with you? What if she makes you feel the best and worst of you all at once? I love her so very much, with every beat of my heart — I love both my kids. But I feel so lost.

Sitting here on this strange bed, in this hotel room

thousands of miles from home, I allow myself to breathe. To be.

Am I happy? Is anyone ever happy all the time? I don't think so. It's the whole sunshine and showers thing, right? You have to let it all in to make the rainbows.

For the last few weeks I have thought of nothing else but sitting on this bed, of being in Peru, of being up those mountains and doing my best Julie Andrews impression as she swings her arms in the air and twirls in a beautifully carefree manner. It has kept me going, it's given me something that is mine away from the family. That is what I have been yearning for and why I so desperately wanted to go away with my best mates. I pushed for us to be out here. Then, the night before I left, I sobbed as I packed my suitcase, causing Nick to have a little chuckle before pulling me in close. I think it was part relief that I was actually doing this and that we were leaving, but more than anything it was guilt that I could have something for me. Something that was my own. Something that I wanted besides my family.

Then the kids were distraught as I said goodbye to them. They gripped hold of me in a way that only children can. Right around the neck, pulling me in like little koalas, really doing their best to unknowingly rub in and embed that guilt I was already feeling. Nick had to pull Chloe off me and usher a sniffling Barnaby away from my taxi. With his hands full he was only able to briefly turn back with words of encouragement, the smile on his face unable to hide the fact he was trying to keep his emotions at bay, probably for the kids. 'I'm so proud of you. Have the best time,' he whispered in my ear before giving me a quick peck on the lips.

As tears threaten to fall again I realize that I need to get up and get out. I don't want to sit here and wallow. This trip will be a total waste of time if I do that.

I get up and walk out of my hotel room, another simple act that feels so strange without other people to ferry and organize. I don't even take a bag – I just pop my key and phone into my back pocket and exit quickly.

Even though I know I'll be early I decide to head straight to the meeting room for our briefing. It's one floor down in a little conference room, with a sign for 'Gap Adventures' placed outside to welcome me in. Glasses of red and white wine have been laid on the table; I happily grab a white and take a quick gulp.

'Get it in now, there'll be none on the trip,' a voice with a Cornish lilt sounds from behind.

I turn to see a young man, maybe early twenties, smirking back at me. He sweeps his unruly mop of hair away from his bearded face before busying himself with paperwork and leaflets on the desk in front of him.

'I'm Vicky,' I announce. 'Victoria Albert.'

'Yeah, great,' he nods, stopping to tick my name off on a list before carrying on. 'We'll do proper intros in a mo. For now, I'm Scott – feel free to look around.'

'Thanks, Scott,' I smile, watching him playing with his papers before ambling across the room to a poster giving info on the local area. I know I'm early, but seeing as

I've travelled across the world to be here and spent a ton of money doing so, you'd think this dude would give me a little small talk.

His beard makes me think of Nick. When we were younger he'd often try and grow one but I always contested the idea. The roughness irritated my skin, especially when we used to spend so much time 'getting off' with each other. Do they call it 'getting off' these days? Making out? Necking? Either way, when we used to do it and Nick hadn't shaved or was in a beard-growing phase I'd come up for air with a huge red rash around my mouth. I used to prefer him cleanshaven, not just because of my skin reaction, but because without the hair I could see the curve of his lips. Lips that I used to love watching as he talked, laughed and slept. Chloe has his lips, Barnaby has mine.

I like Nick's beard now, with its flecks of grey that shimmer in the light. He's turning into quite the silver fox.

Scott's beard, however, like the rest of him, is unkempt. From his shoulder-length hair that's curly and wild down to his dusty sandals and knee-high socks, he looks like he went off on a gap year and never returned to real life. I imagine he wakes up each morning, reaches for the closest pile of clothes and chucks them on in the dark.

As though he's aware of me looking at him he brushes a hand over his T-shirt, blue with the company logo embossed on the front, and reaches over to grab a woolly hat, which he plops on his head.

'Aren't you boiling?' I ask, the words firing out of my mouth in the same way they do when the kids do something questionable, like deciding they're going to rehome every single worm and snail in the garden.

'Erm,' Scott sounds, raising an eyebrow at me before breaking into a smile. 'It's a local design. You'll have seen loads of the locals wearing similar patterns.'

'I'm not talking about the pattern, I'm talking about the fact you've just put a woolly hat on when it's super warm and we're inside. I'm boiling.'

'I thought you were hot,' he nods, looking at me seriously.

'I'm here with my two mates, Mike and Zaza,' I reply, aware of his innuendo.

'I look forward to meeting them,' he says, placing the information packs he's been sorting on to chairs which have been positioned to face his desk.

'We're from London. Used to live together before I met my husband and had kids,' I say, really punching out the words.

'Nice,' Scott replies, although I'm not sure he's still listening to me.

I pick up one of the leaflets.

'Lares Trek! That's the one we're doing. Wanted to do something a little different. Although I'm sure Inca is as good as they say it is. Mike, my friend, he does this sort of thing all the time, said the Lares was the one for us,' I say, aware that my mouth is still moving and that there's a steady stream of words tumbling from it. 'Where do we start from? Is it really high the first day? Should I get altitude tablets?'

'So many questions,' Scott laughs. 'I'll go through all of that in a second.'

'Fair enough,' I nod, managing to shut my mouth.

'But you're lucky.'

'Lucky?' I frown.

'I also prefer the Lares route, and you've got me accompanying you this week.'

'Oh. Nice,' I say.

'Calm down, Mrs.' He chuckles before waving to four other men who've come in, all wearing the same company uniform. 'We'll be starting in about ten minutes or so, so hang, take a seat and enjoy your wine,' he says before going to join his team.

My cheeks burn bright red as I sit down, feeling like a complete and utter tit. He seems like a nice enough guy but I really don't want to be made to feel this way all week. It's uncomfortable. I bury my face in the leaflet.

Slowly a few more people come wandering in. As they look equally curious and nervous, I hazard a guess that they're part of the team trekking the Inca Trail. I smile at everyone I catch eye contact with, I even exchange pleasantries with two older women while they're waiting to sign in. It feels like I'm on my first day at school as more and more people filter into the room and I'm there grinning like the Cheshire Cat. One older man looks straight at me and my smile for a good five seconds before turning away without reciprocating. Before I can feel embarrassed or put out by the rejection, Mike and Zaza finally appear.

'You didn't shower?' Zaza asks, taking in my clothes, the same from our flight, when they finally arrive.

'I . . . no,' I shrug. It didn't even occur to me that I should.

'Well, I found a pube,' she hisses, sitting in the chair next to me.

'Er, gross!' I whisper back.

'And she claims it wasn't her own,' Mike adds with a smirk as he sits.

'You saw how long that was – there's no way that belonged to me!' she laughs, giving him an elbow.

'Our Zaza takes care of herself,' I remind Mike. 'Do you not remember how long she would spend preening and pruning before dates? Me on the other hand, well, it's been so long one pube would look like a nest. A fricking big hairy pube nest, fit for a family of ten thousand chicks.'

'Hey!' Mike says, looking up at a figure behind me.

'Sorry, didn't mean to interrupt your . . . chat,' I hear Scott say. 'You must be Mike and Zaza. Victoria was telling me about you. But, as you were. Carry on. I'll be starting in a bit.' He shuffles off awkwardly.

Mike and Za can't contain their laughter.

'I think you made him blush,' giggles Za.

'Am I still here?' I ask. 'I'm pretty sure I asked the ground to swallow me up.'

'Must've spat you back up again . . . maybe it choked on your bush,' Zaza's laugh booms across the room before she covers up her mouth to try and suppress it. No use.

The three of us sit there, our shoulders bouncing up and down while tears stream down our faces.

'Hey everyone! I'm Scott, this is Kevin,' he says loudly, as the man next to him gives a little wave. 'We'll be leading the Lares Trek – and Martin, Nando and Nigel will be leading the Inca Trail – but as we're all starting as one I just want to get you up to speed with the plan over the next couple of days and our time together . . .'

While everyone else is hanging on his every word the three of us take some time to get a grip and act like sensible adults. This is not an easy thing to do. There's something about having to hold in the laughter that makes the situation even more hilarious.

As a rush of exhilaration runs through me, I look at my mates through my laughter-induced tears and am so thrilled to not be the one in charge right now, to feel carefree.

18

Mike

My friends have been so tightly wound with apprehension over this trip, I'm amazed either of them made it all the way here. The endless calls to check what to pack, the inability to strip down to just 'essentials' and travel light, the difficulty in being able to switch off and let go. Although it's understandable when Vicky has kids and Zaza is juggling wedding plans, getting away from it all is what I've loved about my previous travels – immersing myself in something new and sacking off the stresses and strains of life at home. Going at the pace of a new culture and seeing what else the world has to offer besides a nine-to-five job and the monotony of living for the weekend, only to find you're actually too knackered to do anything when the 'time off' arrives.

They'll get there.

'I feel good now. I feel excited,' Vicky declares, grinning at us both and looking down at the leaflet in her hands that she's scribbled further details all over. She hardly looked at Scott while he gave the briefing and her cheeks still haven't lost their pinkness.

'The toilets sound dire,' Zaza says, her lips curling.

'I've done worse,' I shrug.

'All right, Bear Grylls. I think I'd rather dig a hole,' she tuts.

'Don't think you'll feel that way when we're up in the mountains and you need a crap,' I warn her.

'Eesh,' sounds Vicky, screwing up her face. Scott, however, laughs before patting me on the back.

'I can tell I'm going to have fun with you three,' he says, Kevin and the rest of the team smiling along behind him. 'See you in the morning.'

'Yes,' blushes Vicky.

'Yes sir, we won't be late, sir!' chimes in Zaza.

'He's going to hate us,' mutters Vicky.

'Right. I think it's time we do what we do best,' I declare, putting my arm around Vicky's shoulders. 'And I don't mean whining and moaning.'

'I don't know what else I'm good at,' Vicky replies, looking up at me with a worried expression.

'Oh you do. I'm talking grab your jumper, your rucksack or your bumbag – let's go find somewhere to eat and drink.'

'Finally!' announces Zaza.

'This I'm definitely good at,' chuckles Vicky.

We exit the hotel and walk along the narrow streets towards the main square we drove through earlier. Maybe it's due to the time of day, almost six in the evening, but the streets are mostly empty with only the odd car or bike travelling by. As a result every pedestrian chooses to walk along the cobbled road rather than on the pavement, and just weaves in and out depending on traffic.

The streets are lined with orange, yellow and white buildings, some proudly built with local grey stone, the hanging signs offering anything from a hostel to coffee shops and local tours. Inviting as they are, the padlocked grilles covering the windows and doors give off a different vibe. Above our heads tangled wires travel along the streets and between the buildings – a troubling sight if it was in London but here it highlights a country still getting to grips with modern technology. Or, at the very least, seeing functionality as the priority and not really paying close attention to risk assessment.

Eventually the tight road leads into the vast square, where it feels like everything small has been replaced by everything big. Big streets, big walkways, as well as the view beyond. The opening of the space has afforded us a view of the huge mountains surrounding the city, a reminder of the magical adventures to come and the rich history of the Peruvian Andes capital. The Sacred Valley and the renowned Incan ruins of Macchu Picchu are nearby, maybe adding to the calmness that I feel as we walk through this busy place.

The Plaza de Armas glows orange thanks to the disappearing sun, highlighting the beauty of its huge cathedral that takes up the majority of one side of the square. Elsewhere restaurants and bars call out to us, beckoning us away from the decorative grassy verges in the heart of the square, all of which have been lined with benches for people to sit and absorb the local sights.

'Anyone hungry?' I ask, after we've meandered around for a while.

'Starving!' declares Zaza, her arm looped through Vicky's who clutches her bag tightly.

'Let's head a little out of the square. That guy on the front desk recommended that pizzeria up here, remember?'

'I thought you'd want us to try the local cuisine,' says Vicky, looking surprised and relieved.

'It does both,' I smile.

'I'm good with pizza, wine and bed!' declares Zaza.

'I could sink a beer or two,' I nod, not really wanting a cloudy head in the morning but knowing it'll help me sleep. I can't remember the last night I went to bed and my mind and body agreed to take a break so I could get some good shuteye, but maybe a drink and a different bed will help.

We head through the crowds, a mixture of locals going about their day, stray dogs, and tourists taking photos of every single thing they lay their eyes on – including the stray dogs and the locals going about their business – and up another narrow street. Within minutes we're sitting in Chez Maggy. I might not've chosen local cuisine for tonight, but everything about this place shouts local – aside from the Coca-Cola fridge that's sticking out in the corner. Wooden tables are crammed into the space and the wooden benches lined around them have been upholstered with traditional Peruvian fabrics. Next to where we're seated a chef hangs freshly prepared pasta over wooden rods, where it waits to be ordered and cooked. It's rough around the edges and because of that it's homely and welcoming. Although I'm not too sure the others feel the same when I look up from the menu to see them sharing some of Vic's anti-bac hand gel.

'Want some? You can never be too careful,' she says, proffering the bottle.

'I'll feel dirty if I don't now,' I laugh as she squirts some on my palm.

We place our order and the drinks arrive in a speedy fashion — much like they're drunk. The food, however, takes more than a while to come out, meaning we're on our way to being quite drunk by the time it arrives. Once it does, though, the table is covered in different dishes for us all to share: a margherita pizza, vegetable calzone — both cooked in the wood-fired oven — and a carbonara, because seeing the pasta hanging there was just too tempting. We all tuck in hungrily, sitting in silence as we chuck it into our gobs.

'Do you think the others think we're in a three-way relationship?' Vicky ponders.

'Who?' I laugh, almost choking on my drink. 'And where did that thought come from?'

'The others on the trek! The ones we're with for a couple of days. I was thinking about them and what they're all like — there's the mum with her teenage sons, those two girls who look like they're actually travelling properly, not just dipping in and out like we are, then there's the older couple who are so cute but I'm not sure how they're going to take on the trek, and the American family too, the two women who must be in their seventies and the man on his own, who looks to be in his sixties – I think I heard one of the guides call him Derek. I did smile at him but he didn't take the bait. Anyway, I was just thinking about what must've brought them here.'

'Speculating and judging?' says Zaza.

'Exactly! I was doing just that because everyone must have a reason for wanting to take on this challenge, and I suddenly thought, I wonder what they make of us,' Vicky says, taking a giant bite of pizza.

'They probably just think we're a bunch of mates,' I say, rolling my eyes at them.

Zaza giggles into her drink before reaching for her phone after it pings.

'Is Liam still up? That's love right there. I forgot about the time difference and called Nick earlier. Accidentally woke him up so told him to just go back to sleep,' Vicky says with a grimace, causing Zaza to look sheepish. 'Oh shit, I forgot to get our altitude tablets!' she gasps, her hands covering her face in despair.

'I thought you added them to your big Amazon shop,' Zaza says, her focus shifting to her phone.

'No, that was the electrolytes that were mentioned on that travel blog, remember?' she says, referring to what's become her hobby over the last few months – looking up Peru in the location setting on Instagram and making a note of what every tourist has said they've found useful. 'You said you'd go get them and I said not to bother because I had to go to the pharmacy with Chloe for more Calpol anyway. I just forgot.'

'Don't sweat it,' I shrug.

'Sorry, guys,' she says with a frown, her frustration visible.

'We'll get them here,' Zaza says into her phone.

'Pharmacy will be shut by now,' I say, looking at my watch to see it's nine o'clock already and that we've managed to sit in this spot for hours. I've no idea how we've all managed to stay awake when we were ready to crash when we first arrived. 'We'll go before we leave in the morning.'

Zaza stuffs her phone into her bag after quickly tapping away on it. 'Hmm?' she asks, her mind having been elsewhere.

'The tablets,' says Vicky.

'We might not even need them anyway,' she replies.

'Fail to prepare . . .' Vicky sighs. 'I've read it can get pretty bad.'

'That's why they gave us that tea at the hotel, and I bet they offer us a mug before we leave here too,' I state, looking around for the waiters who've been rushed off their feet the whole time we've been here. 'They'll be loading us up with that on the trek. The guides do not want us all getting sick. That would be a massive ball ache for them!' I add, remembering the amount of moaning I heard some people do while I was travelling around with Pia and how it really killed the vibe for everyone else.

'That tea was not tea. Tea relaxes you and is a remedy in any life situation – that was a bitter attack on my taste buds,' states Zaza, her nose turned up. 'Worse than green tea. Properly hit the back of my throat and made me want to gag.'

'Certainly an acquired taste,' I agree, finding her disgust at most things she's encountered on this trip so far hilarious. 'But it's what the locals believe helps with headaches from the altitude.'

'You mean the fogginess I'm feeling isn't just from jetlag?' Zaza asks. 'I feel like I'm on a boat. My head is swaying.' She holds her arms out either side of her, and gives an energetic sway, managing to whack another diner in the arm as they pass. 'Sorry,' she calls as they turn and grunt at her.

'Probably that too,' I agree, watching the person continue on their way to the loo. 'The tea is made from coca leaves – the raw ingredient used for cocaine.'

'Shut up!' Vicky gasps, as though I've just told her she'll be snorting lines of coke all the way up the mountain. 'Are you joking?'

'No! It's a banned substance in most other places around the world,' I tell her, unable to stop myself from smiling. 'You'd literally never make it through customs if you tried to smuggle some home.'

'It's illegal?' she gasps. 'Oh I don't think I can have any more of that!'

'It's not that bad. It has to go through a whole process before it becomes the white stuff.'

'Shame!' says Zaza, her phone pinging again from her bag. This time she ignores it. 'Fuck, I really need to stop drinking now or I'm going to be no use tomorrow!'

Tomorrow.

I'm aware of excitement fluttering around inside me at the reminder of the adventure we're on and the things we're going to see over the next week. Something inside me is reawakening, a comforting feeling to experience after living without it for so long. Like a hibernating bear waking after a dark, bleak winter.

Tomorrow we're starting with a trip to the Sacred Valley and to meet some locals. Although I've been laughing off Zaza's desire to not socialize with anyone other than our team, I do wonder how much of a tourist I'm going to feel when we're travelling around in the bigger group and jumping off a coach to take in a site. Tourist and traveller are two very different experiences. Guess I'm used to exploring local cultures in a slightly more intimate way. Smaller, more personal and at a slower pace. Being here and seeing how busy it is, I'm so glad we went for the Lares and not the Inca. I would've been doing peace signs in front of cathedrals before I knew it. This is much better for us. I just want to get on with the trekking now and immerse myself.

'What's up?' asks Vicky, giving me a gentle nudge with her elbow.

'Nothing,' I shrug, taking a gulp of beer.

'We wish she was here too,' she says kindly, squeezing my hand.

I can't tell her I wasn't thinking of Pia because the truth is I usually am, but any time I'm not consumed by dark and tragic grief I feel guilty, like I'm somehow forgetting her by daring not to think about her every single second, or for attempting to carry on without her . . . I feel like I'm cheating on her with life and the living.

I put down my beer and pat the back of Vic's hand, wondering when I'll be free to think of anything beyond what has passed and land in the present – never mind the future, I just want the now.

19

Zaza

I shouldn't have drunk so much last night. Any fool would've known it was a bad idea but I was excited to be out of my normal routine and somewhere new. Now, as I sit on the bus, Vicky tucked in next to me and Mike behind, I can hear the relentless nattering of the girls in front. From my seat I've been able to overhear their conversations with others and have learnt that Claire and Sammi are in the middle of a gap year where they're trying to travel as much as they can in a purse-friendly fashion, with loads of sofa-surfing with 'safe' online friends thrown in to keep costs down.

It is vaguely interesting, but the pair just don't stop yapping even when someone isn't asking them questions. Even though they've spent the best part of six months together they still have a million things to talk about. Clearly. I have to resist the urge to grumpily yell at them to shut up. We don't all want to know what's been going on in Billy Buskin's private life – even though it *is* wonderful to know he's going to be a dad.

I remember being young and feeling like life was too short to be quiet, that silence wasn't something to grab hold of but rather shirk against. I remember having to vocalize every single thought that entered my head even if it was banal and completely and utterly boring.

As we turn a corner we're greeted by another incredible view, pulling my focus from my grizzly hangover and the girls who aren't doing anything to specifically annoy me personally but are just the same, reminding me to make the most of this trip I'm on and what it might teach me. Which is hopefully more than the fact I'm just a truly grouchy sod who can no longer handle the morning after a night out – which wasn't even a night out-out.

I pull my phone from my orange Oliver Bonas rucksack (which is not my main hiking bag but my everyday travel one – even I know fashion must be sacrificed when scrambling along valleys) and go to take a photo of the cascading hills surrounding us. I'm greeted with a message from Albie.

> Your desk is looking so sad today! Dare I say it, the office isn't the same without you. Might have to order a life-size Zaza cutout. Can't guarantee it'll stay in the office though.

The side of my mouth curls into a smile. I can't help it. Then I think of Liam and reprimand myself. It might be harmless and innocent flirting but Liam would be crushed if he saw our exchanges.

'Albie is a cute name,' Vicky says, cutting into my thoughts with a shock. 'We almost went for Albert for Barnaby. That or Herbert. Albie or Herbie. Cute names.'

'Barnaby is such a Barnaby, couldn't imagine him being anything else,' I say, holding the phone back against my chest.

'I know what you mean. They grow into their names or their names are such a huge part of who they are they can't possibly be anything other than that,' she sighs, her eyes softening at the thought of her kids. 'And my Barnaby is so fricking cute.'

'You OK?' I ask, holding on to her forearm.

'Missing them today,' she winks, screwing her face up in the way I know she does when she's trying to stop herself from getting emotional. Her eyes remain watery, but thankfully the dam doesn't burst. She lays her head on my shoulder and I cup her cheek before kissing the top of her head. 'So who is Albie?' she asks.

'Someone from work,' I say, acutely aware of how I pitch my answer, willing for it to sound casual and nothing to cause any alarm yet aware of how defensive I feel over our exchanges.

'Oh,' Vicky says, raising her head and looking over at me, taking in my face. 'I don't remember meeting him.'

'He started a few months back,' I shrug, coughing as I put my phone back into my bag. 'He's a friend.'

'Of course he is,' she nods in return, a forced smile appearing on her disapproving face as she looks down to her hands.

'What?' I snap.

'Nothing,' she replies, surprised that I'm challenging her.

'Mike is a man and he's our friend. We are allowed to be friends with the opposite sex, you know. Doesn't mean we're all sneaking into the stationery cupboard for a quickie behind our boss's back,' I state, although I definitely dreamt about it a few weeks back.

After completely ravishing each other amongst the office supplies, our sweaty bodies pressing against one another, slipping and sliding in the sexiest fashion – all while his hot breath caught warmly on my ear – I woke in a state of confusion, as though my senses had been opened to a whole new world that I'd blocked out previously. My chest felt open, between my legs wet and sticky.

Turning in bed I found Liam lying next to me already awake, a big morning grin on his face. Guilt hit instantly.

Arriving at work a few hours later I saw Albie sitting at his desk. Catching his gaze made my cheeks flush with embarrassment as I walked on by. I had to pretend I'd suddenly remembered something and was distracted.

'Everything OK?' he asked later on, letting me know I hadn't been able to act as nonchalantly as I'd hoped.

'Yeah, of course,' I stammered back.

'You've been off all day,' he said, touching my arm as he spoke.

It took everything in me not to stiffen at his touch, my mind instantly going to his hot, sticky flesh on mine.

Thankfully things were only awkward for the one day. I rationalized that you can't help what happens in your dreams, it's completely out of your control, and seeing as mine have been chucking out all sorts of craziness over the last six months I had to accept it as just another part of that. Sure, having sex with a co-worker isn't quite the same as standing waist-deep in sea water chatting to your dead mate, but it's my mind making sense of things and processing all that's been going on. They mean I miss my mate and am aware that Albie is attractive. It doesn't bode well to dive deeper into my dreams than that. I've come not to trust them anyway. That little snippet of make-believe sexy time was lovely while it lasted but didn't prompt me to jump into bed with him, or grab him so that I could orgasm against the piles of paper and pens in the cupboard. No thanks. Not that I haven't revisited the dream a few times since then though. The thought makes me clench my jaw.

'I know that,' Vic stammers, shocked by my crude remark, taking me back to our conversation.

'I'm sure Nick has loads of female friends at work!' I state, trying to move my mind away from that stationery cupboard.

'What's Nick got to do with it?' she frowns, taken aback.

'I'm just saying,' I say, heat spreading across my chest and cheeks. 'He has female friends and I have male ones. I bet you don't go snooping when he gets a text from work.'

'OK,' she says softly, glancing around at the other passengers. She's never been one for creating a scene.

Vicky has always been the sort to want to know

anything and everything about a situation. *What's that?* and *Are you OK?* are two of her favourite phrases as she needles out something she deems to be the problem, which she then goes about fixing. Not everything needs fixing.

'What's up?' Mike asks, poking his head between our two head rests, his face looming between us both.

'Nothing,' Vicky sniffs, without turning back to face us. I roll my eyes at him.

'She was just sticking her oar in. As per,' I state.

'What?' she shoots at me, her head whipping round as the words come out in a whisper.

I inhale to speak but nothing comes out. Even I know I've pushed this too far and been a dick. I look back to the view outside, unable to look at the hurt and betrayal on Vicky's face.

With my back to them I'm aware of Mike sitting back down into his own seat and Vicky gathering her bits before moving elsewhere on the bus.

I feel shit. A shit friend and a shit human.

I close my eyes and try to block it all out, but now all I can hear is the female chatter in front from Claire and Sammi, nattering away about someone they know who might, or might not, have put on a few pounds over winter.

Who gives a crap.

20

Vicky

I find a spare seat on the bus, next to the mother with the teenage sons, and sigh as I lower myself into it. I've no idea what's got into Zaza but there was no way I could sit there and take any more of her crap. I haven't travelled across the world and away from my family to become someone else's punch bag. At least Barnaby and Chloe are children who don't know any better, a five-year-old who's learning about boundaries and buttons, and a toddler who has no idea how her words and actions might affect others. Zaza is a fully grown woman who should know better than that. I'm so annoyed at her for transferring her foul mood over to me, especially after I'd already said I was missing the kids.

And why did she have to mention Nick? Why did she have to say anything about the women at work? Women that are able to give my husband their undivided attention, women who are able to hang on to his every word and converse with him as much as the job allows, and maybe a bit more over lunch and a glass of wine? Women who are able to enjoy him in a way that I haven't been able to in years – as an individual who they're not looking to for help with the bins, a bit of DIY or any chore around the house to make their own lives easier. Women who can just listen to him and find interest in all he says, hanging on his every word, rather than hoping he'd just shut up so that the telly can be watched and some downtime enjoyed. Women who would love to have him want them, rather than avoid any situation of intimacy.

I push him away so much. I know I do. Every time I rebuff one of his advances it hits me, the ways in which I have fallen short. There's the guilt that I've failed him, the shame that I'm stopping us being together the way we used to be, the fear that I'm so changed and altered, and the dread that it's one rejection too many.

It's not just when I'm tired or stressed. It's every time aside from a quick birthday or anniversary bonk.

There's a block in me, and I've no idea how to fix it.

I know where I fall short in our relationship, and I've read enough books and watched enough daytime TV to be aware of the warnings, 'if he's not getting it at home he's getting it elsewhere', but none of it makes me want to throw myself on the kitchen table and wantonly do the deed.

I try not to be the jealous type. And even though I know I struggle being at home with the kids and having almost zero adult interaction, I could never let paranoia and jealousy in. It's not how Nick and I have ever been and I don't normally look enviously at the women he works with. There doesn't seem to be much point.

I resist looking over at Zaza but wonder what's got

into her. Something niggles at me. For the first few years of our friendship she always had a string of boyfriends; some were complete douche bags who really hurt her, and others were pretty nice guys who seemed perfectly pleasant. The jerks left her broken and somehow returning for more, yet the nice ones had her seeing flaws we couldn't see. She'd bemoan parts of their personality the rest of us found endearing or 'normal'. She never seemed to stop looking beyond that decent person in her bed and keeping an eye on what else life had to offer. Not in a terrible way – she never cheated, but she was aware, always questioning what else the universe could have in store for her. That all seemed to change when Liam came into the equation, even though he was, and is, undoubtedly one of the good guys. It was as though she finally allowed herself to feel happy, or maybe his quirks were more bearable than the others'.

It's not beyond Zaza to feel dissatisfied with what she has, even when she's finally got something she's longed for, and I hope the arrival of this new guy in the office isn't causing her to doubt what she has at home.

I almost laugh at myself as those thoughts bubble in my brain. It's like I'm forgetting my own reasons for coming out here. I haven't been discontented with life and the way things have panned out, but I've definitely needed a break from it.

'You been married long?' the woman next to me asks. You can tell her children are older and that she hasn't had to spend all her time focused on getting them up, fed and dressed this morning. Her blonde hair has been dried into glossy waves, her makeup is more than just a pinch of her cheeks as she rushes out the door – she actually has lipstick on, and her baby blue sleeveless shirt hasn't got a single stain on it.

She looks at me expectantly, nodding over at Mike.

'Oh no! No,' I laugh, knowing I was right about us all eyeing each other up and jumping to conclusions from our observations.

'Sorry, I saw the rings and just put two and two together,' she says, shaking her head with embarrassment. 'I'm Bronagh, by the way. That's Josh and Ben over there, my sons,' she adds, pointing across the aisle to where her sons are sat heads down, their faces sullen while their eyes are transfixed on the gaming devices in their hands. They could be anywhere right now.

'Well, hello, Bronagh, I'm Vicky,' I say. 'And that over there is Mike, one of my best mates, and so is Zaza in front of him,' I say, stopping myself from saying anything else about Zaza and realizing how silly it looks with us all spread out and me opting to sit next to a stranger rather than one of them. 'My husband is actually at home with the kids.'

'You have children?' she asks, her eyes widening.

'Yes, two. A very energetic boy and a cheeky little girl,' I say with a grin. Even thinking of them makes my heart swell with pride as their faces come into my mind.

'And you left them to do this?' Surprise flickers across her face.

'Yes . . .'

There's a pause as she processes the information and works out how to respond.

'Well, good for you, taking some time for yourself. That's good. More mums should be doing just that, putting themselves first,' she says, reaching across with her own ringed hand and giving my hand a pat. 'I couldn't do it myself, I'd never last a week without them even at this age, but it's great that you are and can.'

The words instantly sting, making the apples of my cheeks hot as though this woman has just slapped me right across the face.

'I'm with them every day. You know, stay at home,' I state. 'I don't have a nanny or anything. My youngest isn't even in nursery yet.'

'Oh, so young,' she smiles. 'Bet they've found this separation incredibly tough.'

She's not being bitchy exactly, but she is. Her comments are loaded with judgement and they crush me.

'Where's your husband?' I ask, looking down at the patting hand as she pulls it away.

'He died very suddenly a couple of months ago,' she says with a pursed smile, looking down at her hand.

'I'm so sorry to hear that,' I say, instantly regretting having asked and therefore making her have to reveal information I imagine she'd rather she didn't have to tell a complete stranger on a stuffy bus in Peru – especially one who has left her very much alive husband and children back at home by choice.

'Depression is an awful thing,' she states. 'It's why I feel I need to be with them, my boys, making every second count.'

I nod, feeling even shittier as the bus comes to an abrupt stop. Suddenly the chaos of a morning school run after dodging chucked Weetabix and wrestling to put socks and shoes on little feet doesn't seem too awful. In fact, I'd welcome it compared to the start of this day where I'm putting my foot in it left, right and centre.

'OK, you two, time to turn those off now,' Bronagh sings at her teenage sons, both of whom completely ignore her and continue playing with their games. She laughs in response. I'm not sure whether she's laughing because she genuinely finds their lack of enthusiasm for where we are funny, or whether it's out of embarrassment at me witnessing their apathy. Either way, it's good to see I'm not the only one who has kids with selective hearing.

Scott stands outside, waiting for us all to get off the bus so we can hear what he has in store for us. We all stand around, and rather than heading over to Mike and Zaza like I usually would I faff around with my bag and retrieve my camera to start snapping while I wait.

'OK,' Scott calls to the group, making everyone fall silent. 'This morning we've brought you to meet a local co-op of women who don't do things the way we are all used to.' He turns and gestures to the women behind him who are either stood in their stalls or gathered round preparing to get to work on creating something. There are children happily running around their feet or hanging from their mothers' backs in slings; it's a very calm and tranquil environment. 'You can see from the traditional way they dress that they're not buying their clothes online at Gap or H&M. These clothes are made to last, they're made to keep them warm and to be functional, they're made in the most sustainable way possible – from the land around them.' Scott's good at his sales pitch, pausing in all the right places and breaking it down so that we all have a moment to look at the women in awe over what they're able to do with their hands, all while taking in the matching outfits they're wearing. The red-rimmed hats with thick straps looping under their chins, the white blouses with a frilly detail running down the front, the bright red cardigans embroidered with a delicate white-threaded design of plants travelling up the front panels to their shoulders, the same cardigans then piped with a punchy green trim, the cuffs and pockets a vibrant blue with the same white-threaded pattern. Their black skirts are just as pleasing to look at, the red trim just hitting their knees – the look finished off with flat slippers that look comfy and practical. The women look impressive, especially gathered in a group, and I can't help but wonder if they dress like this normally or if this is more of a uniform they're wearing for our benefit. I've definitely seen women wearing similar items and wearing the colourful wool blankets to carry their young while we've been travelling around, especially in central Cusco, but the fact they're all completely matching makes me think this is a little more contrived. This is a tourist destination after all, even though we'd all like to believe we're on a completely unique journey on a previously untrodden path.

'This morning they'll show you how they work,' continues Scott. 'How they weave local alpaca wool, and then you'll be given the chance to buy some of their hand-made crafts. I strongly urge you to, because your input makes a huge difference to these women and their families in this ever-changing world. It helps keep their culture, their language and the traditions of the Inca alive.' Scott raises his eyebrows at the group. 'Right, off you go. Let me know if you have any questions.'

Definitely a sales pitch and I find it hard not to be sceptical about the set-up, but the people before us look happy so I venture over to a group of women sitting in a circle, weaving individual blankets that all hang from one metal rod set in between them all. They look up from their creations and smile, nodding as I hold up my camera in an attempt to ask if I may snap away. It's therapeutic watching them work, the repetitive action, with the back-and-forth, up-and-down motion of the thread.

I keep walking and find another group of three women, this time sat in a huddle. Two look like they're using a method similar to crochet, the other like she's knitting a pair of gloves. In front of them sit a dozen baskets, each containing bundles of wool, the dust from the sandy ground which blows in the breeze covering everything it finds, yet unable to disguise their vivid colours.

I make my way to the stalls beyond the women crafting which are framed by the Inca stone we've already become accustomed to seeing with wooden beams finishing the structure for straw to sit on top. Inside them bundles of dyed alpaca wool hang from washing lines. Stringy piles of khaki, orange, purple, yellow, red and maroon sit drying before they can be used to create new garments for us tourists to buy.

While I'm browsing at a collection of hats I look up to see a little girl of about four years old playing around with multi-coloured wool that's been woven around two rods. Unlike the women the children aren't in traditional clothing, but that doesn't mean their outfits are any less cheerful. On her feet are little black wellies which she's teamed up with a wool-lined denim jacket and cerise pink jogging bottoms which have been rolled up to stop them trailing in the dirt. The pink highlights her rounded grubby cheeks and makes me think of Barnaby and Chloe. Their cheeks always rouge up in this way when they're teething, poorly or have been outside in the fresh air for long periods of time.

The little girl looks up and meets my eye. Her head tilts to the left. I smile at her, but her gaze is one of indifference. She's adorable. I hold my camera up to my face and the sound of the shutter closing and opening as I take a snap causes a little smile to creep across her face. She turns her cheek, her chin lowering so she's left looking up at me bashfully. She lets out a little giggle before running to her mum who looks over with her own smile.

The girl motions for another child to come over, and when the other little girl joins her they whisper and giggle. The first girl motions for me to use my camera, and as I start clicking away the girls start striking innocent poses, both letting out cheeky chuckles as they smile for me. They then run to the camera, wanting to see what I've taken in the viewfinder, before heading off again so I can take some more. It's not long before they're joined by more children, all wanting to be part of the fun. I'm happy to be capturing their joy and this moment.

Whatever the cynical part of my brain wants to tell me, this co-op, these stalls selling handmade arts and crafts are an investment in the future of these children and their generation.

Before Scott starts rounding us up and getting us back on the bus I select gifts for the children, matching hats and gloves, and a blanket for me for those nights curled up on the sofa with a glass of wine. As I'm handed my plastic bag of gifts I feel a surge of excitement at the thought of handing them to Barnaby and Chloe, and telling them all about the children I met here in Peru.

A pang of longing hits me at the thought. Being a parent is complex. I spend so much of my time longing to breathe, and now that I have that space I long to be wrapped in their arms and legs, pulled in tight for warm hugs and sloppy kisses.

21

Mike

I'm very used to female drama and the complexities of being friends with women who absolutely adore each other but also irritate each other from time to time. Isn't that the beauty of friendship? Having those who see us for who we are and completely accept us for every flaw and foible, but are also willing to challenge us in moments of questionable behaviour, or when we're on the receiving end of their messiness?

Following the frosty encounter on the bus I watched as Zaza and Vicky avoided any sort of contact for the rest of the day. They didn't look at each other, walk together or even sit together at lunch to enjoy the traditional offering of ceviche – a dish made of raw fish marinated in chillies, onions and lime juice. While Zaza and I sat in the sunshine trying to enjoy our food, with small talk about how refreshing and light the meal was and that we'd have to try and recreate it at home, we avoided the whopping big elephant of their earlier exchange. Meanwhile Vicky opted to sit with Gillian and Betsy, the two women in their seventies who we have found out are from Manchester and have been best friends since they were born, thanks to their mothers being neighbours and inseparable. She looked thoroughly immersed in the conversation and I couldn't catch her gaze to encourage her to come and sit with us at all.

It's funny how we've come away from home and I'm still clinging to the security of having my mates near. This isn't how I used to be on my trips with Pia; I've always thought of myself as someone who can easily slot into any situation, but I realize now we always had each other during those adventures. We had the security of never being on our own, of having a teammate. I wonder if there's only so much change we are able to comfortably deal with in life. Not that any change in the last year has been at all comfortable.

Vicky keeps her distance again for our trip to the Sacred Valley, opting to stick with Gillian and Betsy, and I get separated from Zaza here too; while she ends up with Claire and Sammi, I walk with 'the kids' Josh and Ben who have come away with their mum. Josh is as tall as me and Ben isn't much smaller. Age-wise they're not far off Claire and Sammi, yet because they're with their mum the group seem to be collectively referring to them as 'the kids'. I recognize their hunched-over stances and moody faces from my own teenage years and can't help but feel drawn towards them.

'You guys having fun?' I ask at one point.

Josh shrugs and Ben nods politely.

Only once we move the conversation on to gaming do they really perk up and become more animated as we take in the new environment around us. We're bowled over by the giant, endless steps that hop down the mountains they've been chiselled into, a visual representation of a whole lifetime of stories we learn of through fables and folklore. It's the perfect mixture of rich history and nature, the manmade cuttings covered in the greenest of grass and lined with Inca stone. The effort to get it all there must've been immense.

Even though Zaza and Vicky have spent the majority of the day apart, trying to avoid each other at all costs, they have met a dead-end because a mishap with the hotel booking system has led to Scott asking if the three of us mind sharing a room. Neither of them was cold enough to argue against the idea and as soon as the door to our double bunk-bedded room is shut, and I've already jumped up to one of the top bunks like a big kid, Zaza decides to address the situation.

'I've been a twat and I'm sorry,' she declares, holding Vicky firmly by the shoulders so she can't avoid the situation by shrugging it off. Instead of a verbal reply Vicky just looks back at her and sighs. 'Of everyone in the world I know you always have my back,' Zaza continues, her face folding into a frown. 'I know you never have anything but love in your heart for me and I'm sorry I chucked that in your face. I was tired, grumpy and a bit hungover. I know you didn't mean anything by it – we're all nosey when it comes to each other's lives. That's what friends do, and should do.'

'Gillian and Betsy said they once had a fight that

meant they didn't talk for three months,' Vicky pouts, the sight of her eyes welling with tears dissolving the tension, her words making Zaza pull her in for a hug.

'Must've been over something huge,' I chip in, leaning over the wooden railing of the bed which is more comfortable than one might assume on first inspection, thinking about how united the older pair of women seem.

'Nope. Not really,' she says, shaking her head. 'Betsy was late for a lunch they'd planned. When she arrived thirty minutes later Gillian wasn't there.'

'Harsh!' Zaza mutters.

'Pre-mobiles and Betsy had no way of letting Gillian know the bus she was on had broken down. Both were upset and both thought they'd been stood up so they waited and waited for an apology. One didn't come and the months rolled by with them not talking.'

'How'd they resolve it?'

'Betsy had her handbag pinched while out shopping one day and was pretty distraught. The security team took her in and offered to phone someone for her. There was only one home number she could remember off the top of her head, she says. Gillian went marching down there to help and her anger at the guy who attacked her mate eradicated anything that had come before.'

'Blimey,' I state.

'I'd beat up a thug for you any day,' Zaza states, squeezing Vicky.

'That's a lovely notion, but please don't,' Vicky pleads before we all chuckle.

An hour later we're on the last excursion of the day and visiting a local home, owned by relatives of our Peruvian guide Kevin. It's vastly different from what we're used to. The house is one square space with a table at one end, a fire in the middle, bowls of food and water scattered around the floor and a bed in one corner. We're surrounded by Inca stone walls that are home to goat, or alpaca carcasses, which are hung like artworks. While I'm trying to avoid looking too much at those my gaze lands on an alcove in the wall that holds a vase full of yellow and purple flowers. Before the more palatable image can take my mind away from the dead animals, I spot what's below it. Under a blanket, as though they're spying on what's going on in the room, are three human skulls sitting side by side.

'Jesus,' mutters Zaza.

'My ancestors,' Kevin says, appearing at my side. I glance over to see his expression is one of affection as he looks ahead.

'Oh,' I reply, turning back to his family, unsure on the politest way to respond.

'We don't tend to do that back home,' manages Vicky.

'Here it's seen as good luck,' says Kevin, nodding his head. 'They protect my aunt's home and are good company for her. They conjure up good things. Love, affection, and they're good for the memory of what came before. No one is forgotten,' he adds in such a way it's almost impossible not to see the beauty in the tradition, even if it is eerie.

I don't think I'd take great comfort from Pia's skull being displayed in this way, but each to their own. I guess we all take comfort from different things and process death in our own way. Imagine if I did want to do that though. Where would I have put her? In the bedroom? The lounge? Would I have moved her around, wrapped her up and carried her with me to meetings each day, chatted away to her while I was on my lunch break? Still included her in every bit of life I was still here to live?

I think about the contents of my backpack. I really do need to talk to the girls.

'Weeeeeee!' Zaza squeals with a jump, just as the room starts squeaking and dozens of guinea pigs run across the floor.

Having heard about this tradition my own shock is more due to the collective hysteria within the group.

'Waaaaaaah!' shouts Sammi, suddenly clinging on to Zaza's arm, much to the amusement of Claire who seems unperturbed by the little feet scurrying around and decides to capture the moment on her phone instead.

'That's a lot of pets!' shouts Gillian, her arms crossed protectively in front of her as though they might be about to run up her body, something I've never seen a guinea pig do, but you never know . . .

'Where are they all coming from?' asks Betsy, bending over to have a good look below the bed they've all disappeared under, being far braver than her best mate.

'Why are they here?' adds Vicky, pulling a grimace.

'Dinner!' Kevin laughs.

'Sod this,' Derek mutters, the unsociable pensioner, grabbing for his cigarette packet as he walks out of the house.

'Gross,' Zaza mutters, clutching on to my arm as though they're about to attack her.

'A slightly different culture to ours,' Vicky gulps just as Scott joins us, cupping one of the furry creatures in his hands like you would in a petting zoo.

'I know it's strange for us to think of them as food when we're so used to seeing them as fluffy little things you'd have in a cage at home,' Scott says, stroking the furry animal. 'But they actually originated here in South America before the Spanish took them back to Europe and declared them to be pets. It's not that bad once you get your head around it. And it tastes all right, actually.'

'Wait. Have you tried it?' Vicky gasps, looking horrified, clearly forgetting what she'd just told Zaza. 'I thought it was just a locals' thing.'

'It's become a thing that people have to do when they come to Peru. So yes, I have and I've done it more than once,' he nods proudly. 'It would be rude not to eat what you're offered when welcomed into someone's home.'

'Does it taste like chicken?' asks Gillian, a serious look on her face.

'A bit more like rabbit, actually,' Scott says thoughtfully, as though he's recalling the taste in his mouth. 'But squeakier.'

'Eeesh,' sounds Sammi, her face screwed up.

'You're sick,' declares Zaza, also unable to hide her disgust.

I can't help but smirk at their reactions.

'Vegan?' Scott asks, matter-of-factly.

'No,' she says, rolling her eyes as he shrugs his shoulders at her response.

'You know, they're higher in protein and lower in cholesterol than chicken, pork or beef,' he reasons. 'They'll be lining the meat aisles in your local supermarket before you know it.'

Zaza shudders at the thought, causing the owner of the house to look over at her.

'Sorry,' she whispers with a curtsey, causing me to laugh.

'You can take the girl out of the city . . .' I tease.

'Oi,' Zaza blushes, her elbow prodding at my ribs. 'Are you drinking with us tonight?' she asks, turning to Scott.

'You're off out drinking?' Scott says, raising his eyebrows at the three of us. 'Again?'

'Not just them, we're all going,' chimes in Betsy, who was the one who suggested we all go for one last hurrah just in case she breaks a hip in the mountains and has to be airlifted out – this seems to be her main concern.

'We need dinner,' I state, knowing this really will be the last proper dinner we're going to have before we officially start the Lares trek tomorrow.

'We'll only have the one, sir,' Zaza says, a cheeky expression on her face while Betsy raises her hand in a fist, her fingers slowly unfurling to show she's not going to be sticking to just the one.

Scott doesn't manage to stifle his laughter.

'After your hangover today I think that might be for the best,' I jibe to Zaza.

'Actually I might be super naughty and go for a Diet Coke,' she says excitedly.

'Well, enjoy. I have to do the last bits for tomorrow to make sure we're all good to disappear off into the valleys for a few days,' Scott says. 'But for my lot – the bus leaves at five-thirty tomorrow, just make sure you're on it in time for me to chuck some breakfast in your direction.'

'Deal,' we all nod.

'The rest of you aren't my problem,' he shrugs, causing great laughter amongst the group.

22

Zaza

Despite my less than friendly attitude towards them at the start, I'm sad having to say goodbye to the other team as we split off to take on our individual treks. Up until this point it's been a nice bit of sightseeing with the occasional 'walk' thrown in along with some steep stairs, but over the next few days our challenges are going to ramp up a gear and I can't help but wonder how they're all going to get on. I'm sure Gillian and Betsy will master anything thrown their way, that Sammi and Claire will be talking non-stop and the kids will find some time to actually talk to their mum away from their devices, but at the same time I would've loved to be with them cheering them on. I'm sure the rest of the group will do that. All except Derek who will probably be too busy puffing on a cigarette to get any words out. He's a funny one, as while everyone has got on with mingling and getting to know each other he really has kept himself to himself. He's hung to the back of the group every time we're out together. Although maybe that'll be me when I'm in my sixties. I was reluctant to be with others before arriving here but I also know that society dictates that antisocial behaviour leaves you looking like a dick, so I did put myself out there and got to know the other people in the group – something I've actually really enjoyed doing. If, however, I didn't care what people thought of me I would definitely be more Derek. I can't help but wonder how he's going to handle the next few days and whether the team will see a different side of him.

They're still loading their rucksacks and daypacks into their minibus when we pull away from the hotel, so we frantically wave before settling back into our seats. I look down at my trekking get-up. It's definitely a case of all the gear and no idea. I basically bought everything that was on the kit list, even the optional stuff. My walking boots feel clunky on my feet and, although I know I should've walked them in properly beforehand, they feel surprisingly comfy. Just huge when compared to the flimsy flipflops I've been wearing. I opted for my gym leggings over hiking trousers because I reasoned that if I can manage an hour spin class in them without any chafing or rubbing, then they're probably going to be good for a bit of walking. The one bit of kit that does give me joy is the bright orange bomber jacket, which I'm thankful for right now as the air is fresh at this hour.

'Breakfast,' Scott yells, chucking some plastic-wrapped croissants in our direction from the front seat he's sharing with the driver and Kevin. 'There's fruit too, bananas and aguaymanto,' he adds, passing back a tub for us to share.

'I need something in me, I'm shattered. Feel like I

could've slept for hours more,' says Vicky while rubbing her eyes with the back of her hand.

'Know what you mean,' agrees Mike, an unwrapped croissant already shoved into his gob.

'You are such a terrible snorer,' I say, grabbing some of the cherry-sized fruit and popping one into my mouth.

'I've been told,' Mike nods, still chewing.

'No, not you,' I laugh, pointing at Vicky.

'Oh no. Am I? Please tell me you're joking,' she says, looking mortified with her hand on her chest like I'm breaking her heart. 'I've never been a snorer. Surely Nick would've told me.'

'Oh,' I stammer, taken aback. 'It was dark and I was so out of it. Must've been you, Mike.'

'Sounds about right,' he nods. 'Wake myself up sometimes.'

We fall into silence, Mike goes back to sleep (and yes, he does snore) and before long the minibus is coming to a stop in a place called Ollytaytambo. I look out, expecting to see an exciting, inspiring, awe-inducing sight – an incredible view of the mountains we're about to conquer or maybe a big shiny sign declaring the start of the trek, but instead we appear to be in the corner of a dusty playground or football pitch at the base of a mountain, with chain-link fencing surrounding us. Several houses surround the space we've entered with an opening in the fence leading out to them.

'Thank you so much,' I hear Vicky say, holding up her camera. Looking over I see that our bags have been taken off the minibus and the heavier ones, the ones with all our sleeping bags and camping gear, are being strapped to two sad-looking donkeys – although I've never seen a happy-looking one. Kevin goes over to the three Sherpas and chats away in hushed tones as they load them up. It's clear they all know each other and are very used to tourists coming along and taking snaps of them while they go about their daily job.

'I'm so sorry, but I really need the loo,' says Vicky, looking sheepish as she admits as much to Scott, who must hear that request so much he's beyond being embarrassed by it. When you think about it it's a rather strange thing for us all to be shy about when we must take a dozen loo trips a day, at least. I guess we haven't asked to go since school though.

'Want to get your last proper toilet trip in?' Scott chuckles.

I shudder as I remember how he described the Portaloo tent we're going to be enjoying while we're in camp – other than that we're going al fresco and letting the Peruvian air get to our bits.

Scott calls over to Kevin who takes Vicky off to one of the local houses.

'I'll come!' says Mike, running after them.

'Get a move on,' I shout after them while at the same time questioning the strength of my own bladder and if I should actually squeeze one out just for good measure.

While I'm pondering that thought a group of five children, four boys and a girl, walks from the front of one of the nearby houses and up to the fence, just in front of me. Three of the boys sit down on a little ledge a few feet away from me but still the other side of the divide. I can't help the desire to take a photo of them and the smallest one at the back offers the biggest grin. He really makes me laugh. The other two are inquisitive. They sit and watch me, while one of them removes his sandals and starts scratching his feet, the sound alerting me to just how dry they must be.

They're layered up. A mismatch of colourful clothes – anything from gilets to fleeces, jeans to more traditional Peruvian items, baseball caps to a fisherman's hat. The bobbles on the fabric and the way the dirt is embedded into it shows just how much mischief they've been up to, and fun they've been having, while wearing them. Whether they're dressed this way out of necessity or style, it puts a smile on my face.

To my right I'm aware of the other two children, a girl and a boy, edging their way towards me. Venturing closer to see what the strange lady is up to, maybe attracted to my big hair or my skin.

The girl holds out a hand, her eyebrows raised. When I'm not forthcoming she uses her other hand to point into her mouth.

'You want some food?' I ask, pointing at my own mouth.

'Sweets,' Scott calls over. 'Now that they've got a taste for sugar they try it on with every group that comes here. They can't get enough.'

'Oh I hear ya, sister,' I say softly to the little girl. I giggle as I take off my daysack and open up the top, diving into a pouch I put in there for the darker, more difficult moments ahead. I've called this my energy-giving stash, which is mostly a bunch of Cadbury's chocolate eclairs. My thought was that if it all got a bit too much then a good suck on a toffee filled with chocolate goo would make everything better again. I take out a couple and hand one each to the girl and the little boy who has leapt to her side now he knows I'm going to deliver. They inspect them, twirling them in their hands and watching as the sun bounces off the golden goodness.

Just as I'm about to hand some through the fence to the three waiting boys, all of whom are now enthusiastically up on their feet, I spot the girl pop her sweet into her mouth while it still has its wrapper on.

'Oh noooooo . . .' I say, holding out one of the toffees in my hands and showing her that the foil might be inviting but it's definitely what's underneath that counts. 'Like this,' I say, popping it into my own mouth and grinning back at her.

The boys copy me straight away, needing no encouragement; she, however, watches me with such an adorable look on her face, like she's enchanted by the action of me eating sweets. She's like a little Disney character with her big brown eyes and two messy braids hanging over her shoulders.

'Mmmm . . .' I sound, gesturing for her to do the same

with her own. I'm surprised she hasn't scoffed it yet, but maybe they're used to getting wine gums or jellybabies – sweets that actually look like sweets.

She does as I have done and her eyes widen as the sweetness hits.

'Just you wait, it's going to get a whole lot better than this,' I say, even though I know she doesn't understand me. 'Just keep sucking.'

She giggles in response and I feel a swell of warmth.

I've always been one to see children in my future, but the practicalities of that, the realization that most people my age were already jumping on that train while I was still single, meant that it was somewhere I never really let my mind go to. The idea of having kids has lingered on the horizon, especially since meeting Liam, yet I've never really let it come into focus. Recently I've pushed it even further away. With everything going on, with losing Pia, it's felt like one hope too many. One beauty of life I've really not dared to dream about.

But human connection . . . isn't it something we all deserve? Isn't it something to be celebrated, not feared just in case the unthinkable happens?

I think of Liam, and for the first time in a long while I allow myself to let the softness towards him in.

'You're not giving her sweets, are you?' reprimands Vicky, interrupting my thoughts as she finds her way back from the loo. 'What about her teeth? Her gut?'

I adore my friend, really I do, but it takes every ounce

of restraint not to bite back. Instead I focus on the sweet warmth of chocolate escaping my toffee and the smile on the face of the girl in front of me.

I take a handful more from the pouch and hand them to the girl, gesturing to the other children and for her to share them out. She does exactly that, and the five of them all huddle together behind the fence. Still watching us, but chewing, sucking and picking out bits of toffee from their teeth while they do so.

'OK guys, we're about to head off,' Scott calls, just as Kevin makes his way around to the three of us offering out coca leaves.

'Oh no!' Vicky gasps with a panic, her hands on her head. 'I didn't get altitude sickness tablets. I was going to, I was meant to, but we never got to the pharmacy.'

'These will help,' Scott gestures.

'Take lots,' smiles Kevin.

I look at the hesitancy on Vicky's face and have little doubt she's linking it back to what Mike told us about them and cocaine.

'It's what we've got now,' reasons Mike.

'I guess we've been up high for a couple of days already. Maybe our bodies will have already adjusted,' I say to Scott, in a way that is very much a leading statement. The hope being that it'll stop Vicky frantically worrying about not getting her tablets for the next few days.

'Yeah,' Scott replies in a tone that doesn't say he totally agrees. 'Just get chewing and store it in your cheeks like tobacco. They're sharp though, so just remember to spit, never swallow.'

I swear I see Vicky blush as she reaches out for the leaves and places them into her mouth.

'The big thing I want you to remember when we're out there,' continues Scott, looking completely oblivious to the effect he's had on my friend, 'is to hydrate. If you're standing still, hydrate. If you're walking, hydrate. You're going to be sweating for a long time and your body is going to need its resources restocked, so do just that.'

'I have some energy tablets to pop in your water,' says Mike, working his way into my bag and getting out my fun water bladder and plonking them in. 'I've already done mine and Vic's. Might make it taste better as well.' He tucks it back in and gives my bag a tug to make sure it's secure.

'You all ready?' shouts Scott.

'Yes!' we all shout.

'Then let's go.'

I wave to my new friends as we head off in the same direction as the Sherpas and donkeys, although they've already sped off into the distance, used to taking on this walk.

23

Vicky

I pull my phone out of my fleece pocket and check it again. No signal, just as it's been for the last few hours. Scott warned us this would be the case so I snuck in a quick call with Nick and the kids as we started walking – they were about to head to the park for ice creams so all rather giddy, but now there's no chance of phoning home and speaking to them. I take a deep breath to calm myself but I can't break the unease that I feel. These visceral feelings have been deepening since I got here, the worry of the unknown, that maternal pull that seems so real it's almost physical. A tug on my gut that tells me I'm not where I should be. I've only spent one night away from them both since Chloe was born, and that was for a friend's wedding which was only an hour and a half up the M40. I would never have considered travelling so far away from them this time last year, and the reality of that distance is really hitting home now. What if something were to happen to one of them while I'm up in the mountains and unable to get to them or I didn't find out until afterwards? What if something happens to me and I never get to go home to them?

I take a deep breath and concentrate on my feet as they walk one in front of the other, the repetitive action of my boots hitting the dusty ground giving a steady beat for me to concentrate on. I'm here now and have to make the most of the adventure. I have to park those worries until I have a reason to have them. I have to use my missing them as some sort of fuel to keep me going and see it as part of this challenge, otherwise what's the point of even being here?

There's been a tightness in my chest for most of the morning. I was worried it was because I have become incredibly unfit (running around after the family is the only working out I manage to fit in these days), but it turns out we've all been feeling it. We've travelled a long way already, and with that has come an increase in altitude, which affects the oxygen in the air. Our lungs are having to work harder. I find myself occasionally having to take a deep breath just to top myself up. I've never experienced anything like it before.

The small towns and villages disappeared from view as we walked and before long we found ourselves trekking along a narrow path that's been cut into the mountainside. It's a well-trodden route despite it feeling like it's in the middle of nowhere. In the distance, for as far as I can see, are mountains. They roll, cascade and climb invitingly. The expanse of it all, the silence of it, making me and my worries feel small.

As we walk in single file I can hear Mike and Zaza behind me, asking Kevin lots of questions about the history of the place and the beliefs of the Incas. While I'm listening to his answers I focus on Scott's legs and boots in front, my mind starting to drift off. I can't help but wonder how many mornings he's pulled on the same pair of boots. How many times he's taken on this trek and many others. I wonder how far he has travelled and what it's like to be him with his carefree existence, taking on the world in this way. It must be breezy and cheerful being Scott. Easy. Stress-free.

'So what do you do?' I hear Scott ask from in front, the actual words getting lost in the daydream of my thoughts. 'Vicky?' he prods.

'Oh! I'm so sorry!' I laugh. 'I heard you but I was in such a daydream.' I don't add the subject matter of those thoughts. I've been embarrassed around this guy enough already, I don't need more material to cringe over.

'Right.'

'What do I do?' I repeat, thinking how to answer the question I hate more than most. 'Raise kids?' I say, instantly hating how I turn it into another question, like it's not enough or I'm looking for some sort of confirmation and understanding that it absolutely is. Like I want him to validate my life with his awareness of how bringing up little humans to be good ones is definitely an important full-time job involving more unpaid overtime than any civil rights lawyer would want to be faced with.

'Really?' he asks, the rhythm of his feet changing, almost skipping a beat as his heel scuffs along the floor.

'You seem shocked.'

'I thought you were unattached and devoid of responsibility,' he says.

I remember my thoughts about him a few moments ago and let out a laugh.

'I didn't think I gave off such a relaxed vibe. I worry about everyone and everything and am most definitely the most considered and hesitant one of us three,' I state, realizing that he definitely wasn't listening to me when we first met. He's clearly not observant either, I think, looking down at the band on my wedding finger – a simple circle of silver, having decided to leave my engagement ring at home for safe keeping.

'Yeah,' Scott shoots back before nodding and stepping out of the way to allow a local farmer to walk past before looking back to ensure the rest of us do the same. 'I didn't really pick that up,' he says, walking again. 'I knew something was on your mind and taking you elsewhere. Kids though, that's a big one.'

'Yeah . . .' That's the understatement of the century, I think, before we fall back into silence.

'Remember guys,' Scott calls out as he walks. 'Keep drinking. Even if you feel like you don't need it – little sips every so often.'

'Yes, sir,' Zaza giggles before going back to the chat.

'What did you do before you were a mum?' Scott asks after a while.

'I was a TV producer,' I say, a familiar feeling of pride washing over me.

'No way. What kind of shows did you work on?'

'Daytime,' I say, enjoying his surprise.

'News based?' he asks.

'No!' I laugh, thinking of the more formal content that would land on other channels while we were creating a mash-up of being informative with a light touch while also bringing in the ridiculous – like when we got our main presenter to celebrate the start of spring by doing the whole show from the middle of a working farm. There's a reason they say don't work with animals, but it was cracking for live TV. Especially when one of the goats tried to eat the presenter's skirt, causing quite the panic – she was fine after brief hysterics. So was the goat. 'I tried my best to make a bit of telly that would leave people laughing and feeling good. Although sometimes we'd flip that on its head and create something that informed viewers about something they might've previously thought was a little scary,' I say.

'Like what?'

'Bowel cancer,' I reply without skipping a beat. 'Turns out lots of fun can be had when talking about poo and it can save lives too.'

'All while people are eating their breakfast.'

'Exactly,' I say, nodding at myself with a sense of achievement because it's not like he can see me as we walk.

'And what was it like to walk away from that?' he prods.

'I don't think I ever thought I really was. I was off to

have a baby, it was really exciting, but I thought I'd go back. There wasn't a doubt in my mind that I would. It was such a huge part of who I was and the life I led, I couldn't see myself not doing it. And then maternity leave was ending and I just couldn't imagine going back to the studio every day, leaving the house at four in the morning in time to get everything sorted before that day's show or, if I had a later start, hopping on the Tube with hundreds and thousands of other commuters like a swarm of little ants and huddled together in a tiny space. What was exciting to me before simply wasn't any more, and I just didn't know how I felt about leaving my eldest with someone else or missing out on parts of his child-hood. It didn't sit right with me. So I just didn't go back. I told myself it was a short fix, that I'd get back out there when Barnaby was a bit older and maybe in pre-school, but then I fell pregnant with Chloe and that was that,' I say.

'That sounds very final.'

'It's very full on, this parenting malarkey. I don't know how I'd find the space to add anything else in.'

'And how does that make you feel?' Scott asks. 'When you look back to the person on the show doing her thing, being all sassy and loving life?'

'I feel so far removed from her,' I sigh. 'It's not like I was in fancy suits and heels every day, I was always in trainers and comfy clothes, but it's the interaction, the connection that you feel with others you work with, that's what I really miss. That and the fact I knew when

I'd done a good job. There was a sense of achievement with work that I simply haven't had since becoming a mum. Nothing is ever complete or right – I'm constantly getting things wrong and beating myself up over it. It's so isolating being at home. I look back at the laughs we used to have at work and I feel so sad not to have that in my life still.'

'Hmmm . . .' he replies.

'It's not that I'm not happy being at home with the kids, it's just sometimes it's not what I thought it would be. You see all these images online of mums smiling with their children and everyone looks like they're having so much fun. I see them and wonder why that's not us. I rarely just lose myself in the laughter like them. I feel like I spend most of the day frowning and saying no. How'd I go from a people pleaser to a matriarchal dictator whose sole purpose seems to be ruining their fun?'

Scott gives a little laugh. 'I'm sure they don't see it that way.'

'I don't think I know who I am any more. And that's terrifying.'

'Or exciting,' he offers. 'Everything that was waiting to be discovered before is still there, and it sounds like you'll be rediscovering what you had previously discovered with fresh eyes anyway. Eyes that saw life being brought into the world. That's pretty cool.'

'Maybe,' I say. 'Sorry, I'm chewing your ear off now . . .'

'No, you're not,' he says firmly. 'You know, the best people to bring on trips like this are people who've got a bit more life under their belt. The kids that come, they're fun and all that but they're doing it because it's the done thing. They want to take the snaps of them looking all enlightened and full of thought while sitting with a contemplative pout at the top of a mountain – which they'll probably post on Instagram with an Erin Brockovich hashtag to really show how inspired or inspiring they've become, but it's all performative,' he continues, turning occasionally to check I'm still listening, which I very much am. It's so nice to simply talk and listen to another adult without having one of the kids nipping at my heels wanting my attention. I've lost count of the amount of times I've headed home following an afternoon of broken and unfinished conversations. Aside from Mike and Zaza, this is the longest adult conversation I've had in absolutely ages, and I'm including Nick in that. We just don't seem to find the time any more. This is a nice reminder of how important that time just chatting is.

'People beyond that have a more inward journey while they're here, and they're all the richer for it. That's what I do these treks for. So that people like you get to step away from life for a bit and ponder,' he says, stopping so the others can catch up with us. He looks directly at me when he continues. 'So ponder, Victoria. Let the thoughts come, let the words out.'

I'm thankful when his attention turns to the others as I'm aware of the sting of threatening tears. It's nice to have someone listen to me, to ask questions and actually hear what I have to say back, to challenge what I say and dig deeper. The words keep tumbling out of my mouth here like I have verbal diarrhoea. Maybe it's the fresh air, but it feels good to be afforded the space to speak and be heard. It's something I don't want to let go of now I've rediscovered the joy of it.

24

Mike

I was ravenous before lunch thanks to our first proper experience of the challenge, the terrain and the altitude. As we came over and round the final bend of the morning it was awesome to see that the staff who'd run off ahead with the donkeys at the start of the day had created somewhere comfortable for us to eat within the scenic setting. In a huge clearing they'd erected a white tent on the dry grass, with a smaller bright blue tent placed 100 yards from it – the toilet. I braced myself for Zaza's reaction, and sure enough her disgust came, although nowhere near as bad as I'd presumed. More grumbling than actually voicing her dislike, but by that point we were both wiped out from the morning and hungry. Zaza is never herself in such conditions, even though we both had a great time distracting ourselves with Kevin as we walked. What was strenuous to us didn't even make him sweat, let alone run out of puff. He was bouncing around like a mountain goat completely unfazed as he continued with our conversation.

Arriving in the clearing we were all happy to dump our bags, which might be only day bags but the amount of water I've brought (I always carry a little extra, just in case), along with the snacks Vicky's packed and toilet rolls and potions Zaza couldn't manage without, were really adding to the strain of trekking.

I took a breath before walking into the food tent, feeling slightly dizzy from suddenly stopping after the continuous moving of the hours before, not to mention how much higher we'd climbed already this morning.

Finally feeling steadier I took myself inside and my hungry eyes were instantly satisfied with what they saw. The white tent had been partitioned into two, with the chef working away on one side and a table laid out on the other for us all to sit around, already laid and set for lunch.

The food did not disappoint. Maize soup with garlic bread to start and then quinoa, chicken and broccoli to follow, all rounded off with copious amounts of coca tea to wash it down.

Walking out of the tent half an hour later my stomach feels rounded for the first time in months, almost painfully so as my insides stretch to accommodate the volume of food I've just put inside me as easily as inhaling air. I forgot what it was like to feel that hungry, and then to over-eat to this extent. I might actually have to loosen my belt before we get walking again.

Eating has been a pretty functionary activity for quite some time. It's not been something I've taken any care over. Cooking for one is very different to the joy that comes with creating a meal for two. I always loved those meals where we'd come together and talk about our days while eating the food we'd prepared along with a bottle or two of wine. We loved sampling new dishes, trying out new recipes from our mums that they'd unearthed from old recipe books, both trying to keep traditions alive in our mash-up of cultures.

Food hasn't been the same for me since. I've slowly made my way through the meals placed on my doorstep or in my freezer by people wanting to show they're thinking of me, but I couldn't tell you what a single meal tasted like in that first month or so. I just forked it in because I knew I had to.

Putting food into my mouth, tasting it, allowing myself to enjoy it, feels like an act of self-care I've overlooked.

'Thank you so much,' I call out, turning back inside and poking my head beyond the hanging sheet and into the other side of the partition. Chef Jonny politely nods at me with a smile before continuing with his work, scrubbing at a pot in his hands so that it can be packed away with everything else he's already organized. I duck out and let him get on with it. I know offering to help is seen as an unacceptable thing to do, so I resist the urge – unlike Vicky who almost had to be wrestled out of the tent a few moments ago after trying to do the washing up. You'd think she'd be happy to have a break from the endless chores she has to endure back home but she's a doing person and hates just standing by and watching someone else get on with a task if she can help. She was the same when we lived together, so it's really not something she's picked up since becoming a mum. Switching off might be longed for when it all gets a bit much, but it's not so easily achieved in practice.

'You've got a while before we have to get moving again,' Scott says to the three of us, following us out into the sunshine. He takes off his cap and smoothes back his long hair before putting it on again. 'Rest your feet, take it all in, and make sure you go to the loo.'

Zaza eyerolls back at him.

'There's always the bush,' he shrugs. 'Although the next part is a bit tougher to navigate, so you might not want to stray too much from the path. Could end up falling off the edge of a cliff mid-flow.'

'Cliff?'

'I might've exaggerated,' Scott smirks as he walks off, Kevin following behind him. 'Just go to the bog.'

'He's such a git,' Zaza says, smiling back at him, plonking herself down on the ground, her face basking in the sunlight while her arms grab at her puffer jacket to keep out the chill of the breeze. I join her, grabbing my day bag to use as a pillow.

Seconds later I feel Vicky do the same the other side of me.

There's no distant sound of traffic, no sirens speeding past, no people shouting or music blaring. There's only the sound of Chef Jonny clearing up and one of the donkeys braying while they rest ahead of being loaded up again.

'Must be so weird for Kevin,' Zaza murmurs next to me.

'In what way?' I ask.

'This is his life. What he's used to, what he's been brought up to believe and worship. Then he's got tourists, people like us, coming in and asking a million questions about it, almost questioning the fabric of his beliefs. Must be odd to get his head around,' she says.

'Maybe, but there's a sense of pride when he talks,' I reason. 'He never seems caught out by the questions.'

'You don't think that's because he's heard them all a million times before?' asks Vicky.

'No, actually,' I say, thinking of all the various locals I've met in other corners of the world and how they're always full of interesting facts and stories so different to my own. Some of my favourite moments when Pia and I were off on our adventures were born from having the time to sit, talk and listen. Something that's robbed from us back at home with our fast-paced lives. It gave us a new appreciation for others and the lives they lead. It's why we had the let's-just-go bag – to get away from the nonsense and actually immerse ourselves in life and different environments and the situations people are living in away from the nine-to-five mentality so many of us have had engrained into our psyche.

'I think he genuinely likes to pass on the traditions that, if his generation and the ones that follow stop sharing as guides, will die away. Then Peru and the Andes will be no different to the rest of the world. While we're here we should learn all we can about their beliefs and their way of life, because, for me, that's the beauty of being here – seeing what little nuggets I can take home with me. I don't think we're all going to go back and start adding guinea pigs to our Sunday roast menus, but we'll definitely leave feeling inspired by some parts of their lives and will adjust ours in some way, maybe without even realizing. I think that's what guides like Kevin love about talking to losers like us.'

'He really is a talker,' Zaza notes.

'I ask a lot of questions,' I laugh, aware of part of myself that's felt hidden starting to free up. My interest for life. For living. 'How do you think the others are getting on?' I ask, wondering how different their view will be to ours and if their trail is, as Pia and I were once warned, far busier than this one.

'Ooh. I had a weird pang of missing them then,' she says, her hand on her chest while she looks confused by the feeling.

'And you were reluctant to even mix with them!' I remind her, knowing that friendships made on such trips are often formed quickly and intensely through the shared experience and everyone being away from their usual creature comforts.

'We made friends,' laughs Zaza.

'I'm sure they'll all be in one piece,' Vicky smiles.

'OK, I can't actually control it any more,' Zaza says, jumping to her feet. I watch as she pulls out a see-through pouch from her bag which appears to contain wipes, anti-bac gel and some sort of spray. 'I'm off to use the loo. Wish me luck.'

'So prepared.'

She looks down at the items in her hands and back up at me. 'Fanny spray,' she nods. 'I like to feel fresh.'

'Good to know.'

She chortles as she walks towards the blue Portaloo tent, turning to give us a comical grimace before stepping inside and zipping herself in.

Vicky and I laugh at the sight of our friend before lying back down on the ground.

'Do you have suncream on?' she asks.

'I'm all right,' I respond, remembering how much my blatant disregard for skin health used to upset Pia. I would say it was ironic that she's the one who went on to get cancer after worrying so much about my health, but I'm not quite there yet. It wasn't irony. It was pure shit.

'Zaza gave me this one, really good SPF for your face . . . we're so high up and the sun will catch us without us even knowing with this breeze. Your cheeks are looking a little rosy,' she presses, massaging some lotion into her hands before sweeping it across her face.

'Go on then,' I say, holding out my hand as she squeezes some on.

I copy her action and rub the lotion through my hands before smearing it across my face haphazardly. I've never been one for 'self-care' like this. I'm the get-up-and-go sort, not the kind to spend hours looking at myself in the mirror while preening myself like a hedge.

'I forgot to say – Bronagh, mum of the kids, she

assumed we were married,' Vicky says, raising her eyebrows at me.

I laugh at the thought.

'I mean, it's not that funny,' she says with a tut.

'It was that look,' I explain.

'I did say they'd be speculating,' she says, putting the lotion back in her bag.

'You did,' I nod.

'It's nice that you spent some time with the boys.'

'They were sweet kids,' I shrug. 'Typical teenagers, moody and smelly.'

'Did they tell you about their dad?' she asks.

I look up to see her biting her lip.

'No . . .' I say, unsure if I want to hear the answer.

'Died a few months back,' she says, just holding my gaze.

'Shit . . .'

'Yeah.'

'Well, no wonder they were quiet,' I say, wondering whether I should've asked them more questions or gone deeper with the chat. Would they have even wanted that? I doubt it. It's been so hard to have normal conversations with anyone once they find out about Pia, and I imagine they've been experiencing the same. Everything awkward or forced. I know how difficult it is to navigate grief and I'm in my thirties, I've lived a bit of my life at least. I can't imagine what it must be like for them. Not that grief is ever something that should be compared. 'Life can be so cruel,' I say, aware of a bitterness in my mouth as I say it.

My friend moves next to me and squeezes my hand firmly, not letting it go.

We sit in silence.

'How are you feeling?' she asks quietly.

'I hate that question,' I say honestly, feeling relieved I didn't know about the boys' dad and wasn't put in a position where I asked them the same thing.

'Why?'

'Because when I'm asked and I'm feeling fine I suddenly feel like I shouldn't be, or it makes me question if I really am. It makes me wonder if I'm doing a pretty good job of pretending to be fine when actually I'm not. I wonder if I'm doing the whole fake it till you make it thing.'

'Sorry, Mike,' she says, looking embarrassed, like she's done the wrong thing and I'm calling her out on it.

'No, you don't have to be sorry. You care. You're my friend and I know you want to ask me that and I know you want me to tell you I'm fine – you want me to be OK. But being OK makes me wonder if the hurt is getting less. And if the hurt is getting less does that mean that I'm forgetting? Am I dishonouring her somehow? I think my "fine" has forever been altered, all of ours has. We're all just very good at plastering over the cracks and making ourselves presentable so that we don't fall into a million pieces or self combust.'

'I hear you,' she exhales as we fall back into a silence.

'Isn't the view stunning,' I say, breathing it in and wondering what Pia would've made of our choice of adventure.

I wish she were here with every inch of my heart.

Vicky leans over and gives my shoulder a tight squeeze. Then she stands and strolls towards her day bag, busying herself with repacking it, replenishing her 'sweet pocket' and getting more water.

'Has she been mothering you?' Zaza whispers, having returned from her loo trip with a relieved look on her face, attempting to stuff her toiletry bag back inside her day bag.

I shrug in response, needing to take a moment. 'She's just trying to do what she does best – care.'

'All right, don't make me feel bad,' Zaza says, looking over to our friend.

I often wonder if we would've ended up as mates had we not gone into a flat-share together. Despite Zaza's observations on Vicky mothering me, they both do it, though in very different ways. Yes, Vicky is in your face, always wanting to know you know she's there whenever you might need her and fretting about 'getting it right', but Za has been just as present. Her relaxed approach does make her easier to be with sometimes. Where Vicky's emotions are like a tap and ready to pour at any given moment, Za has always been more controlled with hers, unless she's hungry, tired or hungover. I often wonder if her stoic attitude is just a piece of armour she's scared to remove, but who am I to say anything about anyone doing what they have to in order to keep it together.

'Well done for surviving your first Portaloo wee,' I say, nudging her knee.

'Don't even get me started,' she says, turning to me with a serious look of horror on her face while continuing to wedge her belongings into the tight squeeze of her bag. 'I really wasn't made for this outdoor stuff. Oh fuck!' she shouts, as water flies up from the water bladder in her bag and squirts her entire face. 'How'd that happen?' she gasps, wiping it away from her eyes.

'Karma,' I say, unable to stifle the laugh that erupts, filling up every part of me that felt so empty just moments ago. It spills out until I'm curled over on the ground. I look over and see Zaza follow suit, her head tilting back and her mouth opening as she lets out the loudest laugh I've ever heard from her.

'I've got to stop,' I gasp, tears of laughter streaming down my face. 'My tummy hurts,' I add with a giggling squeal, my body confused by the feeling of being full and this noise spilling out of me.

Zaza leans over and nudges me in the arm, her way of telling me to stop laughing at her, although I know she doesn't mean it in the slightest. I laugh harder. So does she.

It feels so good.

25

Zaza

When I thought about this trek I imagined us meandering along a well-trodden path, taking in the sights and breathing in the fresh air with gusto and uplifted spirits. The weather, however, has changed drastically in the last few hours as we've travelled higher. I did not imagine us freezing cold in the fog, unable to see beyond each other or where we are, and feeling pretty miserable as we practically scramble our way up a mountainside. This is more physical and strenuous than I'd envisaged – not that I'm opposed to hard work, but there's the tiniest possibility I overlooked how tricky putting one foot in front of the other on a trek can actually be when up a mountain in Peru. I might sweat my butt off on our Peloton back home, but at least I can get off after a forty-five minute session and have a nice soak in the bath. What I'm doing right now requires a different skillset altogether, namely stamina and endurance. I'm beginning to doubt my reserves of either.

'Here,' Mike calls out, reaching hold of my hand and literally pulling me across a rocky patch.

'Thanks,' I mumble.

'You OK?'

'Yeah,' I lie, falling back into the silence which has eerily descended upon us for most of the afternoon, and feels noticeably different to the jolliness we started with.

'Everyone stop where you are for a moment. Catch your breath, have a drink,' calls out Scott, who has been leading the way and helping Vicky along up front. 'Remember, if you need some motivation, time to try some rehydration.'

'Am I tripping?' I mumble to Mike.

'Nope, he really did use a rhyming couplet,' he sniggers.

'Wow,' I say, trying to stifle a laugh.

Scott shrugs. 'I keep trying to come up with new ways of getting people to drink.'

'Noted.'

'You can come up with a new drinking slogan for me if you like, but until then – drink.'

'You know what,' I say, putting the mouthpiece of the water bladder to my mouth and taking a swig, 'I actually think that last attempt had a bit more oomph about it.'

'It made you drink, that's all I care about,' he says, before turning to the others with a satisfied face as he sees we're all doing just that.

We start walking again and I'm relieved when we stop going up and start plateauing out on level ground. That comfort lasts only a few minutes as we then start going down. You'd think heading in a downward direction would be easier, gravity is on your side, yet the opposite is true. My body naturally wants to lean forwards so I can see what's going on, but doing so makes me too fast and throws me off balance, so I lean backwards into the ground behind me as I go.

'Not long now,' Kevin says behind me.

His words fill me with relief and excitement, foolishly leading me to be clumsy with my footing. My right boot goes down on a loose rock which wobbles and falls away, my weight is thrown off-balance as a result, and my arms flail helplessly as I land heavily on my backside, my body skidding down the mountainside.

'Fuck,' I scream, curling into a ball when I stop. I take a breath of relief when I realize I'm safe and not still plummeting down to my death.

'Shit,' calls Mike, rushing over to help me just as Kevin does the same. In the foggy distance I see Vicky and Scott stop where they are and turn back to see what's caused the commotion.

'I'm OK!' I shout, leaping to my feet before anyone can get to me, giving myself a dusting off and gesturing for us to keep going.

'Slow down,' urges Mike, holding me by my shoulders to steady me further.

'I just slid down, that's all. I'm good,' I protest, aware of how much my body is already aching from the heavy impact of my butt on the ground, and not completely sure why I'm shunning help when I'm in pain and feel like bawling my eyes out.

'You sure you're OK?' asks Mike, rubbing me down before easing his grip.

'More than sure,' I say, as Scott comes bounding up to us, his experienced legs not faltering at all on the terrain.

'I just felt like going for a slide. Thought it might be quicker,' I joke. 'I scraped my arm,' I admit, looking down to see only a little graze whose sting makes it feel worse than it looks.

'Need to sit down?' he asks.

'No.'

He looks me up and down.

'Let's take a moment.'

'I'm fine,' I whine, hating the fact we're having to stop because of me.

'Insurance says I need to check you're OK,' he shrugs.

'And I've said I am.'

He looks at me for a moment or two.

'Any other injuries?'

'I might have a scraped bum too.'

He raises his eyebrows at me.

'No, I don't need you to check it.'

'As if I would ever suggest such a thing!' he says, mockingly, looking over at the others and rubbing his eyes before turning back to me. 'In all seriousness, do you feel fine to carry on?'

'Do I actually need to tell you I'm fine again?'

'Come on then.'

'You've got this, Za!' shouts Vicky as Scott starts

moving back towards her. She hasn't moved from her spot, although I'm guessing that's because she's scared about falling over too.

When we start going again, this time even more tentatively than before, the ache and stiffness worsen, and a wave of relief washes over me that I wasn't seriously hurt. I feel a bubble of emotion swelling inside. Usually I'm able to push this down and park it, but as I walk I feel the tears fall down my face. Big, fat streams of tears falling uncontrollably. Not a wail of despair, but sadness, dripping from my insides, no longer willing to be contained and suppressed. Even when Pia died I didn't allow the tears their freedom to flow. Mike needed us, Vicky needed me. I couldn't let myself go there. So I squashed it, held it in as much as I could, and pushed Liam away so that this weakness couldn't be found out.

The realization sends fresh waves of tears. They don't feel debilitating, though, as I've always feared they would. They feel freeing, happy to be noticed and validated.

As we come to a few rocks that need more thought to navigate around, Mike turns and offers a hand across. Our eyes lock as he takes in my tear-stained face. I notice his jaw tighten. He squeezes my hand with his, his face showing a look of understanding and determination. Once I'm across the rocks we return to walking as before, the silent look between us speaking volumes.

A little while later, just as my tears have dried up, we walk over a ridge into a flat valley. With the fog having cleared, we can see that over in the far corner is our camp for the night.

'Thank fuck for that,' I mutter.

'Amen to that,' winks Mike, chucking an arm around me and pulling me close, kissing the top of my head.

'Race you!' shouts Vic, who's already 100 metres ahead.

We don't even hesitate. Arms and legs that only moments ago felt too knackered to carry on find a renewed energy.

*

Our little red tents might as well be five-star luxury hotels, which I know is rich coming from me, but whatever comfort they have to offer I'm grateful for. Just the thought of getting out of my boots and putting my tired feet into a pair of sandals feels like a blessing. The reality is that they have to be yanked off, with Vicky giving me some extra help to set my feet free before she starts rummaging through her bag so she can have a quick refresh with a wipe wash.

'They must've swollen!' I say, suddenly groaning as I grip hold of the soles of my feet and give them a squeeze, something that makes the muscles ache even more but feels oddly satisfying. Peeling off my socks I let out a gasp.

'What?' Vicky asks.

'Might have to say goodbye to my strappy footwear this season,' I say, waving them in her direction. Both heels have been invaded by the biggest blisters, as have my little toes, and one has randomly appeared just under my right big toe.

'Shit,' she says, her face screwing up while tending to her armpit with one of the wipes. 'Do they hurt?'

'They didn't but they do now I've seen them,' I admit. 'I'll let them breathe and then wrap them up in the morning,' I decide, feeling surprisingly OK about the state of my feet that I usually take such good care over.

It's for a purpose.

Plus, although I've not mentioned it to anyone at all since, I'm grateful that my body didn't get more of a hit when I took a tumble. A broken bone or a twisted ankle would've been miserable.

Seeing Vicky reach for her phone makes me grab mine out of my pocket.

'Fuck,' she mutters, her face full of worry.

'What's up?'

'Still no signal,' she says with a frown.

'Not too surprising, I guess,' I say. We are, after all, in what appears to be the middle of nowhere. That said I can't help but look at my own phone with a disappointed pout.

'Were you hoping to message Liam and let him know you're safe?' she asks. 'Or maybe Albie?'

'Vic—'

'It's none of my business,' she says, flapping her arms about as though she's literally batting the conversation away.

'You brought it up, but I agree. It isn't,' I state.

Thankfully the conversation is left.

Dinner couldn't come quickly enough and it certainly didn't disappoint. The main meal was another taste of local cuisine with a marinated beef stir-fry known as *lomo saltado*. The steak was cooked to perfection in soy sauce, chopped red onion and tomatoes and came with some fluffy white rice. It was delicious. I never have white rice at home, we always opt for brown, and because of that it always feels like such a treat to have it.

By the time dinner has been and gone I'm shattered and longing for bed. I'm ready to let my feet breathe ahead of Scott wrapping them up in the morning (his offer), but thanks to Vicky's constant mission to keep the kids entertained she produces a pack of UNO cards.

'UNO?' asks Scott, walking the remaining empty plates round to Chef Jonny. 'I was right about you three, you're wild.'

'Ha-de-har,' Vicky giggles before pulling a funny face at him.

'I can't remember the last time I played this,' I say. 'I know we played it in the flat a lot, but I don't remember it being fun.'

'Don't try and be the cool one,' jokes Mike, raising his eyebrows at me.

'You know I am, though. Right?' I smirk.

'Are we all playing?' Vicky calls out, motioning for the whole Lares Trek team to join us.

'Are you sure?' Scott asks, sounding surprised yet keen. 'You don't just want to play the three of you?'

'Don't be daft!' I say, looking back at Mike. 'If *I'm* having to endure this so are you lot.'

'Smooth,' he laughs back.

I watch as Kevin looks over to Scott and the others. Clearly this isn't standard practice as there's such an awkwardness about whether they should or not. I imagine Scott and Kevin joining us is one thing as they're with us all the time, but wonder if some guests put a distance between themselves and the rest of the team, as they don't get to know them while walking.

'Come on!' Mike calls, beckoning everyone over and getting us to squidge up so there's space for us all to sit. Chef Jonny and the two Sherpas, Pedro and Rafael, do so, looking apprehensively between us all.

'Everyone knows the rules, right?' Vicky asks, dealing the shuffled pack.

I'm not entirely sure how much English the team can speak, but they take their cards and hide them from each other, whispering behind their hands for further clarity of the rules.

'You ready?' asks Vicky, before putting down her first card, and we're off.

We start slowly with us guiding those not in the know on how to play and what their cards mean, and once everyone is ready there's a shift in the air and a competitiveness builds, namely because Vicky, Mike and I stop being helpful and instead start focusing on the cards in our hands and how to get rid of them.

It's tense with lots of dramatic intakes of breath when someone puts down a card that requires a big pick up – something Kevin seems to be getting the brunt of thanks to the novices beside him each gaining some beginner's luck.

Very quickly I find myself with only one card left, and it's a wild card plus four, meaning no matter what, I can put it down.

I try to keep the look of glee from my face until it's my go.

'I win!' I say, placing my final card down on top of the pile.

'You didn't say UNO!' remarks Vicky.

'UNO!' I repeat.

'Not now, you're meant to say it when you have one card left in your hand so we all know!'

'I forgot,' I shrug, looking around at the rest of the table who are either still looking down at the cards in their hands in order to play on, or at what's happening between me and Vicky.

'But that's the rule.'

'Well, I can't turn back time,' I laugh, suddenly remembering why Vicky always loved this game and I didn't so much. She's not the best loser. In fact, UNO is a tough game for anyone to lose, that's why people find it addictive.

'You can't do that?' smirks Scott from across the table, leading to him and Mike singing a line from a classic Cher song.

'You cheated,' declares Vicky, deciding not to let the matter go.

'I did not!'

'All right, all right!' chimes in Mike, still laughing from his musical outburst. 'Vicky, she would've won anyway with that card. And Zaza, try not to be such a naughty girl next time. Let's carry on.'

They do so while I watch.

'UNO!' Vicky calls when it's her turn.

I catch her eye, and she rolls both of hers to the ceiling.

Kevin, Chef Jonny, Pedro and Rafael excuse themselves after a couple more games – Chef Jonny won the second game and Mike won the third – leaving us alone with Scott.

'Come on then, Scott, tell us more about you,' I prod.

'What about me?'

'Where are you from?' I ask.

'I grew up in Cornwall.'

'Nice,' I note.

'Love it there,' nods Vicky.

'And?'

He laughs. 'What more do you want?'

'Happy childhood?'

'Are you wondering if I do this because I'm running away from something?' he asks, raising his eyebrows.

'Aren't we all?' Vicky chuckles, her response seemingly taking her by surprise.

'I don't think I am. Mum and Dad were pretty chilled growing up,' he says, tapping the cards on the table as he talks. 'We surfed every day, even in the winter, and life was bliss.'

'And then?' I ask.

'My mates went to uni and I just knew it wasn't for me,' he says, looking up at me. 'Thought I'd rather spend the three years travelling the world and spunk money that way rather than sitting in lectures every day with some boring old dude droning on at me about a subject I wouldn't end up pursuing anyway.'

'Fair point,' Mike smirks at Vicky and me, knowing none of us three is actually working in the field in which we studied. I've definitely fluked my way on to the beauty desk.

'Right?' nods Scott.

'So, it was the whole university of life thing?' I say.

'I guess. Felt more appealing.'

'How'd you end up here doing this?' asks Vicky. 'Because I'm assuming you're older than twenty-one, right?'

'I look like I might not be?'

'It's hard to tell with all that hair,' she jibes.

'All right, Mum,' he says, taking his cap off and shaking his mane out.

I look to Vicky and see her cheeks have pinkened at his remark.

'I'm twenty-six,' he admits. 'I did three years' travelling, earning as I went, then went back to find all my mates had jobs and proper responsibilities and thought "nah". It wasn't for me. Not yet.'

'And you thought you weren't running away from anything?' I laugh.

'Are they intimidating you yet? They really like to get stuck in there with their interrogations,' Mike says to Scott, his fingers turning into claws while gesturing at me and Vicky.

'You're good. Although I am going to call it a night,' he says, suddenly standing up and moving a black kettle so that it's placed between the three of us. 'Grab a coca tea before bed.'

We do as he says, filling our mugs before stepping out of the dining tent.

I take a gulp before resting my mug back on the table.

'Did you just drink that without screwing up your face?' Vicky laughs.

'You've changed,' Mike joins in.

'I have, haven't I?' I nod. 'This is a whole new me.'

'You'll be moving to the country to live on a farm before we know it,' smirks Mike.

'Didn't realize coca tea and farm life were so linked, but I'll take it,' I say.

'Come on,' Vicky says, grabbing her mug and stepping out of the tent.

'It's flipping freezing!' I say as soon as we're outside, pulling my puffer jacket around me just as my shoulders creep up to below my ears. 'That's some bloody temperature drop.'

'Look up,' says Mike, shushing me.

'Wooooah . . .' whispers Vicky.

I look up and see the sky is awash with stars. Millions and millions of bright lights shine and twinkle. It's beyond anything I've ever been able to see in my back garden before.

'That's the Milky Way,' Mike says, his hand sweeping to where the sky is filled with the densest cluster. It almost looks like one solid light source.

'It's so beautiful,' I say, my arms looping through Vicky's and my head resting on Mike's shoulder.

'We're definitely just small fry,' says Mike.

For a moment or two we each get lost in looking at the expanse of sky above. It's incredible to think that each star is a sun like ours, with possibly its own version of earthlings spinning around it.

'Thank you, Pia,' I whisper, giving the other two a squeeze.

'Yeah . . .' sounds Mike.

'It's probably a bit strange to have a favourite when it comes to her Rules of Death, but this is mine,' Vicky adds.

'Feels like we're putting life back into life somehow,' Mike adds. 'It doesn't just stop. There's no way it can even if it sometimes feel like it has.'

Silence descends on us once more as we take in not only the view, but the idea of us continuing with life. I can't help but be reflective of how my life has changed over the years since meeting Liam, and then what a huge shift has occurred within me since losing Pia. I've been feeling like the world has let us all down, like I can't possibly enjoy what I have when there's such devastation existing so close to me, inside me – but maybe that's Pia's point by making us come here, or Mike at least. Let's not forget we just tagged along. Maybe this trip was meant to be her way of allowing acceptance to occur. Her blessing for letting life back in and moving on with our lives again.

Maybe.

'We never do this any more,' sighs Vicky, forlornly.

'What do you mean?' I ask.

'This. Hang out.'

'We do hang out. This trip got booked when we were hanging out,' Mike notes, chuckling to himself, his eyes firmly fixed above.

'It's nice,' Vicky says, squeezing my arm. 'We need to do more of it.'

'Hmmm . . .' I say.

'You don't agree?' she laughs, nudging into my side.

'It's just, there are certain life events that have stopped us from getting together as much,' I say. 'It's a shame that death is the thing that made us all put life aside so that we could regroup properly.'

'We were still seeing each other!' she says.

'I think I saw you a handful of times when Mike and Pia were away travelling,' I remind her.

'I was there if you needed me,' she frowns.

'I know!'

'We do better than most,' interrupts Mike. 'I was hardly seeing Reece and AJ at all before, unless I had time to sign up for their weekly football game, and they're my best guy mates.'

'Life gets busy,' I agree. 'People move away, get married, maybe have kids. Priorities change.'

'Pardon?' Vicky asks, pulling herself away from me in a way I didn't expect, her body turning to look me square on, her eyes squinting at me. 'Are you saying I became a crap friend?'

'No, I'm not. Not like that. It wasn't intentional. You got married and had kids. Your focus shifted,' I explain, aware that I've touched a nerve and wanting to put my words back into my mouth. 'Like Scott just said, responsibilities come along . . . you met Nick and had kids and didn't need us so much any more.'

'Just because you avoid responsibility like it's the plague doesn't mean I'm wrong for taking some on,' stammers Vicky.

'I didn't say that,' I say. 'What is going on, Vicky?'

'It's you talking nonsense,' she hisses. 'I was always there, have always been there. You're too busy swanning off, chatting up men who will do nothing but hurt you and constantly blind to what you have at home.'

'Blind?' I ask, her words hitting with a shock. 'What about you constantly being in everyone's face and mothering them? Maybe people just want to be left to sort their own shit out. Maybe having you constantly reminding them that there's something to worry about isn't actually helpful. Maybe it's actually so unhelpful that it can cause harm.'

'You won't be saying that when you've chucked away all you've got with Liam for some little fuckwit from the office. You'll want my mothering ways then to sort yourself out,' she declares.

'OK, that's enough now, guys,' Mike says, stepping between us.

'More than enough,' I say, storming off back to the tent. I get inside and hastily climb into my sleeping bag, trying to ignore the fact I've not brushed my teeth or washed my face after a day of sweating and getting covered in dust. I just can't look awake when Vicky comes inside. I can't deal with her right now and the confusing stream of conflicting emotions that are swirling inside me.

26

Vicky

My head pounds as I try to force open my eyes following the worst night's sleep since I brought Chloe back from the hospital as a newborn. I can handle being sleep-deprived, it's my natural state these days, but my sleep was so broken last night. Not only was I suffering from a feeling of unease following our unexpected fall-out, it then felt like I was sleeping on a block of ice, even though I'd folded up my puffer jacket to use as a pillow, alongside my blow-up travel one. The result is a sore head and a groggy disposition, which is a sorry state to be waking up in on what is supposed to be an enlightening and uplifting trip.

On top of all that I'm desperate for the loo and have been for quite some time. I've tried to ignore it. Firstly because being inside my sleeping bag has to be warmer than being out of it, and secondly because I haven't really fancied taking the trip to the loo tent in the dark. However, I can see it's lighter outside now and I really can't hold it for much longer. My bladder has taken quite the bashing since becoming a mum and holding it in feels like an uncomfortably testing place to be.

I look over and see Zaza completely curled into her sleeping bag with not even the top of her head poking out.

My tummy knots as I take her in. Deciding not to torment myself further, I wriggle ungracefully out of my sleeping bag, crouch over to my boots and shove them on without properly doing them up and just twirl the laces in loops around the top so I don't trip over them.

Trying to be as quiet as I can, I grab my water bottle before pulling on the zip of the tent door (quickly learning there is no silent way of working one) and walk through the opening before not-so-quietly shutting it behind me.

Standing up straight I take in the view around me, which is so different from what I am usually greeted with first thing – a wailing child, a stressful dash to get out of the house and on the school run. I take a deep breath. The fresh air hitting my lungs is such a welcome feeling.

Once I've relieved myself I stand outside and stretch my arms over my head before giving my puffy face a rub. My head still throbs.

I let out a long, slow exhale before sitting on a nearby rock and pulling my knees into my chest.

I'm so confused by what is happening with Zaza right now. One minute we're behaving normally, the next we're upsetting each other with random digs and hurtful words. This isn't the first time we've argued. We once had a blazing row over why I felt the need to put vinegar on our communal chips. It resulted in us telling each other all the things we did that irritated the other. We were in our early twenties and very drunk, needless to say, and the next morning I just climbed into her bed and the whole silly thing was forgotten – although it became a long-term running joke any time there was a bottle of vinegar placed near us.

This has been building though, and I know that I've fed into that. There have been times in the last few days when I've said something I shouldn't without thinking, and have then taken her words to heart. I'm sure Pia would've just bashed our heads together and told us to grow up last night. She was always the calm and collected one when it came to dramas and squabbles, always asking people to look at the bigger picture and if the situation really called for battle lines to be drawn. The only time Pia really dug her heels in and declared war was when anything competitive was involved. It didn't matter if it was a game of beer pong at a party, or rounders in the park on a hot sunny day – Pia would be there, a stickler for the rules, telling people what they'd done wrong whilst also getting her elbows stuck in for the win. If anything I'd say she welcomed a bit of bickering in those moments, knowing that it never really meant anything. It seemed to be the time she was released from being the rational, level-headed one – and she relished that freedom.

I shouldn't have said what I did to Zaza last night, or have been chipping away at her over the last few days. Truth is I'm proud of her. She's thriving while out of her comfort zone. I think I heard her complain more in the hotel than she has on this trek. I have no idea why I'm sniping, why I'm interfering or why I feel the need to say things that might upset her. Is it a friend calling out questionable behaviour because I'm worried she's seriously going to do some damage to her life? Possibly. Mostly. But also it's nothing to do with her at all, and all to do with me feeling on edge and unsure how to process my feelings.

I rest my head on my knees, trying to let the complete silence of where we are calm me.

A tent unzips. I look up to find Scott clambering out with a big yawn, his arms stretching wide to the view before him. He's rugged, worldly-wise. He's capable, able and strong while light on his feet. I know because I've watched his calf muscles contract and relax rhythmically for hours as we've walked, his feet never misjudging the ground below.

His focus is completely different to my own, which is consumed with the motherload with no time for anything else. Whereas I have a million and one responsibilities he seems to run on a different frequency.

A quick, sharp pang of desire hits.

For Scott?

Surely not.

Maybe.

If I weren't me right now, if I too lived my life in a different way and had taken another path, maybe I would be more spontaneous, more feisty, more fun. That version of me would glide over to Scott right now, my arms looping around his waist from behind in a seductive manner before teasing him back into his tent for a bit of hanky-panky.

Jesus.

Hanky-panky?

I've turned into my mother.

He turns and I startle at his eyes on mine.

His hand goes up and I wave back. Hoping he can't read my mind and therefore isn't aware that I've just used an old-fashioned rhyming compound to describe what sex with him would be like.

'You're up early!' he practically shouts, causing his voice to echo around us.

'Got a headache,' I say, tapping the side of my head, my face screwing up to let him know just how much discomfort I'm in.

'Stay there. I've got something for that,' he says before disappearing back into his tent.

Thankfully, intrusive thoughts of going over there and diving in behind him don't come back, and within seconds he's out and walking towards me swinging around a first-aid kit.

At this point I see Chef Jonny wandering out of the dining tent and wonder how long he's been up. Maybe I was wrong to think I was the first to wake up.

'Headaches are such a nightmare up here. Super common because of our altitude but that doesn't lessen the pain,' he says, unzipping his pouch and rummaging inside.

'Here we go – super-strength painkillers. They should do the trick but let me know if your symptoms worsen and I'll see if there's anything else I can do for you.'

He pops two tablets into the palm of my hand.

'I should've remembered the altitude tablets . . .' I say, placing them both in my mouth and chugging back some water to wash them down.

'You thought you'd do it the hardcore way,' he shrugs.

'No, it was me being forgetful.'

'Vicky, it sounds like you have a lot of things to remember. Give yourself a break.'

'Yeah . . . my head feels so groggy,' I say as a sharp pain attacks.

'Morning, guys!' Scott shouts, as Kevin, Pedro and Rafael appear.

They all wave in return, immediately tending to the donkeys and checking in on Chef Jonny.

'Hopefully some breakfast will help, but chew on these in the meantime,' he says, handing over more coca leaves. Chewing on them makes me feel like a pirate. The thought makes me think of the kids and how hilarious they would find it that Mummy is chewing on leaves. Although maybe I shouldn't tell them about that, they don't need further encouragement to stick things in their mouths that they shouldn't. I had to rescue a worm from Barnaby a couple of years ago, and Chloe has a thing about mud.

'I heard you guys last night,' Scott says, perching on the rock next to mine. 'All OK?'

'I'm sure it will be, but it was a bit shit,' I say, slightly embarrassed that he overheard us.

'Treks can cause emotions to run high,' he says, his hand tapping on my knee in a way I imagine is meant to be comforting but makes me jolt in surprise. 'You're away from home, away from your kids. Your husband. Away from everything you know your life to be. It's overwhelming to be asked to exist like this while pushing your body too. It's not easy. Emotions do all sorts when we're pushed.'

'I have been feeling a bit out of sorts,' I confess.

'I'd better keep a close eye on you today then.'

'Thanks,' I say, fully aware of my cheeks blushing.

'Morning,' calls Zaza.

'You're up!' shouts Scott.

'You weren't exactly keeping it down,' she replies before turning her back and heading to the toilet tent, doing so with a slight limp which I'm guessing is due to the massive blisters on her feet. I don't know how she's walking on them at all they looked so sore, but she's barely complained.

'Let's hope your headache goes so you have one less thing to worry about,' he says, getting up. 'And if you need anything at all, anything, just let me know. It's what I'm here for.'

'Hmph,' I say, not really able to formulate a proper word as my head just shifted back to *that* place. What on earth is wrong with me? I don't want to have sex with my husband but thinking about doing it with this near stranger makes my body the most switched on it's felt since Chloe arrived.

That's the point though, isn't it? I know nothing will come from these embarrassing thoughts, it's not like when Nick and I met and literally couldn't keep our hands off each other.

After finishing work on the South Bank one Friday afternoon, a few of us decided to head out for a drink. One turned into two, turned into three, turned into me being at the bar when a tall hunk of a man arrived next to me. He gazed at me, a smile cracking as our eyes met and it was like dynamite was exploding everywhere. Physically, emotionally, mentally – something about his being just had a hold over me straight away.

'I feel like I should say something profound, witty or memorable,' he said, having to crouch down to talk into my ear so I could hear over the noisiness of a Friday night in London.

'And why's that?' I asked, looking back up at him, my eyes wide, imploring him to feel what I felt and for this to be more than just a quick poke in the dark before a taxi ride home.

'Because I hope this is a meeting I'm going to be telling our kids about.'

Boom.

Mic drop.

Right there.

I was his and he was mine.

No mind tricks, no squabbling over lines being blurred or hearts being tampered with.

I took him straight back to mine (much to the hilarity of Zaza, Mike and Pia who we had to stumble past to get to my room) and we made love five times that night. And let's be clear – it was making love, not like any sex I'd had before. From that point there was a clear distinction in my mind – one is a simple case of getting kicks, the other is that feeling of fulfilment. Of becoming complete in the arms of another. Of having every inch of you touched, caressed and cherished like there's nothing more divine and reciprocating than that feeling and action for the other – not done out of duty or obligation, but because of the desire and need running through you. It's a feeling of being one.

Our connection was instant, and I've never doubted the firm pull between us.

But.

I don't like myself right now and therefore it's a huge ask to accept that someone can love me in the same way they did before. I don't recognize my body or my mind, my emotions betray me constantly – what could he possibly see in me now?

I'm failing him. Just like I constantly fail my kids. Just like I've clearly failed my mate.

Push.

It.

Back.

I take a deep breath to still the thoughts, to stop my heart from drowning in what my mind is trying to tell me.

I get up and attempt to shake it off – moving my head, my arms and my legs. Trying to get the blood pumping and the noise to stop.

'Breakfast in fifteen,' Scott calls over.

I give him a thumbs up in reply and make my way back to my tent. Zaza's bag seems to have exploded across the floor and in the middle of the chaos she's attempting to stuff her sleeping bag back into its sack.

'Such a fucker,' she says, the bag appearing to be growing rather than shrinking, the air filling it working against her efforts.

After last night's 'chat' I know better than to steam in like her mother and take over. Instead I tend to my own corner of the tent, which is an organized little haven in comparison. I quickly change from my thermals into my trekking gear and begin clearing my belongings away. Once that's done I start rolling the air out of my sleeping bag, as well as my incredibly disappointing travel pillow and mattress, and squeeze them all into my bag. It's an effort but I'm finished within a few minutes. Only my toiletry bag remains out, and I'll need that.

'I just don't see how it's all meant to go back in!' Zaza huffs, glancing at me with a desperate look on her face, her sleeping bag now sitting comfortably packed while the rest of her belongings are still on the ground around her. 'Can you help me, please?' she moans, looking crushed as she recognizes my progress.

'But that would be mothering, and I think that's a trait of mine you can't stand,' I state.

She pauses her efforts to look up at me.

We just stare at each other.

'I've decided that we're both going through some stuff right now that we need to talk about,' she acknowledges, her voice soft.

'Agreed,' I nod.

'Stuff that might not actually be to do with us and our relationship, but stuff we need to process and reach out on.'

'Double agreed.'

'Now, however, is not that time,' she reasons, her lips pursing together.

'Now is the time to get your messy arse organized?' I suggest.

'Exactly that!' she nods.

I crawl over and take control of the situation.

'Next time we do this I'm not bringing so much stuff,' she says, sitting back to look at her gear. 'I have a lot of crap here that I really don't need.'

'Next time?' I ask.

'Just so you can try to beat me at UNO,' she teases before letting out a laugh. 'As if I'd cheat at a game I don't even like that much. I was simply the better player,' she grins.

I jump on her, wrapping my arms and legs around her body. We wrestle over the floor of the tent as she tries to break free from my hug but I just won't let her. We laugh, our bodies shaking uncontrollably as the laughter bounces through us.

Finally we run out of steam and just hold on to each other.

'You know they weren't truths,' she says, giving my body a squeeze.

'They were a bit,' I reply, feeling a sting at my own words.

'We're just a bit broken right now,' she whispers.

I nod my head, and as I do so the tears start falling. My body convulses with the emotion that begins spilling out. Stuff that I've kept in for so long, that I'm no longer able to control now it's been allowed to run free. I squeeze my eyes shut, willing it to stop.

Not now.

But I can't hold them back.

'Hey!' she says softly, wiping my tears.

'I'm so broken. So completely broken. I've wanted it to stop. All of it. I've wanted to –'

Her strength stops me from uttering the words.

She holds me like someone who would do anything to make their friend feel whole again, to ease the pain of whatever it is they're going through, who wants them to know they're loved and seen.

I welcome it, enjoying the feeling of having someone else know how much I ache.

27

Mike

I expected the girls to be at loggerheads this morning and for last night's drama to bleed into today, yet the opposite seems to be true. From the moment they step into breakfast together there's a tenderness between them, with Zaza stuck to Vicky's side and continuously checking in on how she is.

'Still got that headache?' asks Scott. Having already eaten he's up on his feet and ready to get going.

'Yeah. It's banging.'

He grimaces at her.

'I'll be OK though,' she says with a smile.

'Course you will. You're a trooper,' he says, grabbing her shoulder, filling all of our mugs with coca tea before leaving.

'Is it just me or is he always plying us with this and then making a swift exit?' I ask.

'Sounds like a good plot twist in a movie,' Zaza adds, tucking into her breakfast of porridge made with quinoa, topped with banana, sprinkled with chocolate powder – a starter to the apple pancakes that are simply delicious. It's energy-building food for a tough day ahead. I tuck in and accept seconds when I'm offered.

Our trekking day starts slowly and unlike yesterday we have a horse and horseman with us. Nothing is said, but I imagine it's an indicator of what's to come and how much is being asked of us. Vicky isn't the only one who had a bad night or is feeling the worse for wear thanks to the altitude. I'm not ashamed to say I feel rough around the edges today.

I chew on my coca leaves, willing them to give me some energy, but instead I'm feeling breathless every few paces, like the wind is literally being taken out of me. It's gruelling and disheartening when I know I'm fit and capable.

'I can't do it,' Vicky says quietly.

We all grind to a stop.

I look over and see her lip wobble as she bends over and puts her hands on her knees.

'You're OK,' Zaza says, rubbing her back.

A few seconds later Vicky takes a few deep breaths. She stands upright and looks at the path ahead. My gaze follows hers, taking in the next part of the challenge that looks even steeper than what's come before.

'This is really hard,' I say, reaching for her hand to give it an encouraging squeeze. 'It's not easy.'

'Think something's up with my lungs!' says Zaza, her hand on her chest.

'Same,' says Vicky.

'I know we're feeling it today, guys,' Scott says,

watching us take a moment to pause in our efforts. 'This is the toughest day. Last night we slept at three thousand, six hundred metres – which is quite a height. This morning we're going higher, to four thousand, eight hundred metres.'

'Fuck me,' mutters Vicky.

'We're not going to be sprinting it,' I remind her, trying my best to stop her mind from spiralling. 'Every time we catch our breath, we walk. Every time we lose it, we stop.'

'Give me your bag,' Scott says, removing it from Vicky's back and taking it over to the horseman so that it can be strapped on to the saddle. Scott and Kevin remain a few steps away from us as Zaza and I watch our friend gather her thoughts.

'You can do this, Vicky. I have every faith in you,' I say, feeling my words ricochet off her and back to me. As though I'm saying the words I need to hear and am taking strength from them myself. Even though this is hard, I take comfort from being back in this role of support giver, rather than being the one that's constantly having to receive it. I feel the confidence in myself building with every word of encouragement that comes out of my mouth.

A sensation swirls in my chest. The realization that a little part of me has come back, and that it feels OK. It feels good.

'We've got this,' I say.

'Come on,' says Zaza, grabbing her other hand so the three of us are linked as one.

'Can I just say before we start,' I say, turning to Vicky's tear-stained face. 'I have never seen you looking more like Chloe than you do right now.'

'I feel like her!' she says with a mixture of a laugh and a cry. 'I want to throw one of her wobbles. I want to just scream and cry as loud as I possibly can.'

'Then let's do that,' I shrug. 'Let's toddler tantrum our way up this beautifully picturesque mountain and not give two hoots who sees or hears us doing so.'

'Go on then,' says Zaza.

'Euuuuuurgh!' Vicky shouts. 'Eurgh! Eurgh! Eurgh! Euuuuuurgh!'

Words are unnecessary here. And I can identify with every guttural sound that blasts from my friend's mouth.

'Raaaaaaaaaaaaaah!' adds Zaza, her chest concaving as the noise leaves her, as though she's literally getting all that's in her out.

'Yaaaaaarrrrrreeeeeeeeeeh!' I say, joining in, feeling the rip through my body at the power that lies within.

Then all three of us go at the same time. The sound is raw, uninhibited, and as it bounces off the surrounding mountains it builds, as though every single bit of life around us is with us in this moment.

Alive.

I am alive.

I'm allowed to feel alive.

I'm allowed to enjoy feeling alive.

We stop, now breathless for a very different reason but with a fire in our bellies.

We enjoy the silence that follows.

'I can see why she enjoys that so much,' Vicky says, rubbing her eyes with the side of her arm, not letting go of either of our hands. 'Maybe I'll just join in with her next time.'

Another breath is taken, this one to steel herself.

The three of us turn and look ahead. Vicky raises her right foot and, before it can connect with the ground again, Zaza and I join her. We start putting one foot in front of the other. That's all we can focus on. The simple act of walking. Together. As one.

Every so often I look up from my feet to the path ahead, to the saddle between two mountains that we've been told we're aiming for. When it feels like we've made good progress I look up, only to see we still have a long way to go. Yet we continue, squeezing each other's hands when we need that extra boost, muttering expletives when we need a chuckle, getting the job done.

When we hit the saddle and see the path widen to an area we can stop and sit in, we regroup. Our arms fly around each other in euphoria.

'Well done, guys, that was quite something,' Scott calls over our heads. 'Take your time here and grab some lunch.'

When we finally let go of each other we take in what's around us. Firstly, looking back to the route we've taken is quite the sight to behold; it looks like we've been walking for miles. Then looking to the way we're heading, we see a beautiful deep green lagoon, the edges tinged with a touch of turquoise. The mountains continue to roll around it, the sun poking through the clouds causing huge shadows to dance across them. Up ahead the snow-capped Chicon Mountain stands, glistening in all its glory. Although being so high up it doesn't seem as mammoth as it might from below.

'Wow,' I breathe.

'Stunning,' says Vicky.

'Beats the view from the window at work,' laughs Zaza.

'Worth it?' grins Scott, pulling lunch out of a container that was hidden for us behind a rock.

'Absolutely,' Vicky smiles, pulling Zaza and me back in for another hug.

We huddle close, getting battered by the wind while we take some photos, before settling down for some food – cheese and ham sandwiches accompanied by a chocolate nut bar and a banana. While we eat I look at the beautiful view ahead of us.

Pia.

She appears in my mind as though she's here.

She would love this, that us mates are here together, that we're feeling challenged and pushing through, and the breathtaking views surrounding us.

I decide that it's time.

'I haven't told you guys something,' I say, once we've all finished our food.

'Sounds interesting,' says Zaza, shuffling to face me.

'All ears,' adds Vicky, with an expectant smile.

'I was going to tell you sooner but it never felt like the right time. Now it does,' I begin.

Pia never talked about what should happen with her when she died. We talked about everything else, hence the Rules of Death, but not that. It was a topic neither of us wanted to broach because we didn't want to make it any sort of a reality, as though if we addressed it we were truly allowing her dying to be an option when neither of us wanted it to be. Yes, we could talk about material things like clothes and belongings, and she clearly felt she could write about me going on a hypothetical trip at some point in the future – but talking about her body in death felt like a different ask altogether. I didn't want to think about her body when she was no longer using it. It felt like a betrayal of all the hope I had been clinging on to, no matter how many times the doctors said there was nothing more they could do for her. That the cancer had outsmarted their drugs.

When she eventually did die the idea of organizing either a burial or cremation felt like rubbing salt into newly exposed wounds. Both seemed barbaric and cruel. Either burying her in the ground or burning what remained – it didn't seem fair. I knew she was gone, that only her body was still on earth, but all I wanted to do was take care of her. Fix her.

There's no mending the dead.

Pia's parents came to our flat in the end and took the decision out of my hands. Unlike my own family, who for religious reasons always buried, Pia's family leaned heavily towards cremation. She was their little girl, their child, and I decided to follow their wishes. As a result I've had Pia placed on top of the fireplace in an ugly urn ever since, like she's just another ornament I've collected in life. Every time I've caught sight of her perching there my chest has tightened, uncomfortable with her remaining confined when she deserves to be free, as free as the wind, as Patrick Swayze would say.

'On Pia's birthday, the night we started planning this, I went back home and saw Pia's ashes sitting on top of the fireplace. I wanted desperately to talk to her, to tell her that we were doing it, we were doing as she asked and all going on an adventure together. So I took her and placed her on the coffee table,' I say, taking a breath as Zaza reaches across and touches my knee. 'I sat next to her and I tried to talk. I tried to think of her in there like a little genie or something, sitting there waiting to hear my voice. I couldn't talk. Nothing was coming out,' I say, aware of a tear falling. The sight of which sets both Vicky and Zaza off. 'I suddenly realized that her being trapped in there isn't something I wanted. Not Pia. She's not a little genie or even a borrower, she's Pia. Fun-loving Pia who loved the world and everything in it, who wanted to explore and absorb as much of life as she possibly could.'

I pause, pulling a Tupperware box from my bag.

'So I've brought Pia with me,' I say.

'Oh my,' whispers Vicky.

'Some of her,' I correct myself. 'I know this trip means

something different to each of us, that we've all needed it for different reasons, but there's one person to thank for us being here.'

'Absolutely,' agrees Zaza, a solemn expression on her face.

I nod and look down at my wife's ashes. 'I want to take her everywhere – places we've been, places we wanted to go. I want her to be a part of my adventures to come.'

The thing I have hated most about losing Pia is the thought of leaving her behind when every inch of our future was meant to be spent together. By taking her ashes and scattering them in far-off places of natural awe I feel like I'm giving her new life in the wind she's blowing in, the streams she'll run down and the earth she'll be embedded into that'll grow new life.

'So this is only the start?' asks Vicky.

'Yeah. I mean, I still have to work, I won't be hotfooting around the globe for the rest of my life, but I feel like this is a way for me to honour Pia, what we had, and that I should make it a yearly focus,' I say.

The night I got home and tried talking to Pia one thing felt clearer than ever before. We were both stuck in our individual prisons, an urn and grief, and getting out of either felt impossible. Three months ago I couldn't imagine me going on a single trip like this, but now I feel empowered at the thought of doing more. The let's-just-go bag must remain.

'I think it's a lovely idea,' says Vicky.

'Agreed,' says Zaza before tilting her head at a new

thought. 'I just can't believe you've been carrying her around at the bottom of your bag the whole time. In Tupperware!'

'I know,' I shrug, a tiny laugh escaping, remembering how I looked around the house for ages pondering over a suitable way to bring her with us. I came to the conclusion that this might not be the prettiest, but it was possibly the safest.

I turn and look at where feels best, before deciding where we are is perfect.

Standing up I start to unclip the lid.

'Do we say something?' asks Vicky.

'If you want.' I hadn't really thought beyond getting her here and hadn't wanted to over-romanticize this particular moment. 'We don't have to though . . .'

'Pia,' says Vicky with a punch. 'The world isn't the same without you in it, but it was made a better place because you were. Thank you.'

'If I'm honest I'm still trying to figure shit out,' says Zaza, looking out to the mountains ahead of us, occasionally glancing at the tub in my hands. 'I don't understand why you're not here when I am. It seems so wrong when almost everything about you was so good – for fuck's sake, you wore the same sandals for a decade! That's angelic behaviour right there.' She pauses while she exhales, playing with the zip on her jacket. 'I miss you. I hope you know how much we all do.'

I place my hand on top of the box.

'You always were the sparkle in my life. From the

moment we met you just shone brighter than anything else I'd known before. You weren't a saint, although these two would like to say you were, I know how much that would annoy you,' I say, causing Zaza and Vicky to tut in agreement. 'I know the times you struggled, the times you got frustrated, the times your temper would flash – usually because I'd tested your patience. And not just because of cancer, because of life. Life happens and we all have to use the tools we possess to get through. Meeting you gave me a whole new set of tools. I wouldn't be who I am today were it not for meeting you when I did. It's something I'll be forever grateful for.'

I lift the final clip of the box and remove the lid. The thought of what I'm about to do hits and sends a chill through me. I hold the container out and start shaking it gently, allowing the wind around us to start gliding over Pia's ashes and carry her away.

'I love you, Pia,' I call after her, my heart feeling a little lighter seeing her reunited with the world, wanting to imagine her walking on sunshine for the rest of time.

28

Zaza

The morning has been a heavy one, yet somehow I feel lighter as a result, as though I'm starting to unload a weight that's been with me for a while. I'm still unpacking the thoughts and making sense of them, but a hope has started to appear. That's more than I can say for the weather, however, which is looking less than hopeful. Just like yesterday the sunny spells have passed along with the blue skies, and instead a miserable drizzle has set in around us as we've been descending through the valleys that were waiting for us on the other side of this morning's steep climb. Walking-wise it's been a lot more enjoyable, with the arrival of tall trees giving us something different to look at as we take in the view, along with rivers that we have to carefully cross and be sure we don't fall into. Apparently slipping in and ending up with a soggy boot really will add a hellish element to the trip.

Our ponchos are out. Not only do their bright colours make us look like we're in a Uniqlo advert, we also rustle as we walk. With our hoods up over our heads we can hardly hear each other, and so the walk is mostly silent, which after the events that've happened today might not be a bad thing. We all need some thinking time.

The weather is not getting Mike's spirits down. If anything, since he set a piece of Pia free there has been a newly acquired spring in his step which is uplifting to watch.

Vicky I've been keeping close. A protectiveness has switched on within me now she's spoken. I knew she was finding things tough, but it hurts me to know this has been running far deeper than I cared to realize. How did I miss how far the situation at home has been pushing her? Does Nick know? Is that why she needed to get away and come here? To give her some reasoning that life is to be lived? To relieve her of her load and help her see clearly again?

'You OK?' I say for the millionth time as she stops for a drink and to grab a snack bar.

'I think I'd feel better if it weren't for this headache,' she replies.

I nod and reach for her hand through our plastic layers. Now isn't the time to talk.

'You'll see camp around this corner,' offers Kevin with a smile.

'Really?' I ask, the joy his words bring audible in my voice.

He nods with a big smile.

'And there are llamas!' calls Mike as several appear in a clearing next to us, looking up to see what the commotion is. Even though I would love to take a photo of them to show Liam just how cute they are, I cannot be arsed to fight through my layers and pockets to find my phone to take one. I take a mental picture instead and work on getting around the bend to camp.

Kevin's right. As we turn the corner we can see our tents in the distance. The only sticking point is that they're absolutely tiny, letting us know that the hard work isn't quite over yet.

An hour and a half later, though, we stroll into our camp, which is in the courtyard of a farm in the valley. Small and enclosed, as well as home to several llamas and alpacas, it's also sitting three hundred metres lower than last night's camp. So hopefully the Peruvian walls will act as windbreakers to keep out the chill and the difference in altitude will stop us feeling quite so groggy.

'Tents are that way, dining tent is there, and the toilet is just over there,' says Scott, pointing out the obvious. 'Take some time to chill, dinner will be ready in about an hour.'

We all nod at him but the energy has been zapped from me and Vicky. Only Mike gives a more enthusiastic response with a big nod.

'You're not looking too great,' I say to Vicky, who seems to be paler than normal.

Without replying she drops her rucksack and runs off to the loo. When she reappears a few minutes later we're by our tents, unrolling the mattresses and sleeping bags to set up home for the night. Having already done my own I've been working on hers.

'Thank you,' she croaks.

'Need anything else?' I ask, because she really doesn't look her best self.

'Dioralyte?' she asks, scrunching up her face.

'Oh mate . . .' consoles Mike, mirroring her expression.

'To be frank, I've got no idea which way it wants to come out next, so an Imodium might be good to block one end at least,' she declares before giving a groan.

'Shit,' I mutter.

'Exactly,' she nods, her hand over her mouth like she might spew at any second. 'Think I might just need to lie down and see if this settles.'

'OK. Well, do you want to have that tent to yourself for a bit? Have a bit of time to see what's what and try to sleep, it'll make you feel better, I'm sure. I'll only be out here and you can shout if you need me,' I say, knowing that the last place I would want to be when feeling like that is in a tent with someone and being watched.

She nods, too ill to put up a fight and stumbles into the tent, slowly lowering herself into her sleeping bag where she curls into a ball and scrunches her eyes shut with a whimper.

I grab my puffer jacket and close the zip of the tent before pulling out two Double Decker bars. I pass one to Mike.

'Let's go perch over there,' I say, noticing a flattish rock with a scenic view beyond it of the valley we've walked through, the herd of alpacas and llamas happily grazing on the grass in front of it.

'Are you having fun?' asks Mike before our bums have even landed.

'Yes . . . I think so,' I add with a laugh at my own uncertainty, removing the orange and purple wrapper. 'It turns out this is definitely something that doesn't come naturally to me, however, stepping away from everything, stepping away from the comforts – it's been liberating.'

'You did bring half of your bathroom cabinet with you,' he points out, taking a bite of his chocolate bar.

'That is true,' I concede, chewing away. 'But let me tell you that I haven't touched the majority of it. Next time I won't even bother.'

I look over to see him smirking.

'And how are you feeling about everything else?' he asks after a pause. 'About Liam and becoming his wife?'

I take a deep breath, pausing in my chocolate eating. 'Before coming here I had a bit of a thing with a guy from work.'

'Za–'

'No! No!' I interrupt before he can even go down that road. 'Let me rephrase that. A really fit guy started at work and we got talking. Nothing more. But if I'm honest, even before those exchanges, I had already begun questioning a few things.'

'Like?'

'Just, life! I thought I'd been worried about never going on more first dates, having first kisses, that first row that you've got to hope you both know how to come back from,' I explain, with a very slight laugh as I say it, as I remember the first time I got huffy with Liam was on our very first date at the top of the stairs in Wagamama.

'And that feeling got bigger when you realized you fancied this new guy?'

'No. Don't get me wrong, he is very fit –'

'You've said that,' he says.

'But it wasn't going to go anywhere beyond the odd flirty exchange.'

'Well, that's something.'

'I just have had this aggy feeling around Liam. Like I've wanted to push him away,' I admit, playing with the ring he placed on my ring finger. 'So I've been trying to work out why I am the way I am.'

'You're great.'

'Mike, you heard Vicky last night. We all know I've acted in weird ways when it's come to my love life,' I say, stopping his attempts to brush away my behaviour. 'It would be easy to say it's because I didn't have both my parents with me growing up. You know, that love between adults wasn't modelled for me so I don't know how to do it myself,' I say, aware that words are tumbling out that I've never properly acknowledged before, let alone said out loud. 'But I know that's not the case. Mum showed me love. My friends showed me love. You guys did. Yet I've gone through one failed relationship after another. I came away feeling like I wasn't good enough. It's never been about them not being enough, or me challenging their behaviour, it's been me and mine. But Liam came along and made me feel like I was more than enough and treated me with such respect. He flipped it on its head and I've no idea how or why, but he made me believe him.'

'That's a good thing, Za.'

'Then he proposed and I felt elated, but a fear kicked in,' I say, fiddling with the wrapper in my hands. 'I suddenly understood that the doubt I had was silenced because of *him*. Life has been good because of *him*. It's all because of *him*. What about if he's not there any more? How would I feel then?'

'What makes you think he's going somewhere?' he asks.

'Pia did.'

'True,' he nods.

'I got lucky with Liam. And at some point that luck is going to run out,' I say, pushing on. 'It's inevitable and because of that I've been such a bitch. The way I've been treating him . . . I'm pressing the buttons. It's like I'm giving him an out so that it can just happen and I can start preparing myself for the hurt to come. So I've told myself that I miss things, like the firsts – the getting to know someone, the flirting, the kissing, the excitement and nerves that go alongside it, because really I'm just terrified of losing what I have.'

We sit and listen to the llamas and alpacas humming away at each other.

'Actually, I don't think it's this new guy, you feeling like you don't deserve happiness, or Pia's death that's got you thinking in this way,' Mike says after a moment or two.

'No?'

'Nope,' he says with a shake of his head. 'I think it's me.'

'Well, this could get awkward,' I say, unable to stop myself from laughing.

'Don't be soft,' he says, bashing my thigh with the back of his hand. 'I mean, it's seeing someone who had it all, lose it all. You're scared of being me.'

'Yeah . . .' I sigh.

'Nice to know I'm not selling this widower lark,' he says. 'I'll try better.'

'Please do,' I say, taking his hand in mine.

'There's something you should think about though,' he says thoughtfully. 'At some point there's a shift and the firsts are no longer important. It's no longer about finding someone to share all of your firsts with, it's about who you want to be there for all of your lasts. Or your forevers. Because choosing, or being chosen to be that person – that is the real honour.'

'Oh Jesus,' I say, as tears start streaming down my face.

'It's true though,' he says. 'All you have to ask yourself, really, is do you want that person to be Liam?'

'Absolutely!' I say.

'There we go then,' Mike says with a decisive nod of his head, seemingly satisfied. 'The grim thing is that whatever happens, if you are lucky enough to have decades together, one of you will always go first. One of you will always be left. And I will forever feel guilty that that person is me, but – I couldn't bear the thought of her living with this pain.'

'You were perfect together,' I say.

'No, we weren't. We rowed. Abysmally sometimes,' he says, shaking his head. 'I slept on the sofa more nights than I care to remember.'

'No!'

'Yes! She'd kick me out of the bed for snoring after having one too many with Reece and AJ, or I'd go there myself when I was bored of her moaning at me for not doing something I should've,' he says, making us both laugh at the thought. I often forget that he has his guy mates and therefore this whole other life that we're not privy to, not really. 'The sleeping arrangements might've changed slightly when she was diagnosed,' he continues. 'But she could still be annoying, and I was still a dick occasionally. No one person or relationship is perfect.'

'You miss her,' I state.

'So much,' he declares passionately. 'I'm already thinking about running back up that mountain and trying to find the pieces of her I left behind . . . but I have to let her go. And I want to do that in the most amazing way possible.'

I take his hand. 'You can only go to so many places. Don't put too much pressure on yourself.'

'I'm not. It's something I feel I need to do. To feel closer to her, maybe. To feel at peace,' he says, letting me know there's no way he'll be backing out of the plan now that it's been made. 'I've been thinking about those boys, Josh and Ben, too. I don't know how it could work, but I wonder if there's a way of setting up an organization that runs yearly trips for those who've been bereaved.'

'A group scattering-of-ashes session?'

'Maybe, but also a time to walk, process and feel that's away from the pressures of everyday life. I think of what I've been feeling and it kills me that those young kids are going through something similar. It might just help.'

A groan comes from the tent behind us.

We turn to hear Scott asking how she is doing from the tent door.

'Awful!' she whimpers.

'Can you stomach dinner?' he says, his face looking at us doubtfully while he waits for an answer.

'No. I can't move from this spot,' she calls, the pain audible in her voice.

'Drink some water and try to sleep,' he says before turning to us with a pursed smile. 'Ready when you are.'

'I'll just check on her and then come over,' I say, hopping down from the rock before turning back to Mike. 'I love that idea. I love it a lot.'

29

Vicky

I spent the first half of last night toing and froing from the toilet (I debated whether I should make a makeshift loo from a bag and just stay in the tent, but decided against it), shivering with a fever and crying because I felt so flipping awful.

Eventually the Imodium started doing its thing and the loo trips lessened. After downing some Dioralyte, something that always reminds me of being a kid and being handed one by my mum, I managed to close my eyes and drift off.

Mike and Zaza told me sleep would make me feel better, and they weren't lying. Waking up I feel completely different to how I did last night.

'You good?' Zaza asks.

I turn to see her staring at me, her eyebrows nestled into a concerned frown, and have a faint recollection of her tip-toeing in last night. She might've even checked up on me.

'I honestly thought I might die at one point,' I say with a croak, wrapping the sleeping bag around me even tighter. 'In contrast, I feel a million dollars now.'

'Just a shame you don't look it.'

'Bitch,' I laugh, taking my crappy blow-up pillow and chucking it in her direction. She's laughing so much she doesn't manage to bat it away.

'I feel like I'm missing out,' shouts Mike from his own tent.

'You're not. It smells like a rat's arse in here,' calls back Zaza.

'Oi!' I shout before laughing and grimacing all at once. 'I really didn't want to get the squits in the mountains.'

'Still beat running around after the kids all day?' she asks.

'I'm not sure it does,' I say, a sudden pang of missing them hitting me, causing me to bury my face.

'Oh no, I'm sorry!' she cries. 'Wait, I'm coming over.'

I look up and through my watery eyes see her rolling over to me in her sleeping bag. Even though the sight of it makes me want to laugh I can't help the fresh tears that are now a mixture of emotions.

'Have you made her cry?' Mike asks, popping his head through our door.

'I didn't sodding mean to!' Zaza calls, finally stopping next to me and extending an arm out to wrap around me. 'Not this early anyway!'

'Room for me?' Mike calls, hopping in, he too still in his sleeping bag. He makes quite the commotion as he hunches over and bounces through the tent, finally landing the other side of my sleeping bag. Another arm is draped across me.

A sigh escapes me.

'I wanted this trip to be perfect,' I share, staring at the roof of our tent that's covered in condensation.

'No such thing,' says Zaza.

'You're learning,' says Mike across me.

'I just . . . it's not just the fact I've had the squits either,' I admit.

'Go on,' says Mike, his arm holding me firmer.

'I needed to get away, to have some time where no one was relying on me for anything and everything. I wanted to feel free, like me again. But if this is freedom it feels a bit . . . shitty,' I admit, unable to stifle a laugh at my choice of words.

'I like what you did there,' beams Zaza, before giving me a squeeze.

'I thought I'd be running up the mountains like Maria from *The Sound of Music*, singing as I go. But this is hard. It's a strain on my body, my mind doesn't know what to do with itself and my emotions are completely shot,' I admit. 'There are times back home when I really struggle, and when those moments hit I feel completely debilitated. As though I literally can't cope. Then I feel shit because motherhood is such a blessing and my kids are adorable when they want to be. It's shameful to admit that in those moments, though, I feel like other people could do a better job, that they'd be better off without me.'

'You know they wouldn't,' Zaza says.

'I know,' I reply. 'And I really do know that. When everything is going smoothly and I think back to the irrational thoughts that whirled around my head I wonder how I could ever think in that way. But then I spiral again, and those thoughts come back thick and fast. The thing is, I think this week has shown me that motherhood and my children are such a huge part of who I am, and that that's OK. This trip hasn't quite been what I thought it would be so far, but I realize I do need to think about me for a change and process who I've become. Even if I am petrified of who this new "me" is.'

'Does Nick know about any of this?' asks Zaza.

I sigh. 'No. I wouldn't know where to start. I just feel so altered – in every single way: with my body, my mumbrain and my topsy-turvy emotions. I feel so lost sometimes and that freaks me out because I don't know how to be around him as a result.'

'He loves you,' says Mike.

'I know he does, and I love him . . . although I have to admit something rather embarrassing.'

'Go on,' says Mike.

'I've had some inappropriate thoughts about Scott. They've made me feel like a right bitch.'

'Thoughts?' asks Zaza, her head swinging round to face me.

'You mean safe thoughts that you didn't act on?' asks Mike, glancing at Zaza.

'Give her a chance . . . you've seen the state she's been in,' giggles Zaza.

'Thanks,' I mutter.

'Well, that doesn't make you a bad person,' states Mike, again looking across me to Za.

'Maybe not, but it's blooming confusing,' I admit. 'But I know with absolute certainty that I really don't want to break up my marriage for a man who doesn't own a hairbrush and thinks it's acceptable to wear sandals and socks. I don't want to break it up for anyone. I just . . . want to feel alive again.'

'We are all individuals!' says Mike. 'We just have to remember who we actually are! I'm not just a widower, you're not just a mum. You're not just a . . .'

'Super cool human with amazing fashion sense and a banging body?' completes Zaza, leaning over to him with a massive grin on her face.

'Exactly, you're not just that,' I laugh. 'I don't know if this makes any sense at all. Walking just makes you think, and sometimes it's about the things you anticipate thinking about and other times it's total curveballs.'

'I know what you mean,' Zaza nods, her face becoming more serious. 'Before coming here I certainly had a murky attitude towards the future. Now I want to pick up bridal magazines and smooch Liam's face off when we land back home.'

'You do?' I ask, surprised and happy for her all at once.

'Yeah. I really do!' she sings. 'I can't wait to speak to him when we get sodding signal.'

'So, Pia's left behind three humans who were all feeling a little lost,' concludes Mike. 'She nudged us to go on an adventure together so we can feel less lost . . . and in

286

some ways we have done that, but we've also found that being lost is OK?'

'I dunno . . .' I admit. 'I hope to feel a little more unlost before we leave.'

'What can we do to help?' squeezes Zaza.

'We're here for whatever you need,' adds Mike.

'Guys, I didn't want to interrupt . . .' Scott calls, doing just that.

'Morning,' Zaza calls out.

'You sound happy.'

'Yep!'

'How are you feeling, Vicky?'

'Much better,' I say, smiling with relief.

'She's got nothing left in her, that's why.'

'Oi!' I say, my elbow finding her ribs, realizing that even though I tell Barnaby and Chloe off for their poo jokes they'll never stop being funny.

Scott laughs. 'There's warm water for you all to wash in out here and some coca tea,' he calls. 'Breakfast won't be long.'

'Thank you!'

'I guess we'd better get cracking then,' I say. 'Thanks, guys,' I say, aware that the things that have been holding me inside what has felt like an isolating, lonely prison, suddenly seem much more bearable now I've spoken about them.

30

Mike

The morning starts slowly following the pile-on with Vicky and Zaza. We eat a good breakfast – porridge with crumbed granola followed by an omelette – play a couple of relaxed games of UNO (Vicky wins at last, so does Chef Jonny), and then get ready to head off.

Packing up my belongings I feel a wave of gratitude that we'll be in a hotel the next time I'm ready to sleep, and that a nice bed will be awaiting me. I've slept in many places over the years, and camping has never been my favourite. Pia never cared where she slept; as long as we were together she was satisfied. One of our favourite places we visited was Jericoacoara in Brazil. 'Jeri' is unique thanks to the fact it's built on sand, something the town has embraced, with hardly any of their shops and restaurants having traditional flooring. Instead sand has been allowed to do its thing and remain a key part of the brightly coloured town. This delighted Pia, who was in her element. As usual she was barefoot and ready to enjoy the feeling of having sand between her toes, so it pleased her that she was able to do so while we ate lunch.

After speaking to one of the locals about nearby

hidden gems, they told us of a little bay they knew which was secluded and untouched by too many tourists. We set off first thing to make a whole day of some much-needed R&R time after being on our feet for weeks, and we were immediately glad we did. Walking along the white beaches, the clear waters washing over our feet, it felt heavenly.

'Look at that!' Pia said, ditching her rucksack, taking off her denim shorts and running into the sea in her black bikini before I had time to work out what she'd spotted.

Then I saw her destination, a white hammock swinging in the breeze between two driftwood logs. My own shorts came off just as quickly. I ran across the shallow warm sea, seeing if I could beat her there.

'Hey!' I could hear Pia shout over the splashing of the water as she picked up her pace and tried to fight me off. 'Don't you be getting any funny ideas. It's mine.'

But I'm a faster runner with longer legs, so even her head start couldn't get her there before me. I pulled apart the netting and quickly climbed in. When she arrived I had my arms raised with my hands resting under my head, like a male model or *Baywatch* lifeguard striking a pose. Looking back I know I would've looked extremely smug.

'That wasn't fair,' she said two seconds later, slightly out of puff.

Before I could even come back with a response she'd got hold of one side of the hammock's net and lifted it as high as she could, making me topple out the other side and into the water with a splash and a yelp. I imagined I'd come back up to find her swinging gleefully, but she was still standing in the same spot, hands on hips, frowning at me.

'OK, I deserved that,' I agreed, wiping drops of salt water away from my eyes.

'Come on,' she said.

And we both attempted to climb on together. It was clumsy with lots of wobbling and laughter as we tried to balance ourselves, but eventually we were on, with her snuggling up next to me, our arms and legs tangled.

And we talked, about having to head home and back to real life, about shifting our focus on to family life, and about coming back to that exact spot when we were in our eighties, and swinging together in exactly the same way – although maybe with a bit of help needed to get on the blooming thing.

And we dreamt.

And we laughed.

And we slept.

And it was heavenly.

I can't help but smile at the memory. Yes, the sadness is still there, I long for the feel of our legs and arms entwined – her skin against mine, the sound of her laughter filling my ears and the sight of her heart-meltingly gorgeous brown eyes looking up at me. But the fact I have those moments to look back on, that we didn't get so stuck in our nine-to-five jobs and living-for-the-weekend mentality that we forgot life existed beyond those pockets, fills me with joy, reminding me what's important, and what I have to do as I move forward.

Forward.

I retain my glee at the thought of tonight's hotel knowing that although my sleep has been broken here – last night the animals on the farm seemed to be having a party – I've slept far better than at home. If I manage to get some decent sleep in before I get back to my own bed then this might end up being the reset I've needed.

There is a renewed energy as we trek today. There's a collective feeling of lightness as we walk in the sunshine, knowing that this is the last day we'll be walking alongside each other on this route.

I knew I would enjoy my time with Zaza and Vicky, but even I underestimated how much we all needed to be here, just walking, and how much we've taken away from it. There has been a barrage of emotions, a tidal wave of thoughts and discoveries, that have left us exposed and raw, and they've also made us feel closer than ever. Maybe we're all meant to unravel every so often to take stock of where life has taken us and try to rebuild. If so, I want to go on as many of these adventures, and take as many people with me, as possible.

Despite the ground at our feet being unsteady and unpredictable, thanks to the small rocks that roll around underfoot with every step, the chatter bubbles away between us all for hours. There doesn't seem to be a single moment when someone isn't regaling us with a story, laughter isn't spilling out of us, or a song – usually a cheesy number from the noughties – isn't being sung out loud. We've earned the giddy euphoria that has descended upon us, and that feels so good.

Hours later we hit a road, an actual tarmacked road, and it feels like we haven't seen one in years. We skip along it, using up the remainder of our energy on the discovery.

'See that bus up there?' Scott asks, a playful glint in his eye as he points a few hundred metres up the road.

'The one that looks like it's waiting for the England team?' Zaza quips, pointing out the fact that the plush-looking bus does not fit in with its surroundings.

'That's the one,' Scott nods. 'Let's get on it.'

'What?' asks Vicky. 'Have you seen my boots? I'm a dirty mess.'

'You're filthy,' agrees Scott. 'But we'll let you on.'

'Are you kidding?' I ask.

'Mate,' says Scott, his arm on my shoulder. 'I wouldn't joke about taking the load off your feet.'

'So this is it? The end of the Lares Trek?' I ask for clarity, feeling like it's come so suddenly, just with a turn on to a road.

He nods in reply.

I take a moment to look back at where we've travelled from before grabbing Zaza and Vicky, literally grabbing them and hugging them close – a mixture of sadness, relief and happiness washing over me. For all my travelling days this has been the trip that's punched through the most, and I'm so grateful to have had these two with me.

'You're really squishing me,' bemoans Zaza.

I squeeze them tighter, making them laugh.

'I love you both,' says Vicky, before tilting her head back and shouting to the sky. 'We love you, Pia!'

We all join in.

'Race time!' calls Kevin, sprinting off towards the bus.

'Come on, you lot,' says Scott, gesturing for us to follow.

Without even glancing at each other we drop our arms and run. Ready to land in the comfort of the seats on the air-conditioned bus.

*

Half an hour later we pull up outside a small village comprised of only a few buildings. We head straight into one of them, which turns out to be someone's house, with posters of local sites plastered on the walls along with a few string instruments. We're ushered to a large wooden table in the middle of the room and sit down.

'Time to celebrate you all being brilliant!' says Scott, coming over with two of the biggest glasses I've ever seen; they're bigger than his face. One contains a murky yellow liquid, the other a deep pink, with an enormous foamy head sitting on top.

'Chicha!' Kevin sings. 'This is local produce. A beer from Peru.'

'It's made from corn, and there are very precise

methods to making it, but it's something the locals have been doing for thousands of years. This one is traditional,' Scott says, placing the yellow glass in front of us on the table. 'And this one is made up with strawberries.'

'Drink, drink,' shouts a woman, who I imagine to be the owner, from the oven in the corner of the room while she prepares food.

'You two first,' I say, egging Zaza and Vicky on. They never need any encouragement where alcohol is concerned, and to be frank I've seen them drink some vile things in their time. This ought to be nothing in comparison.

They each pick up a glass – Zaza yellow, Vicky pink – and take a gulp.

'Not what I expected,' says Zaza, she and Vicky looking at each other to take in their reactions.

'Same,' says Vicky, sliding her glass over to Zaza so that they can swap.

'Am I not even getting a look in?' I jest.

There's a roll of eyes before another gulp is taken and nods are given. Both glasses slide in my direction.

'Come on,' I say, passing one to Scott.

I take a big mouthful and swallow. Its sourness is what takes me by surprise, that and the fact it's warm rather than cold.

'Wow,' I say, giving my head a shake before taking the pink beer back from Scott and trying it for comparison. I expect it to be sweeter thanks to the strawberries, but somehow it's even more sour.

'Now eat,' says the woman I clocked at the oven as she places a straw bowl in front of us. She gives a warm smile before wiping her hands on her apron and returning to the oven.

'The time has come,' says Scott, taking the straw basket and spinning it so that it lands in front of the three of us.

There is no denying what it is. Guinea pig, with a serving of jacket potato for balance.

Not wanting to be rude, and because I know thousands of people have done it before me, possibly even millions, I take a piece – thankful that it's already been cut and hasn't come whole and looking like a past pet. I shove it straight into my mouth and chew.

'It's all right,' I say to the girls who are watching my reactions like two keen hawks, ready for the faintest gag or flare of the nostrils to betray my response and put them off trying some. When none comes they both pick up a piece and take a bite.

'See? Guinea pig isn't that bad,' says Scott. 'It's something you have to try when you're here.'

'Can't believe I'm eating guinea pig,' says Vicky. 'I feel so guilty.'

'Can you stop saying what it is, please?' asks Zaza, a panicked look on her face. 'I'm fine if I don't think about it.'

Just then the owner pulls out a fresh tray from the oven, containing four freshly cooked guinea pigs – all whole and looking exactly as you'd expect.

'Well, we tried it,' says Vicky, putting her meatless

bone on the plate in front of her, unsurprisingly not going in for seconds.

*

After a tasty meal with our whole Lares Trek team (which thankfully didn't include any more guinea pig, but a barbecue and salad instead), it's time to say goodbye as only Scott will be joining us for the final part of the trip, back to where we started the trek in Ollytaytambo by bus and then on to a town just below Machu Picchu by train. It feels bizarre that the end is here. In many ways the beginning of the trip, when we were dropped off in that sports cage, feels like a million years ago; in other ways it feels like no time at all.

There's no denying things would've been a lot tougher without these guys to help us out. To them we might just be the latest group of trekkers to take on the challenge of the Lares Trek, a route they might even walk daily without any thought, but to us they will forever be part of our team. When we think of this place they will spring to mind. It feels weird knowing it's unlikely we'll ever see them again when we've grown such a good bond this week, even if it has been mostly over UNO.

After lots of grinning, back slaps, and a generous tip from us, we're on our way.

31

Zaza

There's nothing like waking up with a warm feeling of gratitude. My room may cover only my basic needs – a bed, and that's it, but for me that is more than enough. Never have I loved a bed more than I did last night. Coming into the room I did let out one final sob as I stopped and realized how much I stank from days of walking. It's something I hadn't been aware of at all while we were up in the mountains but that became so clear when I was finally standing in an enclosed space and the waft of stale sweat with a hint of urine hit me. It turns out washing with shower sheets, baby wipes or cleaning foam is simply no substitute for an actual shower. As I stepped out of my dirty clothes and headed straight into the cubicle I let out a happy hum as the piping hot water washed over me.

Likewise this morning at breakfast, the sight of the continental bread and jam filled me with joy – and that's after being fed really well by Chef Jonny over the last few days. On reflection, maybe it was the wooden table and chairs that really set me off, that and the fact they weren't foldable and easy to carry. It feels like I've returned after months in the wilderness, and even though I'm not in my own home, surrounded by my own things, I have an appreciation for it.

I might've replaced my trekking gear with a cerise pink maxi dress but the boots have stayed on for now – partly because of their comfort but also because with blisters like mine a switch to gladiator sandals might make them worse. The last thing I need is more hotspots to appear. Plus, I have so many Compeed plasters on it's quite the sight to behold. I have promised my tootsies I'll give them a good airing and some treatments when we get home – although my top priority will be getting them into some decent shoes for Liam's brother's wedding. I'll have to do what I can to sort them out on the flight. That'll give me something to do.

The thought of home makes butterflies dance inside me.

Before we head out and get on a bus, I grab my phone out of my rucksack. I had texted on the way to the hotel saying I'd call when I got there, but then the shower beckoned me in . . . and then the bed summoned me to close my eyes for a few minutes, and that was the last I knew of yesterday.

'You're alive!' he says, picking up the phone in super speed, almost like he's been sitting looking at it, waiting for my call.

I can't help but laugh at the excitement in his voice, a sound that makes me pine for him even more.

'Relieved?' I ask.

'Extremely. How's it been?'

'Erm . . .' I start. 'Well, we still haven't made it to Machu Picchu yet, we're heading there today but the rest of it . . .' I trail off, thinking about the days we've spent together.

'No words?'

'As if,' I laugh, knowing he knows me better than that. 'It was messy, smelly, emotional and fucking amazing. I have had the best time – a tough time, but a great time.'

'I'm so pleased for you, Zaza,' he says.

'I can't wait to get home and be back with you,' I say.

'Oh baby,' he says, clearly taken aback. 'I cannot wait.'

'I love you, Liam.'

'Snap, crackle and pop,' he replies, making both of us giggle.

As we say our goodbyes the tenderness that's been growing towards him grows a little more. As I'm about to put my phone away I notice a load of unopened messages have come through, mostly from Albie. I leave them that way, put my phone in my pocket and head to meet the others.

After being in a small group for most of the trip it feels strange to suddenly be with hundreds of people, all waiting to get on buses to our destination. There's a feeling of cluelessness, of waiting to be ushered somewhere while surrounded by the rumbling of engines and the hissing of hydraulics. Once a bus is fully loaded it heads off, that's as far as the organization seems to go, but it does happen very swiftly with doors flipping shut and wheels turning as soon as a bus is announced full, allowing another bus to arrive in its place.

Once it's our turn to board Vicky and I manage to grab two seats together, meaning we clutch on to each other for the following thirty minutes thanks to the winding roads that seem far too narrow for this wide load to be on, let alone at the speed we're travelling.

'I don't know how long I can stomach this for,' Vicky groans, just as the bus zooms around another sharp corner of the zigzagged route, dodging oncoming traffic.

'I would say close your eyes so you don't have to look, but I think that's even worse!' I reply, having tried that technique moments before and having a wave of nausea hit as a result.

I do not want to be sick on this bus.

Thankfully we make it to the entrance gates of Machu Picchu after thirty minutes of questionable driving. We're thrilled to be back on solid ground and out in the fresh air.

While we're waiting for Scott to sort out our tickets a familiar sea of faces appears in front of us.

'Waaaah!' I find myself screaming, running straight over to Gillian, Betsy, Sammi and Claire, who are just to the side of the rest of the team, and throwing my arms around them.

'Hey,' Sammi says, looking shattered but pleased to see us.

'How was it?' I ask, wanting to hear all about it.

'Long!' says Claire, with a tortured exhale.

'You OK?' Vicky walks over and asks Betsy and Gillian, who are far quieter than usual. They are all a little less sprightly than when we left them outside the hotel.

'We've been up since three-thirty this morning,' explains Gillian wearily. 'I don't mind an early start, I'm used to it at my age – no good staying in bed all day wasting my life away – but they then made us wait an hour and a half before we actually got trekking.'

'It felt like there were suddenly loads of us too,' says Sammi, looking over her shoulder at the crowds of people around us, all milling about for tickets, loo stops and to buy souvenirs before even going inside. 'We were all trying to get through the Sun Gate at sunrise, ready for that magical first glimpse of this place.'

'Was it amazing though?' I ask, hoping for their sake that it was after getting up so early.

'It was so foggy we couldn't see a bloody thing!' says Betsy, placing her hand on my arm, pulling me in so she can lower her voice into a loud whisper. 'You should've heard Derek effing and jeffing about it.'

'Most we've heard from him all trip,' laughs Claire, causing them all to cackle – it's clear they've all grown very close since we last saw them. I'm happy for them, but also, surprisingly for someone who originally said she wasn't here to make new mates, a little put out by the realization that I'm on the outside of their bond. 'I'm being mean – he's actually been all right.'

I look around to see Derek puffing away on his

cigarette, as expected, but rather than standing on his own he's talking to John-Paul, the dad of the American family who I didn't end up getting to know too well. Beside them Mike has joined Bronagh, Josh and Ben. He's animated as he talks, his hand covering his heart. I can tell that he's talking about scattering Pia's ashes. As he talks Bronagh looks between her sons, clearly trying to register their reactions to the idea. I can't imagine the strain there, that emotional pull of just wanting to fix things for your sons, the maternal instinct to want to make everything better while also navigating through your own grief and turmoil.

'What about the rest of your trek? Was that good?' I ask, pushing through the unexpected lump that's formed in my throat and willing them to have had a positive experience despite the hardship of the challenge.

'Oh yeah,' nods Betsy with great enthusiasm. 'Although *she* decided to fall up the steps one day and scare the living life out of me!' She points at Gillian who grimaces in return, covering her face with her hands.

'You know I've always been clumsy,' Gillian says, waving the air in front of her so as to bat away the attention she's getting.

'We promised each other, no dying on this trip,' says Betsy.

'I'm still here, aren't I?' Gillian argues back before grabbing her friend for a cuddle.

'Just about,' she tuts, before tickling an unexpecting Gillian, causing her to jump and squeal in shock.

Sammi puts her arm over my shoulder and lets out a long sigh.

'God, you smell good,' she says, breathing me in before snatching her arm away. 'I can't be around you when I smell this bad.' She pulls her arms into her body and turns up her nose while looking down at her lived-in trekking clothes – a feeling I can relate to.

'Wait until you get to the hotel. Getting in that shower has to be one of the top five moments of the trip.'

She laughs.

'Right, my lot,' calls Scott while flashing a smile at the other team as a greeting. 'We're off.'

We say our goodbyes, knowing we'll be seeing them inside anyway, and follow our leader to join a queue that's formed by the entrance.

'How many visitors come here?' Vicky asks.

'Each day?' asks Scott. 'A few thousand. Roughly one and a half million a year and they're always looking for ways to increase it.'

'Jesus!' I say in reply.

'That's a lot of foot-fall for somewhere so sacred,' says Mike.

'You're not the first to say that,' says Scott, looking like he's about to say something he shouldn't. 'It's changed a lot over the years with these morning and afternoon slots. Definitely more of a conveyer-belt feel to it at times. Although it's the way some guests behave here that's the real problem. Going where they shouldn't, urinating behind rocks, vandalizing stuff!'

'No,' Vicky says, her face screwed up at the thought.

'So disgusting,' I mutter.

Scott's eyebrows raise as he nods his head. 'Just got to split yourself away from it and take what you can. It's a place of massive historical interest and pulls a huge crowd for a reason. Separate yourself from all of that and when you go in and look down remember that people built it hundreds of years ago and there's little known about how. Great big boulders and rocks placed to make a city for the Incas. That is truly mind-blowing and never fails to win me over despite the crowds, the noise and the one-way system telling you where to go.'

'Like Ikea?' offers Vicky, before remembering his point. 'Got it. Ignore all that.'

Despite the gathered strangers around us all wanting to get into the site as quickly as possible, we take Scott's advice and soak in as much of the place as we can while ignoring the busy energy of others. Once we're through the entrance and have made it to the first sighting of Machu Picchu in all its glory we stop and look. Even with the cloudy morning mist that's still slightly covering it, I find it beautifully highlights just how far up in the mountains this wonder actually is. Surrounded by other mountains, which dwarf this one, making them seem like guardian angels, Machu Picchu sits calmly in the middle. Every section of the curved mountain top in front of us has been turned into what once was a habitable home, the focal point of Inca beliefs and values. From its rows of terraces below to the more structured workings of temples and what appear to be living quarters, it's nothing short of majestic to see something of this structure and detail sitting in such a remote location – completely surrounded by nature and exposed to the elements.

Even though we visited other Inca sites at the start of the trip this feels different, suddenly; the pilgrimage people used to make to get here seems fully justified. The idea of doing something gruelling in the hope of being deemed worthy enough to be awarded entry to this place seems more than understandable.

'We need pictures!' I shout, reaching for my phone and passing it to Scott before pulling Mike and Vicky in close to me. 'I fricking love you both so much,' I grin, feeling overcome with gratitude, love and appreciation for them. We hug tighter, the bond between us stronger than ever thanks to us allowing our truths to be spoken, and our vulnerabilities to be seen. 'And you!' I say giddily to Scott, whose eyes are on the phone in his hands. He looks up and raises his eyebrows.

'You love me?' he asks.

'We need a pic with you,' I laugh, quickly asking one of the people walking by if they wouldn't mind taking it.

32

Vicky

It's funny to think of this place as the highlight of the trip, as its focus, but that's because our moment of release came up another mountain a couple of days ago when we scattered Pia into the air. I don't think anything else this trip offers will top that moment for any of us, no matter how much we were all looking forward to getting here. Even though it's busy with tourists and people posing for photos, there's also a peacefulness about it. We find a spot that's elevated above the structures and situated nicely next to two llamas. It's there that we sit in silence for some time.

My mind goes back to home. As it has every time I allow my thoughts some space. I love my children, I love Nick, I love being a mum. However, I have felt buried and unhappy. I need to address that. How can I possibly find time for me when time already feels so short in supply? When I'm already too knackered from doing mum duties, how can I possibly sign up to something else that's going to require my time and energy? I'm not entirely sure, to be honest, but I do know that unless I change things and find a better balance that works for me, I won't be the best version of myself for the people

I love more than anything. I would do anything for my family, and that is why a change needs to happen. To preserve it. To save me. Whatever I've had lurking over me has clouded my mind so vividly that it's been hard to see clearly through the fog. I need to stop being scared and start breaking my way through it.

I think that is a conversation for home, with Nick. The man I chose to walk through life with while facing any adversities and problems side by side.

I need to trust him with this.

I need to let him help me.

I need to be honest.

Gosh, I miss him, I realize. And my bonkers children. I miss the lot of them. I texted Nick as soon as I got signal yesterday, telling him to call me as soon as the kids were up, no matter the time. They were up just after six their time, so I got woken to a FaceTime video call just after midnight, and I couldn't have been happier for the night-time interruption.

'Babies!' I cooed at the phone, smiling at them all lying in my bed.

'Mummy?' grinned Barnaby.

'Yes.'

'Are you coming home yet?'

'Not long. Just a few more days and I'll be with you.'

'Mumma,' said Chloe.

'Yes.'

'Have you seen any bears?'

'No,' I laughed. 'I've not seen Paddington.'

'Oh,' she said, looking sad. 'What about snakes?' she asked, a little more hopefully.

'No.'

'Monkeys?' she tried, looking more and more miffed at my lack of animal sightings – fictional or otherwise.

'No, but I have seen some very cute animals called llamas and alpacas.'

'I'll show you a picture of them after this, sweetpea,' promised Nick.

'Are they cute?' she asked.

'Very,' I told her. 'As cute as Paddington!'

Chloe's eyes widened.

'Can you bring one home?' asked Barnaby, his smile beaming through the screen.

'Not really, baby, they're pretty big. Plus, you know, I'm not even allowed to bring stones home. Nothing.'

Their mouths dropped at my statement.

'What about one of those long chocolate things from the airport?' Barnaby asked.

'Do you mean a Toblerone?' Nick asked him, having bought them one each on the way back from LA.

'Yeah!' he said excitedly.

'I'll have to see,' I smiled. 'How have you been? Have you been having fun?'

'Mumma . . .' Chloe said. 'I went to hospital.'

'What?' I asked, sitting up, aware of Nick whisking the phone away from the kids. 'What's happened?'

'She's fine. Absolutely fine,' he said, firmly. 'But she did slip over and cut her knee open.'

'No!' I gasped, feeling dreadful that I wasn't there when my baby needed me.

'Honestly, I wasn't going to tell you until you got home because she's been brilliant about it and I didn't want to worry you,' Nick said. 'I felt so awful but there wasn't anything I could do.'

'I know!' I said, feeling his pain and knowing it could've just as easily happened with me at home.

'Mumma, I got a sticker for being brave!' Chloe called out behind him.

'And we got McDonalds!' added Barnaby.

Nick pursed his lips at me as he went back to the kids.

'I have a butterfly on my knee now, under my plaster,' Chloe said, pulling her leg out from under the covers and showing me a plaster that covered her entire knee.

'Butterfly stitch,' Nick muttered.

'Wow! A butterfly!' I said to Chloe. 'It sounds like you've been so brave. I'm so proud of you. I really wish I could hug you all right now.'

'Me too!' said Chloe.

'Me three!' grinned Barnaby.

One of them getting hurt without me there was everything I feared would happen, but surprisingly, other than my maternal guilt kicking in, there was a calmness about the situation on the phone. It happened, it was dealt with, even without me there to facilitate everything and take control. It was OK.

I look at the people below now, at them all milling around this place of deep importance that's been linked to enlightenment and spirituality, and I wonder what they're all seeking answers for, if anything, and if their answers have somehow been delivered. There's something nice about knowing I'm not the only one to feel like I need a little encouragement and direction. Maybe that's a bit of enlightenment right there.

We spend the rest of the morning exploring Machu Picchu, with Mike wanting to find out all he could about the historic structures, and then head down to the markets of the town below. The following lunchtime we grab a train to Cusco, back to where our Peruvian adventure started. After dumping our stuff at the hotel and giving ourselves a proper spruce-up we head out to dinner as a collective to celebrate all we've experienced and overcome with our walking boots on our feet.

We're sitting at one long banquet-style table, with Scott joining Mike, Zaza and me down one end with the boys and Bronagh the other side of Mike, and then Betsy, Gillian and co. just beyond from them.

'I'm going for a pizza,' I declare to anyone who's listening, my taste buds already making me salivate at the thought.

'It's your final night to have local food,' Scott reminds me, nudging me with his leg, startling me somehow. Making me super alert to the heat of his hairy leg against my own smooth one, a feeling that remains even when they're no longer touching.

A twinge.

A yearning.

I am not broken.

I can't help but wonder if this is how affairs start up. Someone coming along and unlocking something to make you feel a little more alive. Opening up feelings and sensations that were previously left dormant and neglected or, in my case, that I've become completely closed off to because of the changes that have happened within me, because of how altered I feel.

It's nice to know I'm still in there somewhere. It makes me feel so hopeful about getting my life back on track with Nick, even if it is slightly uncomfortable to be experiencing things moving within me thanks to a man in his twenties whose unkempt ways and travelling life-style are so very different to my own . . . even if he has put on a nice shirt for the occasion along with some inviting aftershave.

'I'm sticking with my first choice,' I declare.

'I'll go pizza too!' agrees Zaza, sizing up the menu in her hands. 'A bit of guinea pig on the side though, yeah? To share!' she adds with a glint in her eye.

'I think I'm done on the adventure front,' I laugh back.

'For now!' chimes in Mike.

'You really should do this kind of thing more. It's been fascinating watching you all this week,' Scott says. 'I'm usually the one rallying people together and lifting them up, but the friendship you share really is something.'

'Thank you,' I say, beaming at my mates.

'Have you all had fun?' he asks, his elbow touching my arm, causing it to tingle.

'Fun is an interesting word to use,' I laugh.

'What do you mean?' he smiles.

'It's been amazing,' says Zaza. 'Although you must be so used to this.'

'What?' he asks.

'Patting us all on the back and telling us we're brilliant for doing what we've done even though you've seen hundreds of people doing it before us and are probably doing it with another team in a few days,' she says, matter-of-factly.

'Don't ruin the magic,' says Mike, nudging into her.

'Look, you're right. This is my job, but every so often a team comes along that I find myself really caring about – and this time that's you,' Scott says, looking earnestly between us. 'You've made my job easy this week. I took a step back and let you get on with it. It's really been something watching you guys be there for each other.'

'You care about us?' teases Zaza.

'Just a little bit,' he says, holding his finger and thumb an inch apart.

'So how close exactly do you get to your trekkers?' I ask, wanting to probe him more now he's opening up.

He looks at me and an expression I can't read flickers across his face.

'We don't want to know about your pen pals! I bet there's juicy stuff!' Zaza states, pouring herself a glass of wine before leaning in, ready for some tantalizing gossip.

Scott smiles at her.

'Must get lonely . . .' she prods.

'Ladies,' laughs Mike.

'It's her now, not me,' I reply, raising my hands in protest.

'Not really,' Scott replies after some consideration, deciding to answer rather than to shut down the conversation. 'I meet people. That's my job.'

'Of course,' Zaza nods seriously. 'But has there been any extra-curricular fun?'

'Straight to the point,' I laugh, aware of my insides churning.

'I meet a lot of people,' he repeats, moving in his seat and causing another brush of our skin, another tummy flip.

'Sure, sure,' she replies. 'I bet you bond with people quickly.'

'Not always . . .' he admits, making me think back to our encounter on the first day and how much of a tit I felt. 'I occasionally might add someone on Facebook, but it gets too much. I'm here to get people through the trek, not become a lifelong mate.'

'Cold!' Zaza frowns.

'No,' he says, his hands splayed in front of him. 'I guess you were right earlier. I don't see all of these treks in quite the same way as people coming out here do. My view has changed over time. My real fascination is with the locals.'

'So you care about us but you don't find us interesting?' Zaza quips.

'You're hard work!' Scott laughs, rolling his eyes at

Mike. 'I've already said I thought you were brilliant. This has been one of my most enjoyable trips in a long time. Even though some of you had your moments.'

I feel his leg push into mine. He's fidgety tonight.

'Do you have a girlfriend?' asks Zaza.

'No . . .'

'Lots of admirers?'

Scott blushes. 'Nothing more than leader lust.'

'Leader lust,' I repeat, unable to stop myself from giggling.

'What?' he laughs back. 'It's an actual thing!'

'Oh I have no doubt about that. None at all. In fact, I'm relieved to hear it,' I add, struggling to get the words out through the giggles.

Zaza joins in. When Scott places his hand on my back to see if I'm OK I laugh even harder.

'It's not that funny,' he declares, his eyebrows knitting together into a frown.

'Oh I know, I know,' I say, catching my breath. 'It's just me being silly.'

'Right . . .' he mutters.

His words and the realization they bring enable me to relax and enjoy the meal. I'm so thankful that I hadn't allowed my mind to go off to weird and strange places – like me running away to live a life in the mountains with Scott. They should put out a warning ahead of these treks about that one though, it would probably save a few panics.

Once the meal is finished the whole group travels back

to the hotel together and, as we're all off at different times in the morning, we linger outside to say our goodbyes.

I spot Mike swapping numbers with Bronagh and think to do the same with the girls, but before I can suggest it Claire is asking everyone for their Instagram handles. I expect Gillian and Betsy to look back confused or, at the very least, say they're not on there – but of course they are.

'Your kids are so cute!' Sammi says to me once she's looked me up, flipping her phone to show me a picture I took at the zoo a couple of weeks ago – it's of me and the kids with chocolate ice-cream smeared across our faces. Our massive grins reveal just how much we loved the day.

See, I do sometimes get it right.

'Right, I'm off to bed to stalk you all,' declares Gillian, her arm looped through Betsy's so the pair of them can leave together. 'Safe travels home, everyone!'

And with that people start disappearing off inside.

'Come on then,' Scott says, walking over with his arms as wide as his grin.

I walk into them and enjoy the squeeze.

Just as I'm letting go he keeps hold of my elbow, his mouth turning to my ear.

'I would totally shag you,' he whispers.

I look up at him open-mouthed. In that one sentence he has confirmed everything I don't want. Scott and sex – not with him anyway.

33

Mike

Pia and I always had this thing about every trip changing us in some way. They moved us forward in life, refocused our attention, and somehow taught us a new way of being. Whether it was locals who lived at a slower pace than us or the realization between us that we needed more focused 'us' time when we returned – whatever the lesson, we'd come back and changes would be made. Sometimes they happened without us even talking about them, just a subconscious part of us knew to adapt. I spoke about it on the trip with Vicky and Zaza, and I'm really feeling a shift within me now it's come to an end.

Growing up I was terrified of change, of changing; it always seemed like the biggest insult to be told 'you've changed'. Like you'd forgotten who you were and had turned into a knobhead who'd forgotten their place in life, causing you to appear above your station. No one wanted those words uttered to them. It was the worst.

Nowadays I'd have to argue that if you walk through life unmoved by significant events – birth, marriage, death, loss, joy, love, connections, success and failure – then that is when you should actually be classed as a knobhead. I would now argue that to be told 'you've changed' should be seen as one of life's better compliments. My reply to it would be a great big thank you. 'Yes, I've changed. Thank you for noticing. Life not only gave me lemons, but it gave me limes, apples, pears, strawberries – and even some dragon fruit for good measure because even though it looked scary it was actually really tasty. It gave me a fruit salad to work my way through. There are sour moments, parts that are bitter and unripe, but now I make sure to take the time to fully enjoy the sweeter offerings when they come. I'm altered because of all I've been exposed to, and that can only be a good thing.'

OK, I wouldn't say all of that.

But still.

I always feel philosophical when returning from a trip. Pia would laugh at me on the plane, looking out the window, headphones on, having a moment while listening to Sigur Rós's *Takk* . . . on repeat, my head trying to process all we'd seen and done. It was always the same. It was like a little ritual I'd created for myself and I've done the same on the flight home from Peru.

I once heard someone say that to step away from your life to just be for a period of time, whether that is for a weekend, a week, a month or a year, is always beneficial, because it's about stepping outside of the fire. When you're in it you have no idea of the scale of it, or how to tackle it – but by removing yourself you get a different perspective.

That's what this trip has been.

The three of us have stepped out of our individual fires and been given the time to reassess and re-evaluate our situations and find where changes might be possible in order to get life under control again.

As I walk through the arrivals gate at Gatwick with both of my bags thrown over my shoulder, I feel like I've been away for a million years, not ten days. Even though this is such a familiar setting for me – the coffee shops, the people standing with signs, the huge displays of affection as people are reunited – everything looks different. I'm different. I've been aware of the spring in my step being restored as we've trekked, the physical presence of hope coming back to me, and it's nice to feel it's still there as I return.

I bounce.

'Mumma!' comes a giddy shriek, just as two little bodies come flying towards us and straight into the arms of Vicky, who is smiling, laughing and crying all at once. She drops her baggage on the floor as she covers Barnaby and Chloe in kisses, making them squeal. Nick follows them over.

'All right, mate,' he says, throwing his arm around me before turning to Vicky and kneeling to kiss her. He mutters something into her ear that makes her look at him with a smitten expression.

After all these years it's nice to witness.

I can't help but watch with a huge grin on my face as I think about the Vicky from only a few days ago who was a weeping mess, and how much she has changed since then, just from stepping away, facing her thoughts, and talking about them. It's only the start, clearly – but each day her renewed strength and self-belief have been visible to see. I just hope that continues and she doesn't fall back into her old ways once she's at home and back into her normal, everyday life.

'Mummy, we made you signs,' sings Barnaby, holding up a crumpled piece of paper and prompting Chloe to do the same with hers. They hold them up proudly, just inches from Vicky's face. She has to back away to take them in.

'Oh wow! Look at them!' Vicky replies. 'What have you drawn?'

'They took a lot of time over them. They were very particular about what they wanted to draw for you,' says Nick, getting back up to his feet and hugging Zaza before collecting Vicky's bags.

'So lovely you're all here,' says Zaza warmly.

'This is you on the top of a mountain,' says Barnaby, clearly eager to please his mum with his creation. 'There's a tent at the top – that's the pointy bit – and you and Uncle Mike and Aunty Zaza are walking up to it. There's one of those animals you said about. Just there,' he says, squinting at his own work.

'A llama?' prompts Vicky.

'Yes! That's it. Llama,' he repeats excitedly, his eyes glancing over to his dad who winks at him to carry on. 'You have sunglasses because you are high and closer to the sun . . . And Uncle Mike has turned red because he forgot suncream.'

We laugh in response, and he smiles up at me before snuggling back into his mum's body, pleased with the reaction.

'I love it.' Vicky kisses him on the cheek, making him squirm even though he's obviously enjoying having his mum back. She turns her attention to Chloe. 'And what about your drawing, sweetheart? Can you tell me about it?'

'This is you,' she says, her sudden coyness making her put her fingers into her mouth, so her words are only just audible. 'You have a big smile. See? And your eyes are shiny because you're happy now.'

'Oh darling,' Vicky says, the words tight in her throat. She squeezes her daughter close. 'I'm definitely happy now I'm back with you.'

'Mummy, say hello to my butterfly,' Chloe says proudly, completely oblivious to her mum's emotions as she sticks her leg in the air so Vicky can see the bandage on her knee.

'Oooh,' Vicky replies, taking hold of the flailing leg to stop her falling over. 'What a brave butterfly.'

'Liam!' Zaza gasps, looking through the arrivals crowd. I follow her gaze and see him stood several feet away, a bunch of flowers in his hands. He takes us all in and then hesitantly steps forward.

'Hello, beautiful,' he says, his smile wide as he arrives in front of Zaza.

'I thought I was meeting you at the wedding! In Liverpool!' says Zaza, her hand on her chest in shock.

'No way I wasn't coming to get you,' Liam replies, putting his arm around her waist and pulling her in for a kiss. 'You OK?'

'I really am,' she says, leaning into him.

I can't help but smile for them all.

It's a wholesome sight, seeing two of my closest friends being greeted with such love by the important people in their lives, those who've missed them while they've been away. Obviously I wish Pia was here to do the same for me, the twinge of sadness is not going anywhere, but I know if she were still alive she'd be walking through the arrivals gate with me, not waiting for me on the other side.

While I'm taking it all in, a grin firmly on my face, a hand rests on my shoulder, giving me quite the surprise.

'All right, son?' says a voice I've known all my life.

I turn to see my mum and dad, both smiling up at me cheekily, with tears in their eyes. My dad is a short man whose talent for athletics makes him slight, and time in the sun makes his skin golden. My mum is also short but less sporty, her softness always giving way to the best hugs I could have asked for growing up, or indeed right now.

'Mum, Dad!' I say, scooping them both up and holding them close.

'It's our tradition,' Mum says, although there's no need to remind me. For every trip Pia and I had ever been on our return was quite the spectacle, with both our families coming to greet us after our extended time abroad. Although all of those trips were for far longer than this one and they had usually spent the months we were away waiting for us to get to internet cafés so we could update them on what we were doing. I think they used to love coming to the airport just so they could check we'd both made it back in one piece.

'I can't believe you're here,' I say, not realizing how much it would mean to have them greeting me until it's happened.

'You thought we wouldn't be here?' laughs Mum, as though I've said the most ridiculous thing. I suppose I did. There was no reason for me to doubt them waiting in arrivals when I walked through, yet I've had to say goodbye to so many traditions. It felt safer to overlook this one.

'And . . .' Dad says, his hand reaching behind him to let others in.

'Hello, you,' says Pia's mum, Anju, her husband Sajan hovering behind her, waving over her shoulder.

We always laughed that all of our parents were pint-sized, as was Pia – whereas I was the only one out of all of us that was taller than five foot seven. Not massively, but enough for it to become a funny point of conversation between us. The thought makes me smile as I look at the group of four in front of me.

'Thank you!' I say, giving each of them another hug, enjoying their squeezes.

'Good time?' asks Dad.

'Really great,' I nod. 'Peru is stunning.'

'I bet,' says Mum, who has never been keen on the idea of travelling herself but has revelled in our stories over the years — I've no doubt she's repeated them all to the girl at the check-out in Tesco, to the local butcher, to their rabbi, to all of her mates and anyone she can stop for a chat.

'And, did you do it?' Anju asks, an expectant and hopeful smile on her pretty face that looks remarkably like her daughter's.

I nod, taking her hand. 'There was a beautiful spot after a particularly tough morning. It was really stunning.'

'She'd like that,' Sajan says with a frown and a nod, something I've learnt is not him showing his displeasure, but rather him trying to keep hold of his emotions.

'I've got photos of the place we chose, I'll show you,' I say, patting the bag on my back.

'We'd love that,' Anju says, gripping hold of Sajan's arm.

'Well done, love,' says my mum.

Dad squeezes my shoulder.

'It's the rents!' laughs Zaza, coming over to greet them all, causing the rest of our extended group to do the same, even the kids.

I take a step back and observe the busyness, the love that's shared and passed between them, and I have an overwhelming sense of gratitude, affection and hope. How lucky I am to still have all of this in my life. How thankful I am to be able to see that again, be aware of it, and truly believe it.

'Come here, you!' Vicky says, prising herself away from the kids and reaching over to me. 'A million thank yous for letting us tag along with you. I know that wasn't really the deal. That wasn't part of her request of you, the Rule . . . but I'm so glad you let us join you. I wouldn't have done it otherwise and, well, I needed it,' she says, her lips curving into a huge smile.

'There's no denying I did too,' I admit.

'Are you two getting emotional without me?' Zaza calls, throwing her arms around us and giving us a squeeze. 'You two are the total nuts, you know that?'

'The total fucking nuts,' I whisper, making them laugh as I look over my shoulder to make sure my mum hasn't heard me. They know she doesn't take kindly to filth coming out of my mouth, even if I am a grown man in my thirties. These two on the other hand, they love it.

'In all seriousness, though,' says Vicky, her face looking a lot more measured. 'There are no two people I'd rather get the runs with.'

'That's love right there,' I laugh.

'I know,' she nods.

'I think we've peaked,' laughs Zaza.

'Well, there's certainly no going back now,' I mutter.

It's strange saying goodbye to them, but Liam, Nick and the kids are ready to whisk them away from the middle of arrivals so they can head to weddings and some fun, which is fair enough. More hugs, more laughter, some promises to see each other next week, and then we're apart. Which, after such an intense trip away, feels incredibly strange.

34

Zaza

'No, there was an actual toilet in there!' I say, trying to help Liam get to grips with the loo situation while unpacking my weekend bag. Having packed it before the trip to ensure I could get up to Liverpool swiftly, it feels weird to suddenly be diving into a bag of things that a pre-trek me had packed. It's full of all the luxury items I realized I didn't need on the trek, and although it was freeing to realize that at the time, it's also exciting to see my toiletry and makeup bags again. It's also incredible to be staying in Thornton Manor for a couple of nights, which is a period house on a massive estate just outside Liverpool. Needless to say it's vastly different from sleeping in a tent with your mate who has diarrhoea.

'So you had plumbing in there?' Liam asks, his face falling into an amused frown as he reclines on the hotel sofa and tucks into the fruit platter that's been laid out for us to enjoy on arrival.

'Nooo,' I laugh, taking out my nude stilettos and putting them in the large wardrobe, wondering how my feet are going to slip into them when they're still covered in the Compeed and zinc oxide tape Scott had shown me how to use. 'It was a tall tent, you walked in, zipped the door up behind you and then there was what looked like a proper loo but a bit smaller and flimsier. Inside it there was a bag of that blue stuff you see in festival loos. No flush. Just go in a bag and leave.'

'And you used it?' he asks, sucking on a strawberry.

'I told you – I immersed myself fully,' I say, standing up proudly to give a little curtsey. 'I mean I really didn't want to use it at first, but the alternative was a totally wild loo trip with my bum out, and that felt far worse.'

He laughs in response.

'Oh God, I haven't told you about the coca leaves yet!' I say, shaking my head as I put my underwear in the cupboard drawers.

'What?' he says when I've filled him in. 'And they perk you up? Are you sure you're not on them now?'

'Oh ha-de-har,' I say with a laugh. 'I'm not sure they worked though, and they tasted horrible.'

'Shame,' he shrugs.

'I'm being annoying, aren't I?' I say, joining him on the sofa with my head in my hands. 'I talked about the trek non-stop the whole way up here and now I'm on to the toilet facilities and the local Class As.'

'You have talked about it a fair bit,' he acknowledges, finding my horror amusing.

'Oh God! I'm a trek bore!'

'No, you aren't. Za . . . it's just lovely to hear you talking about something that's clearly made you excited and giddy,' he says, looking over to me as he visibly searches for the right words. 'It's nice to have you talk to me with a smile on your face.'

I nod in reply and nibble on my lip.

'You can't stop talking *now*!' he smiles encouragingly. 'We can do this . . . talk to me.'

I take a deep breath. I knew this moment would come, there was no way I could come back with an altered outlook and demeanour and not have to answer a few questions about what's been going on with us. Neither would I want to.

'I know I've been a right bitch the last six months or so,' I admit, forcing myself to look at him while I speak. 'I'm not blind to it, I've known every time I've said something too harshly, been too blunt or purposefully been difficult. I've walked away and felt that. I've wondered why and just pushed through, not really wanting to face up to the behaviour.'

'Your friend died,' he says simply, taking my hands in his.

'Yes,' I say, tears filling my eyes. 'Yes. Yes, she did. My friend died. But if she were here now she'd tell me off for being a dick. Although I don't need the heads up. I knew it then and I know it now, it's just the why that's been bothering me.'

'Oh shit,' he says, taking a breath.

'I'm not calling anything off!' I say, leaning forward so he has to look into my eyes and take in what I'm saying. 'That is not happening. I've been pushing you away as a means of coping. I've had to be so strong. I've had to

327

hold my shit together so that others can deal with their grief and therefore I never unravelled. I never lost my way in grief because I didn't let myself go there. Instead, I let the hurt and anger out in other ways, with you. Because really my biggest anger was at the realization that love doesn't always win. That sometimes the love between two people can be so deep, so indestructible, and yet something happens to rip them apart, to obliterate what was between them. To show them that the universe or God or whatever you believe in is bigger.'

'So you've been a bitch to me as payback to God?' he asks, his eyebrow raising as a soft smile appears on his lips.

'Not quite. That would make me totally crazy,' I say, rolling my eyes. 'I didn't fully believe in love until you came along. I thought it a thing in films and books, I didn't believe that two people could slot together in the way that we managed to. I didn't think such respect and understanding were possible. I dated frogs and I dated good guys, but somehow none of them truly captured me. And then there was you and you won me over with a chicken katsu curry and vegetable gyoza.'

'It was a good speedy service,' he recollects with a smile.

'I didn't believe in love until there was you. But now I have it I'm so scared of losing it. And I know that's ridiculous when it's been me pushing you away – it's been me working hard against the love, but I love you so fucking much the thought of being without you makes my heart actually hurt.'

'It does?' he asks, a slight tease in his voice.

'Yeah,' I say, aware of the snot and tears running down my face, quickly wiping them away with the back of my hand. 'I could psychoanalyse myself until the cows come home, think about all the different things that have led me to become who I am and handle things in the way that I do – but the past can only be held responsible for so much of the future. At some point you need to take accountability for your actions and own them. So yes, I have been a total twat but when I look to my future all I see is you. Nothing else comes close.'

'Not even a new Gucci bag?'

'No.'

'Not even the green one you've had saved to your desktop for the last year?'

'That is an absolutely stunning Marmont with the double G on, but no. Not even that,' I say through sobs before cuddling into him.

'It has hurt, Zaza,' Liam says quietly into the top of my head. 'But I see all of you. I knew you were struggling and taking it out on me, and I could've done more to help. Been more understanding, cut you even more slack so things didn't build –'

'Hate to say it but I think I would've found another way,' I say, coming back up so I can see him.

'Very true,' he says sadly. 'But I'm marrying the worst parts of you as well as the best. I don't have the ability to pick and choose which Zaza bits to take and leave, and I'm glad. I'm here for all of it. All of you.'

'You still want to marry me then?' I ask.

'Abso-fucking-lutely,' he says, cupping my cheek.

I kiss him. I kiss him hard. I kiss him passionately. I kiss him to let him know there's nowhere else I'd rather be. I kiss him to let him know he has all of me and that as long as I can help it, I'm not going anywhere.

Something about the need feels new. Like there's been an unlocking within me and all of my firsts have been rolled into one to make something far better.

'Do we have time?' I ask.

'They won't miss us. Not our wedding,' he replies with a coy smile, pulling me on top of him.

*

Although, pre-Liam, a huge sadness engulfed me whenever Valentine's Day would come around and I'd either be single or in a doomed relationship, the same cannot be said for weddings. I have always loved attending weddings – to the point I'd happily be a guest at one even when I haven't ever met the bride and groom. Purely so I could ogle at the day and soak it up. Valentine's Day is essentially a day the shops made up to make money; weddings, however, and the core root of why they exist, have been around for centuries. Yes, it originally came about so a man could take a woman as his property and lay claim to his 'heirs', but it has since evolved into something that I find endearing, beautiful and, perhaps, even idyllic. I know the marriage that comes after that doesn't always follow those characteristics. I know that marriages still have to be worked at otherwise they fall apart. I know that sometimes one party can get lost in the idea that the grass might indeed be greener on the other side but, for that one day, love is allowed to shine through. Celebrating the glory of a bond that has people teary-eyed as they declare their commitment in front of people they love (and me, even if I am the stray plus one) is the ultimate romantic gesture. Walking down the aisle on the arm of someone special, the wedding vows, the speeches, the first dance, the grandparents getting drunk in the corner before taking over the dance floor – I love all of it. They are days that reaffirm the brilliance of human connection, of everyone coming together for a good time.

This wedding is the most spectacular one I've ever been invited to. Liam's brother Duncan and his fiancée Lisa have been together for over a decade, so it's a big deal for everyone that they're finally tying the knot. Even if Duncan protested against the idea of marriage for many years (saying they were happy as they were) he's gone into the wedding planning fully invested. It's a big affair. Huge venue, massive guest list, flowers everywhere, and a firework display to boot, which is a sight to behold.

'Jeez,' says Liam into my ear, his arms wrapped around me as we take in the bright flashing lights in the sky above, the final flourish of wedding magic before we wave off the newlyweds for the night. 'This must've cost a fortune!'

'Did you expect anything less from your brother who

has a different sports car every time he comes down to see us?' I say, craning my neck to whisper in his ear.

'Fair point,' he nods. 'Don't get any ideas though. We might be able to stretch to a few bangers, but this is just –'

'We don't need them,' I interrupt, turning to loop my arms around his neck.

'No?'

'Not even a sparkler,' I smile, kissing his lips.

'You might regret saying that,' he manages, in between the kisses.

'We don't need any of it. Well, obviously I want a mind-blowing dress that's going to show me to be the queen that I am, and the shoes are also very important but . . .'

'But . . .'

'The other stuff can be left at the door,' I say, the crowd around us cheering as another explosion erupts. 'It's not about how loud your fireworks can bang or how many courses you can dish out at the reception.'

'There were a lot of courses,' agrees Liam, conspiratorially. 'The caviar was a bit much.'

'What makes the day special is watching the love between two people being declared.'

'And the dress?' he checks.

'You've got it,' I laugh, realizing that as much as my Peru trip has left me looking forward to stocking up on magazines and compiling a mood board for a dream wedding, the excesses are not really what I'm interested in now. I think back to the kids I met just before we set foot on the Lares Trek, and the delight they visibly felt over a chocolate eclair – a single sweet. The little things, the unexpected melt-in-your mouth moments, they are what make life memorable, enjoyable and worthwhile. I've bought into the man standing in front of me, who already loves me for better or worse, I just want to lose myself in the gooeyness of that.

35

Vicky

'Daaaaaddy! Daaaaaaaddy!' comes a cry from the other side of the landing, making me jolt upright. 'Daaaaaaaaaddy!'

'Coming,' croaks Nick, patting my leg before shuffling off to check on Chloe. I can't recall the last time the kids woke in the night and didn't call for me. When they were younger Nick would try going in and they'd go berserk. It is the one time they have always asked for me over Nick. Yes, the only time my kids really crave me near is during those heavenly hours of sleep. It's something I've often resented as I've stumbled out of the room, barely able to open my eyes through tiredness while a snoring Nick lies completely oblivious in our bed. Yet during my time away they've got used to another person going into their room to soothe them, and now I'm back they're still choosing him over me.

You'd think I'd be relieved but instead the thought sits heavily on my chest.

I lay back with my eyes open. I thought Chloe had woken in the middle of the night but looking around the room, at the sun peeping through the curtains, it's clear

I've already had a decent night's sleep and that morning has arrived.

Oh gosh!

The kids had stayed up for a movie night to celebrate me being back and I must've passed out on the sofa, I don't remember seeing any of *Raya* or waking up to go to bed. Jetlag completely wiped me out! I haven't even managed a proper conversation with Nick yet without a child coming along to interrupt to tell me something I missed while I was away or with a question about the trek. They were giddy for most of the day, a thought that makes me smile. As I was trying to do the washing the two of them had everything out of my bag, trying to work out what the items were used for – which was fine for the sleeping bag and head torch, but less so for the she-wee, even if I didn't end up using it (turned out squatting wasn't that bad). As a result of their interest we popped up a tent in the garden and played explorers for a good chunk of the afternoon.

It was good to feel like they'd missed me, so brilliant to have them engaged in something that I was doing that didn't involve them, so great to feel like I was inspiring their creativity with games.

'I want Mummy! Mummy's bed,' yells Chloe before breaking into a huge sob.

I sit up again, at the sound of heavy feet making their way across the hallway.

'Sweetie,' I say as Nick walks in cradling Chloe who immediately stretches across to me, shifting her weight so that she almost slips out of Nick's arms and lands on my lap. She reaches forward and grabs hold of my neck, holding on tight. I put my cheek to hers, run my hand over her unruly bed-hair, and breathe her in.

'Oh my baby,' I say, enjoying the warmth of her squeeze.

'Mummy! I forgot you were home!' Barnaby sings, a sleepy grin on his face as he comes running in, jumping into the middle of the bed before snuggling into me.

'I'm so glad I am,' I say, kissing the top of his head, a warm feeling washing over me.

Thinking I can't see, Chloe tries to slowly nudge Barnaby away with her foot, irritated that he's interrupted her mummy cuddle. Swiftly, before they can start squabbling, I shuffle their bodies so they're still getting mummy cuddles but also so that Chloe's limbs are nowhere near Barnaby.

'Welcome home,' Nick yawns, snuggling under the duvet on his side of the bed, which is far less crowded than mine. He reaches over and strokes the back of Chloe's head.

'No, Dadda!' Chloe reprimands with a frown, turning to bat him away before burying herself into my chest so she's even closer than she was before.

Nick laughs and rolls on to his back, running his fingers through his hair.

'Come on then, how was it?' I ask, swaying side to side with our children in my arms.

'It was good,' he says, pursing his lips like there's more to say.

'But?'

'No buts,' he shrugs.

'Come on, out with it,' I push.

'Honestly?' he says, looking at the kids before his eyes come back up to mine. 'I don't know how you do it. Even with help it was tough – and don't forget I was still going to work in the week.'

'It's not easy,' I agree.

'You're wonderful.'

'Ha!' I laugh, knowing that when he used to say those words to me they used to refer to very different qualities – when my focus was on him alone and I could surprise him with treats or had time to get saucy between the sheets. 'Well, it's nice to feel appreciated.'

'You really are.'

'Kids, you know what Mummy realized in the mountains?'

'What?' Barnaby asks, his lip curling up in the cute way it does whenever he's questioning something.

'That we are all very small. We're teeny tiny when we compare ourselves to massive mountains and the power of nature.'

'You're not small to me,' Barnaby says, making me wonder how I can explain I mean insignificant. I felt my smallness. The more we walked, the further we went, the bigger the world grew, and the tinier I became.

'Oh I know,' I say. 'But it was a nice thing. It just made

337

me realize that if I am small, then so are the things that make me sad or worried. I might think they're big, uncontrollable and scary, but they aren't.'

'It's called perspective,' says Nick, reaching across to place his hand on my shoulder. I tilt my head and kiss his fingers. 'I love you,' he mouths. I return the affection.

'Perspective,' repeats Barnaby.

'Perpepsteve,' laughs Chloe, making us all giggle.

'Mummy,' Barnaby says quietly. 'Because the trip made you and your worry small, does that mean you didn't miss us?'

'Oh no, I missed you more than you would believe,' I say, ruffling his hair. 'The other thing I learnt is that love is the best thing in the whole wide world, and I have lots of that because of you, Chloe and Daddy. I'm very lucky.'

'Barns,' says Nick, reaching over for his hand. 'Can you please take Chloe downstairs and get her some milk? Then Mummy and Daddy will come and make you some pancakes.'

'Yes!' Barnaby screams, as Chloe looks over at Nick with a very happy grin. I watch as Barnaby climbs out of the bed and walks around to help Chloe down too. Hand in hand they leave the room giggling.

'When did they get so grown up?'

'Scary, isn't it?'

'It is,' I say, sidling up to him under the covers and enjoying the warmth of him as I run my hand over his back. 'I've missed you.'

'You too,' he replies, kissing the top of my nose, his arm hooking around my soft waist.

'Nick,' I say quietly.

'Yes?' he asks, no doubt looking for the rebuff he's become accustomed to.

'I think I might need to make some changes. We need to.'

'Like?' he asks, his hand skimming up my pyjamas and resting on my back like he's supporting me already, even though he has no idea what I'm about to say. At least, I don't think so.

'I have to get over myself and put Chloe in nursery for a start,' I say, gauging his expression for a reaction but, of course, he doesn't even flinch at the suggestion. We'd hardly be the first people to send their child to one. 'I've kept her home all this time because that's what we did with Barnaby. And I know that was because I then fell pregnant with Chloe so was home anyway and it didn't make sense to send him anywhere but, because he had that time with me, just the idea of sending her had left me feeling guilty. I've thought about it and now I think it would be good for her. She needs things that I can't offer her, and that's OK. It doesn't mean I've failed her. She should be mingling with other people, children and adults, finding new things that interest her and enjoying different experiences. Plus, I think having a bit more independence would just empower her so she doesn't feel the need to do things like chuck food at me.'

'The food chucking!' Nick states. It somehow makes

me feel better that it's not just me she's done this to now. 'Where has she got that from?'

'No idea, but she's got incredible aim and precision when she wants to.'

'Oh it's a solid throw,' he says in awe. 'Future shot-put champion at the Olympics, that's for sure.'

'Messy though,' I muse.

'Can we put *Bluey* on?' Barnaby shouts up the stairs. My guess is that he's already got the control in his hand, he's just waiting for clearance.

'Yes!' I yell, turning back to Nick who's looking at me expectantly.

'So that was the first thing,' he nudges.

'I need to work on me,' I say, feeling the sting of tears threatening, relieved when they don't come because I know I must speak, I have to get this out. 'My life has changed so much since the children came along. I know it has for both of us but there's hardly one thing about me that I recognize as me – my day-to-day workings, my body, my mind – all of them have been completely altered and I don't think I've taken any time to process that. When I was away I wondered whether my career was the thing that I needed to resurrect. You know I got such a buzz from it, but that would invariably invite in more stress which, with your job and its demands and overtime, might not be the best thing for our kids. I don't think that would solve anything. So, I'm not heading back into the studio any time soon, although I still wouldn't rule that out in the future . . .'

'Right,' he nods.

'But I need to do something else outside of the house where I can be something other than Mum.'

'I get that. We became parents but you're the one whose life changed completely. Two weeks after pat leave I was back doing what I know,' he says, his hand still firmly on my back. 'For me parenthood was an addition to the life I already had, but for you it was a complete overhaul.'

'Yes!' I say, feeling like I want to cry at his observation. I continue slowly, knowing that I'm about to unload massively and that I need him to understand me. 'And I think the trickier thing for me to address is how it's affected my body and mind too, and how the two of them are so unbelievably connected to everything else. I'm a mum, and that is what I always wanted – you know that – however, there has been a black cloud that's hung heavily above me for quite some time. I haven't felt sexy. I haven't felt gorgeous and frivolous and wanton. I literally haven't felt anything. It's like it's been switched off. There's just a sadness that floors me. Or maybe it's less than sadness . . . sadness feels too giving in a way.'

'But you're gorgeous,' Nick says, moving his hand to stroke my cheek. 'God, I've never meant to put any pressure on you but I know I haven't hidden my feelings of rejection, and I'm sorry.'

'No . . . No. It is nothing to do with you or anything you've done,' I say back kindly, my hand resting on top of his. 'Honestly, at times I've felt like you must think I don't fancy you but it's not that, not that at all. You've been ringing a doorbell to a house where no one lives. And it's that which freaks me out. But how could you know what I'm feeling unless I say so?' I ask, realizing that as important as it is for me to ask for help and share my struggles, it's also not fair to make him feel bad for not realizing what was going on when I've only just started to address it myself. I've wrapped this darkness up and kept it close. I've kept it secret while I've given it a home, and almost nurtured it into growing and taking over my being. I've fed it what it wanted and not said a word because that is what it wanted, because if I talked its hold over me would start to wane. Now though, it's exposed. I'm beginning to see the lies it's told and the shadow it's cast over me. It is an illusion that I have unknowingly bought into – and that realization feels so overwhelmingly comforting.

'All is not lost,' I say to Nick. 'Going out there and trekking, putting my trust back into my body and having it surprise me when I thought I couldn't do something was such a huge boost – to my mind more than any-thing. There's a flicker of light and . . . hope,' I say, the word generating a flutter within me. 'I'm going to speak to my doctor and see what help they can offer, but I've also reached out to Pandas who support women going through postnatal depression.'

'You think that's what it is?' he asks, and I see the guilt flicker across his face.

'Maybe,' I say. 'I could wrap it all up in losing Pia but

the truth is I've been feeling this for a while. I've just pushed through. I've got to the point where I have to stop and hold my hands up. Because I don't want to get lost in that void again. It's scary and I want to get out. I want to be free of those niggly feelings that tell me yours and the kids' lives would be better without me. I want to feel like I deserve to be loved again. I want to believe I'm worthy of that love.'

And with that my husband sees me break.

All at once his resilient wife who organizes everything, who takes charge of the family affairs and is the matriarch of the house, crumbles.

My fractured being is exposed.

I splinter.

And while it takes everything out of me, it is fucking freeing.

'We'll make this work,' his voice wobbles as he whispers in my ear, holding me tight, as though he's trying to hold me together so that I don't crumble apart. 'Whatever it takes, whatever you need, we're in this together and we'll get through it. I love you, Vic. I need you to know that. You have to believe it.'

My chest swells.

I am not perfect and my husband knows that, he knows that and he still loves me.

He loves me.

36

Zaza

Hopping into my bright orange jumpsuit this morning felt like such a luxury. The wedding was incredible, and my long pink maxi was quite the number with intricate lace detailing cut into its full skirt; however, I've created a work wardrobe I adore and I couldn't wait to dive back into it.

It seems I'm not ready to shake off my trip joy just yet as I've teamed up my outfit with black Dr Martens boots, which I'm hoping will stay on my feet far longer than my heels did at the weekend. I was so thankful to be wearing something full length where I could hide my patched-up feet. My DMs are not quite my trekking boots but their chunkiness gives me the same vibes, rooting me to the ground and making me feel like I'm ready to take on the world. Or maybe they're just giving me the extra boost I need to get back to the office and face Albie. His text messages have been coming in thick and fast and he even tried calling me twice over the weekend. Whereas previously that might've titillated me, I found it intrusive and inappropriate. It felt too much. I'm sure our exchanges have always been nothing more than office flirtation for him too, but maybe me being absent and unable to respond has encouraged him to be a bit more forward and pushy with trying to make contact. I really didn't like it though, especially when Liam asked who was calling and I lied and said it was my mum. The deceit made me feel terrible and so guilty.

With an editorial meeting first thing I get into the office early, meaning his desk is thankfully still empty when I arrive. I grab my notepad and pen and dive for a seat at the table as quickly as possible to ensure I'm visibly preoccupied whenever he comes in. As the meeting goes on I become more and more distracted with the idea of it finishing and having to return to the office, knowing the inevitable will happen – our first encounter. When I'm finally back at my desk, I'm aware of my tummy dancing, but rather than butterflies I have an anxious feeling swirling.

'I was worried you'd got stuck up a mountain when I didn't hear back from you. I was going to come rescue you. Even looked into flights,' he says over my shoulder, placing a cup of tea next to my keyboard.

It's all very cosy. All very wrong.

'No, I managed to get myself back,' I say, keeping my body facing the computer so that he might get the hint that I'm not in the mood to talk.

'Something I'm glad to see,' he says, lingering.

'Liam's brother got married in Liverpool this weekend,' I say, the words tumbling out even though I promised myself to make any chat with him short and sweet. 'So I headed up there as soon as I got back. In fact, Liam met me off the flight, which was so thoughtful of him, and we had so much to catch up on. It was a good wedding too, and I just didn't want to be looking down at my phone all the time. I think not having signal when I was away and having to actually look at the world has made me think of my phone a bit differently.'

I look over to him and find his eyebrows starting to knit together.

'Yeah. Of course,' he says hesitantly. 'It's just, I messaged you . . .'

'I haven't had a chance to look,' I shrug, feeling embarrassed as I say it.

'I've messaged you a fair bit, actually,' he says, nursing the mug in his hands.

'Oh right . . .'

Something like a confused grunt escapes his mouth.

There's no denying he's good-looking. He really is a beautiful man and he takes great care of his appearance with his clothes and how he puts it all together. There's also a cheeky glint in his eye and a manner about him that's charming and inviting, hooking you in instantly. The thing about Albie, though, is that he knows the effect he has on others and how to use it. I've dated men like him before and all of this is almost a game they play to lure you in, but really you're just another 'thing' and once they've got you they get bored, finding themselves something newer and sparklier to play with. Of course, he might be guilty of none of those things. I might be judging him entirely wrongly when he'd be a perfect boyfriend for someone – my point is, that someone is not me.

I was truthful to Mike when I said Albie and I have been more like pen pals than anything more sordid, but I wonder if Albie has seen things a little differently. What's passed between us has been in the looks, the daily chats and the frequent messaging, all containing a flirtation that needs to go. I had wondered how to play this one and what to say to draw a line under everything so that some distance can be placed back between us. But how can you break up with someone you aren't even in a relationship with? That seems a bit dramatic and unnecessary. My other approach, the one I've favoured, is to just ignore him and let things cool off naturally. To be civil at work (after all, he hasn't done anything wrong, really) but to ignore any messages that come beyond that. Seeing as we work together and need to talk in order to get our jobs done, maybe it's more about me reinstating the boundaries that I shouldn't have dropped in the first place. He'll soon get the picture.

'Are we good?' he asks, demanding my attention by sitting on my desk and almost placing himself in front of me.

'Huh?' I ask, the 'we' throwing me off as well as the fact he's pulling me up on this so quickly after getting back. I wasn't prepared for this. Suddenly wrapping up what we started and putting it to bed makes me feel even more stupid that I allowed it to begin in the first place.

'Have I upset you?' he prods further.

'All right, guys?' asks Dan from online as he walks by.

'Hi mate!' Albie says, his voice booming back.

I mutter something inaudible, wondering when this little chat will be over.

'You seem really off with me, Zaza. What's up?' he asks, as he leans in closer, forcing me to look away.

'It's just —' I falter, unsure what to say to him.

'So I *have* done something?' he asks, surprise in his voice.

'It's nothing you've done,' I say, turning to him with a sympathetic smile.

'It's not me, it's you? Are you actually going to say that?' he laughs, his hand covering his face as he shakes his head.

'I'm getting married,' I say, a tiny bit more forcibly than I'd intended. 'I found someone I love and admire, and I want to make our lives together as nonsense-free as possible.'

'Am I the nonsense?' he asks, his eyebrows shooting up.

'Not necessarily,' I say, looking down at my hands and the ring Liam lovingly placed on my finger when he proposed. 'I just want to be the best version of me. That's what Liam deserves.'

'I get it,' he nods, rubbing the back of his head. 'I've actually been on some dates with this girl anyway. Good ones too.'

'Oh,' I manage to say, thankful that nothing within me

baulks at the news. If anything, the delivery and timing of his statement leave me having to fight a humungous eyeroll, but that's all.

'Yeah, and she's cool too. Time to focus on that,' he nods, pausing while he takes a gulp of his coffee. 'On her. She likes a good time. Really fun.'

'Oh, good,' I say, knowing not to let him rile me, to let him say his piece and then we can both move on. 'It's really great,' I say, my lips forming a tight smile.

'It is . . .' he says, looking like he wants to say more, but decides better of it. He rises from my desk and visibly returns to work mode – he stands taller, and his expression becomes stony and formal. 'I'll get your pages over to you by midday,' he adds before walking away and returning to his desk.

'Thank you,' I say after him. I might feel like a first-class tit, but nevertheless, I feel relieved our little chat is done. A line has been drawn now and I can focus on what I actually want and, I am starting to believe, what I deserve.

At lunchtime I find myself staying at my desk and scrolling through photos on my phone. Ones from the weekend where I'm dressed up and being giddy with Liam, and then ones from the trek, where I'm more feral than I'm used to being, more challenged than ever, but at peace. I hope the emotions it's stirred within me never fade, and now I understand why people get the travel bug. There's a freedom in it. Not just from everyday life, but there's a freedom to feel everything you've boxed away, to address it and refocus, and renewed energy follows you home. It doesn't just stop when you're back in your bed and no longer trekking hours every day.

Putting my phone down I open my computer and read over what I typed on the way into work today. A little seed of an idea that I hope will help people.

I love working on the beauty desk. I love the way makeup can make you feel good and empowered. I'm not keen on it being smothered on, but I guess that's a personal choice. I've always been so aware of how many products get sent to me here at work, my crap cupboard is full to the brim and that's with me sorting it out regularly. Even though we hold little charity sales for the office every month or so, I have been wondering if there's something better we can be doing with it.

When Pia was going through her treatment her skin regularly suffered bad reactions to the drugs she was on. Even when it calmed down after treatment, she never felt like her face was hers. I used to take different products over to her and we'd have a little pamper. If her face was inflamed we'd do something different, maybe something with her hands and feet, but always there was a little self-care and love. Pia was one person, but imagine if we can go beyond the pages of the magazine and help people when they need it most. When they feel broken, unsure, and could do with a little boost. Obviously it doesn't just have to be about cancer, many people face all kinds of moments of adversity in their lives and part of what can help is simply having someone there to talk to. And so I've dreamt up a little idea called The Chatter Pamper

Club, and I've already managed to rope in some friends who work in beauty to help out after firing out some texts earlier. The idea is to use the products in the cupboard here that would usually go unused, and have regular events for little pick-me-up treatments like pedicures and manicures, but also mini makeovers. Guests can try out different products and looks in an effort to build confidence and feel good, and the whole time there'll be lots of supportive new friends on hand to chat to.

I've made a list of venues to contact which I think might be up for helping out by giving us a monthly space and I'm hoping once the beauty PRs get wind of what we're doing they'll be even more supportive going forward and maybe guests can even leave our get-togethers with little goodie bags too.

I know makeup and all the luxury I enjoy is frivolous, fun and indulgent – it's not a necessity when you look at life's bigger picture. However, it can also bring joy and make individuals feel great. I'm aware we don't need to wear makeup all the time and that finding confidence in our skin is the ultimate dream, but when we feel depleted and spent it's nice knowing there's a way of giving a little boost when it's needed.

I spend lunchtime fleshing out my idea, feeling excited and proud that something good could be coming out of something I love.

The anxiety from earlier has been elbowed out. Now something far more worthy of my attention has taken over: hope.

37

Mike

Getting home from the airport was an intimate experience. All four having travelled there together meant it was quite a squeeze on the way home with me and my in-laws in the back. I might be the tallest but Mum knows her place in the car – how can she possibly keep an eye on Dad's driving and tell him all the things he's doing wrong if she's not in the front? She's very committed to driving from the passenger seat.

We talk all the way up the M23, along the M25, and across the M4. There's never normally a moment's peace with Mum and Anju around anyway, but on this car journey I take great comfort from hearing them nattering away without taking a breath. I take relief from the fact I'm enjoying listening to what they're saying. I feel present.

The five of us head straight to my place so I can show them some pictures. I'll admit there is a twist in my tummy as I put the key in the lock and enter but the banner before me is a bit of a distraction.

'Welcome home,' they all cheer from behind, repeating the banner's words.

Walking through my flat I see not only has it been decorated but the coffee table in the lounge, the one next to our mint sofa, has been covered with party food. From the variety of food on offer I can tell both Mum and Anju have had an input.

'Thank you!' I say, taken aback.

'We just wanted to celebrate for once,' says Mum.

'Put some good feelings back in the flat,' Sajan says, his hand resting on the mantelpiece next to the rest of Pia's ashes, which are waiting for more trips, more scattering and more freedom.

'Your mum and I have been working on our Rule,' says Anju.

'Rule?' I ask.

'You know, from Pia,' Mum replies, smiling as she rolls her eyes at me.

'I didn't realize Pia gave you one,' I say, feeling guilty for my naivety.

'She said she wanted us to teach each other the dishes we love,' says Anju, looking very pleased with the idea. 'So we started.'

'And now we're going to do a weekly swap,' smiles Mum. 'Anju made the challah, I made the paratha. Other than that we've made what we know.'

'Wait until next time, you'll have no idea who made what!' laughs Anju, leaning into Mum as they admire their work.

Pia was one clever woman, I think to myself. The reason for this Rule is simple. At a time when our families could be fractured as we process her death, she's implemented a reason for them to stay together and be entwined. Our mums have such a passion for their cooking, it's what they were always able to nurture in us, even as adults. Her Rule has given them permission to continue with that, and therefore for our families to stay as close as they've ever been.

'I'll get an extra chair,' says Dad. 'We need to hear all about this adventure of yours while we eat.'

I can't fathom what the last couple of years must've been like for the four people here. Anju and Sajan losing their daughter, something that feels so out of the natural order of things and the way life should be. They had to watch her suffer, witness her low moments where life showed itself to be deeply cruel, and then they had to endure saying goodbye. My own parents might not have lost a child, but not only were they close to Pia, having known her since we were teenagers, but they had to watch their son's turmoil knowing there was nothing they could do to ease the pain or fix the situation. I have been so consumed in my own grief that perhaps I haven't allowed myself to truly see this until now.

'We want to know everything. Mostly, how did Zaza handle camping?' Mum asks, whipping off tinfoil and cling film before handing out plates so everyone can tuck in.

'Camping? She almost didn't make it one night in the hotel,' I chuckle, and then dive in with my first story.

We sit and I talk. I give them a full debrief of my time

away. I make them laugh with my tales and it feels so wonderful to feel the connection between us all, and for us to collectively feel something beyond grief.

Once my fridge and freezer have been fully stocked with leftovers and everything has been washed and put away, they make to leave. With the fuzziness of jetlag kicking in I have to say I'm relieved when the door shuts and I'm able to climb into my comfortable bed and sleep.

*

By Monday afternoon I'm back at my desk and working my way through the long list of emails I've received since being away. I'm stoked to discover I've been asked to pitch for a big client off the back of previous work and know I'll enjoy working away on that for the foreseeable – it's the joy of being freelance. One email or phone call can shift your whole working focus.

Just as I'm about to start brainstorming ideas my front doorbell goes. Looking out of the window I spot my father-in-law standing on the doorstep. When I tap on the glass he's caught off guard, he purses his lips and dips his head in greeting.

I run around and open the door.

'Sajan!' I say, a big smile on my face. 'Come in!'

'Oh no, no, I won't stay.'

'Have you come for the dishes?' I ask, already making my way to the kitchen so that I can grab them off the side. When I'd run out of Tupperware the other night

Anju left me some of her serving dishes. Thanks to my appetite fully returning those dishes have been emptied and washed. I messaged Anju a picture of me looking happy with one of the empty dishes last night, to which she replied with lots of laughing emojis and hearts. 'Here you go,' I say, handing them over to Sajan.

'Thank you,' he says, taking them from me and placing them precariously under his arm in a way I know Anju would not approve of. He lingers for a moment, clearly with something on his mind.

'Are you OK?' I ask. 'Honestly, you're more than welcome to come in.'

'No, I really must go,' he says, looking at his shoes before reaching into the back pocket of his trousers. 'Pia . . .' He stops and gives a little cough before continuing. 'If you were ever to go on your trip, Pia said to give you this.'

A small yellow envelope is placed in my hand. On the front Pia's hand has scrawled my name.

'I had it with me the other day but something stopped me from giving it to you then. I wanted her request to stay with me a little longer. It's the last one we have,' he adds, really looking at me as he says it to hammer his point home. If that's true, if this is truly it, then these are the final words I'm ever going to read from my wife that were intended for me to see once she was no longer here.

Sajan grabs hold of my empty hand and pulls me forward, placing his arm around me. Suddenly he steps back and gives a little nod goodbye.

I wave goodbye with my mind on the contents of what I've been handed, waving for longer than is necessary, continuing until he's walked down the drive, got into his car and driven around the corner and is out of sight.

I look down at my hands and turn the envelope.

I lean on the front door of our home, open the envelope and read her words.

> You did it. Now keep going. Remember to always have your let's-just-go bag packed and use it when you need to, and when you don't. See. Hear. Smell. Feel. Touch. Love. Always love. Dive in and keep going. The world is yours, just as it was ours. Live.

I think of my plans, of taking her with me as I see the world, of setting her free, and I know she would approve.

Epilogue – Five Years Later

Vicky

'See you next week,' I shout as I leave the office, getting a flurry of goodbyes from various workmates before I head out of the door of BRB Studios at the end of a busy week. As part of my daily weekday ritual I grab some lunch from Leon along with a coffee and sit down to calmly savour it before heading on to the Tube for the school run.

Me working mornings was the compromise Nick and I eventually came up with, although we didn't get there straight away. When Chloe started nursery I took some time to really focus on me and my recovery. It was only once Chloe started full-time school though, some two years later, that I felt ready to head back to the workday commute into town. This delay was partly because mum-guilt held me back – I have discovered that never truly leaves you, but also because I had to wait for a job I wanted to become available. I had, after all, been out of the game for quite some time by that point. With Chloe settled at school, Nick and I had a big chat about how we could make things work so that our family life wasn't compromised. And that's something we do regularly now, talk! We talk about what's working and what's not, and then we adjust life to strike a balance we're both happy with.

Thankfully working in morning TV has its benefits. I might have to be out of the house at the crack of dawn, leaving Nick to take the kids to breakfast club at school, but more often than not I'm back for the pick-up. Thanks to a Sunday morning batch-cooking session that we all enjoy getting stuck into, dinnertimes have become easier to navigate too. I'm not the only one getting us all organized these days, although I'm fully aware I'm the drill sergeant making sure everything gets done.

'Mum!' Chloe shouts as she's released from her teacher, running over and leaping straight into my arms.

'Hello you. How was your day?' I ask.

'Good,' she says simply, which is always her answer at this time of day. It's only as the afternoon goes on that more comes out of her, like who she played with, what she ate, what fun fact she's picked up that she wants to share. She's transformed since starting school, and even nursery allowed her a fresh environment which she thrived in. She still challenges me (what child doesn't?), but our relationship has so many different parts to it now. Like me and her dad, we talk. I've just had to learn that us talking must happen on her terms and when she's ready, not just when I want to. Kids are complicated, but then I remember being a kid myself and feeling like the weight of the world was resting on my shoulders – even at the tender age of eight years old. I'm just there when she needs me, which I hope she'll always be aware of.

'Hello, Mum,' Barnaby says, already by my side, no longer having to wait for me to arrive to be let free of the classroom. At ten years old he's now above my shoulder in height. Nick's tall so I guess it's not surprising that he's followed suit. I see my children growing as a physical representation of the time that's passing – and that's what gives me pause occasionally. It's going so quickly. When I think back to the newborn stages they seem like a distant dream, and those times of complete overwhelm that followed thankfully feel far away too.

When I do let myself think about that period of time, which I try not to do too often because thinking of myself in that state is too painful, I'm aware of how close I was to darkness. Asking for help, opening my mouth and talking, was the thing that saved me. I don't think I would've done that had it not been for that trip we took to Peru. I would've carried on feeling resentful, angry, buried under the fog, and lost. I was unable to see that there was so much good around me, so much to be thankful for, and to realize it wasn't acceptable to leave myself feeling that way. I wish I had known that help was available to me if I reached for it, and that life would be so much better for taking it. I'm so grateful I found that eventually.

'Where's Dad?' asks Barnaby, tugging on the strap of his rucksack. 'I thought he was working from home today.'

'He has been. He's just finishing up and then getting everything in the car so we can shoot off,' I say, putting an arm around both my children and starting our walk home. As we pass other parents pushing prams, I feel incredibly relieved to be beyond that stage. Though it's tough to admit not particularly enjoying a part of parenting.

When we're on our road we see Nick up ahead rushing out the front door carrying a crate of alcohol and trying to slide it into the boot of the car which is already jampacked. You'd think we were going away for a week rather than a weekend, but with the body boards and wetsuits loaded in it's amazing how quickly it fills up.

'Is that everything?' I ask when we get to him, reaching up for a kiss.

'That's the last of it,' he smiles, slipping his arms around my waist, lowering his head so that our lips meet.

'Get a room,' mutters Barnaby, making Chloe giggle.

'Talking of rooms, run up and get changed so we can get a move on!' I say, sending them inside. 'We're leaving in five minutes!' I announce, following them indoors so that I can get myself ready too.

Forty-five minutes later we're in the car and driving off for a weekend of fun. It might not have taken the old wrestling with socks, shoes and loo-trip negotiations that it did in the past, but my children still need a fair bit of ushering out of the house. They seem to have turned into teenagers already and are extremely slow about getting anything done, even if it's something they want to do.

Now that we're on our way, though, I allow myself to

breathe a sigh of relief. Work and school are done for the week, now we can go on a little adventure and shake it all off.

Zaza

'Are you sure you're OK?' Liam asks for the dozenth time since getting into the car.

'Totally fine,' I say, feeling pretty happy with the weight off my feet and aircon pumping into my face.

'Do you need the loo? Or more snacks?' he prods.

'Honey, I'll let you know if I need either,' I remind him. My bladder might be compromised right now but I like to think I can last more than an hour, which was when he last made us use the services.

'OK . . .' he says, keeping his eyes on the road in front of us. 'But if you want to stop to stretch your legs, we won't be late.'

'Liam. Babe. Chill out,' I say more firmly. 'You're going to stress me out in a minute.'

'Sorry,' he mumbles, making me feel guilty.

'It pains you that they're growing in me, doesn't it?'

'Za, watching you grow our children is the most amazing thing I've ever witnessed,' he says, placing his hands on my bump. 'But not knowing what's going on in there or what you're feeling is so weird.'

'I really feel for you,' I say. 'Must be awful walking around still being able to see your feet, and not knowing that the last time you did see them they were twice the size they were previously, so who knows what state they're in now. Or is it the heartburn you feel like you're missing out on? Or the sleepless nights when even sleeping with the world's biggest pillow doesn't make you anywhere near comfy? Or perhaps it's the piles?'

'You're funny,' he laughs.

'I'm pregnant,' I correct.

He grins like the Cheshire Cat in response, and I can't help but smile with him.

It's hard to believe we're here, that we've made it this far. Five years ago I was pushing him away, too scared of what staying with him might lead me to lose. From there we had the most intimate and special wedding I could've ever wished for, with just our families and core group of mates in attendance (no invites were sent purely out of politeness). The group of kids I met in Peru really did cause the cogs to turn in my brain, or maybe my biological clock started ticking a little louder so I couldn't ignore it any more.

We started trying for our family pretty much straight after our wedding but to no avail. Month after month after month I was greeted with a negative test or the return of my period, and each time it cut deeper and deeper. There were false hopes along the way, heartbreaking glimpses into what might've been before it was cruelly snatched away from us, and then nothing for a year.

Nothing at all.

No periods, nothing.

Not even a cramp to let me know something was stirring, that my body was trying to work.

Nothing.

I tried to bury my head in work and Chatter Pamper, which was building momentum fast and had become a free monthly event for dozens of women to come along to. We had a regular venue, one that we still have, and a pool of makeup artists and beauty therapists to call upon when they were available. However, distractions could only keep my heart from focusing on what it yearned to have for so long.

Many visits to doctors and specialists later and we were on our last round of IVF. Last because it was costing us a fortune, and last because it hurt so much every time my body failed us. With two embryos left on ice we decided to increase our chances and use them both in the final embryo transfer. We didn't expect them both to take. We didn't expect to be so lucky. We hadn't dared to dream it.

'Did you sort out the plans?' I ask.

'Yes, all ready for first thing tomorrow,' he says, taking my hand.

Two hours later, after five-and-a-half hours of travelling thanks to Liam's constant stops, we arrive at the most stunning house on offer in Cornwall's Mawgan Porth.

'I'll give you a hand, mate,' shouts Nick from the house's vast wraparound balcony, and before we know it the whole group is outside, ridding the car of its contents. Even Chloe wanders off with my huge pregnancy pillow in an effort to be helpful.

'It's so good to see you,' says Vicky, her eyes firmly on my bump. 'How are you feeling?' she adds, her eyes flicking up to meet mine.

'Great,' I smile.

She beams in response and does her best to hug me, which is a little awkward given the size of me but nice nonetheless.

'We're all here!' sings Mike, grinning as he places his arms around us both and plants a kiss on my cheek. 'Hello, Twins!' he says with a sudden outburst, bending over so that his lips are against the fabric of my dress. 'Helloooo, it's Uncle Mike here.'

'Be careful one doesn't kick you in the face,' I tease, my smile showing how pleased I am to be back with these two special people.

I manage to get through dinner before the afternoon of travelling catches up with me and I have to admit defeat. Off to bed I go, reminding everyone that we have plans first thing and not to get too carried away.

'OK, Mum,' grins Mike, giving me an eyeroll to boot.

I pick up the nearest cushion and chuck it in his direction.

It's busier than I expected when we arrive at Land's End the following morning, something I maybe should've expected with it being a Saturday, but there's not much we can do about the footfall now.

'If we head up that way there's a lovely cliff and then we can have some time exploring the joys of Cornwall,' says Mike, pointing to his left before heading in that very direction and expecting us to follow.

I glance at Liam and he reads the look in my eye that's telling him our plan is going to fall apart if people start moving away.

'Actually, we thought we'd be a bit touristy and get a picture,' he calls out, pointing at the well-known Land's End signpost perched in front of us, its arrows pointing at different landmarks around the world.

'Oh no, you have to book,' says Vicky, dismissing the idea with the back of her hand before starting to head in Mike's direction.

'But I've booked it!' I shout in panic.

They turn and look at me.

'You have?' Vicky checks.

'Thought it might be nice to get a group photo,' I shrug.

'Oh. You should've said!' says Mike, making me wonder why I thought any of them would've got suspicious if I had told them anyway.

'I'll be two secs,' Liam says, going over to the operator sitting in the neighbouring hut and exchanging a few words, a few moments later holding his thumbs up and beckoning us all over.

'You all stand out front and Rob there is going to take your picture,' the greying operator says in a thick Cornish accent while gesturing to a nearby teenager. 'He's good at finding your best angles, you see. Just got to give him a few minutes – perfectionist, he is.'

'If you all stand in the middle I'll tell you where to go because you don't want to go messing up this shot. You want to be bang on centre,' says Rob, fiddling with his hair before taking my phone.

'Really?' mutters Vicky as we gather before him.

'OK, that's great,' Rob says, holding the phone up. 'Actually, if you can all take two steps that way . . . yep. Oh no, too far. Half a step the other way now. Forward a bit . . .'

'Is he having a laugh?' chuckles Mike.

I stand to one side rather than in the centre, keeping an eye on the operator as he slips around our group and heads to the Land's End sign. He goes to the arrow that the public are able to have personalized and starts changing the words. His hands are quick and he masters our request in seconds. He turns and nods at Rob before going back to his hut.

'Right, I've got one of these,' says Rob, looking down at the phone in his hands. 'But I have one last picture I'd like to do. On the count of three I want you all to turn and look at the sign. Let's see who can read it out the loudest. OK, one, two, three – go!'

'It's triplets!' the group shouts, before stunned faces start looking from me to Liam, to the bump.

'What?' says Vicky, her hands covering her face.

'There's three in there?' asks Mike.

'Three?' repeat both Barnaby and Chloe, looking at my bump like they can't make sense of it.

'Guys,' Nick says, placing a hand on Liam's shoulder. 'Triplets?'

'Yes,' I cry, hormones, emotion and joy getting the better of me as tears start streaming down my face. 'Three squidgy babies. A set of twins, and a little bonus,' I confirm, cradling my bump.

My friends start jumping up and down and the crowd around us starts cheering in celebration.

Love.

Pure love.

I've never felt so lucky.

Mike

'Well, there's no way I'm letting you walk up there now!' I say, shaking my head at Zaza as we walk to an area away from the crowds so we can take a moment to absorb what we've been told. My mate is having three children in one go. Three!

'I'll be OK,' she shrugs, still wiping the tears from her eyes.

'Don't be daft. Pia would come back and haunt me,' I say, knowing she absolutely would.

'So have you only just found out?' asks Vicky.

'No, we've always known . . . but with a bump this big

I couldn't say it was only one and we thought we'd have some fun,' Zaza laughs.

'You should've seen my mum's face!' says Liam, gazing at Zaza with a look of complete adoration.

'Your house is going to be loud, for sure,' notes Nick, his eyes widening.

'Three tiny little bubbas,' Vicky coos, her eyes tearing again.

'Don't you go getting any ideas,' Nick tells her.

'Oh no, no! We're done,' she says, slipping her arm under his and leaning on to his chest.

Five years on from our first trip and we've chosen Cornwall this year because Zaza would've otherwise been unable to join us. That wasn't an option. These yearly trips have remained a boost for all of us, having visited Iceland, the Sahara and the Alps since Peru.

I go off with different groups throughout the year, on adventures with kids like Josh and Ben who've had to face grief at a time when they should be enjoying life. Josh has even started guiding groups with me now that he's old enough, which feels like a testament to what our excursions have meant to him. He wants to pay it forwards. I couldn't be prouder.

Yet these trips with Vicky and Zaza give me something different – time with two people who knew Pia like I did. This year it's turned into a family affair, which adds a bit more chaos than normal, but chaos is never a bad thing. We knew this trip wouldn't be exactly like the others, and have therefore embraced it. This wasn't going to be the same as the long, enduring treks of the past; instead this was simply going to be about being together in Cornwall, a place known for its beauty that's surrounded by the sea.

'I think I want to do it near here, anyway,' I say, looking around us.

'You do?' ask Zaza.

'It's all beautiful,' I say, knowing part of me simply wants Pia to be as close to Zaza and Liam's news as possible, imagining her face as she absorbs the miracle our friends have been given.

We venture further away from the crowd so that there's nothing but sea in front of us, and come to a stop.

Taking a deep breath, I reach into my pocket and pull out the little paper bag. A mixture of emotions hit earlier when I looked into her urn and saw just how much of her has already been scattered. It's what I wanted, of course, but as each particle of her ashes reconnects with the world, it also leaves me behind.

Grief remains the hardest thing I know I'll ever experience. I have no doubt that nothing will ever hit as hard as not being able to stop those final moments from happening and being forced to let Pia go. Yet through her death she's taught me how to live. I still laugh, love, go on spontaneous adventures and make the most of opportunities that come along. It's not the life I had planned by a long stretch, but it's one I've been able to find happiness and purpose in nonetheless.

Years ago I found myself wondering, 'Is this it?', but

now I realize that no one moment is ever it. The world keeps turning, life keeps going, deaths occur, babies are born, hearts are broken and mended again. Life happens and there's nothing you can do to stop it rolling once it starts. In your whole lifetime it only stops once, when you reach the end. Until then you have to be prepared for the lows and highs, the struggle and joy, the hurt and love – whatever you land on, you will keep moving. You will keep going. Because that is the difference between life and death.

I pour the contents of the bag out on to my hand, aware of the fragments that drift away in the breeze.

I close my eyes and I see her face.

My hand closes, instinctively wanting to keep her close.

I hold her for a moment or two.

I hold her.

I hold her.

I hold her.

And then I let her go.

Acknowledgements

In a switch-up of my usual thank you order, I would like to start by thanking the team at Apple, but mostly James and Alex who don't work there but are flipping geniuses. Halfway through the writing of this novel my computer died on me. Being the tit I am I only saved work to my desktop because I figured the Cloud wasn't something to be trusted. Like an even bigger tit, I hadn't sent myself a back-up or saved it to a hard drive for quite some time . . . I was missing 12,000 words. That's seven chapters that for a week of my life just disappeared. In stepped James and Alex like two heroic super nerds and saved the day. There was huge emotion. So guys, thank you. Thank you. THANK YOU!!

Hannah, thank you for always presenting everything to me in the calmest of fashions and always giving me perspective. Thank you for continuing to believe in me, and for doing so for a decade. None of this would've been possible without you giving me that, and it's amazing to know that you continue to spread your belief and encouragement to many other aspiring authors – no matter how busy you are or what you're juggling.

Maxine, what a pleasure it is to call you my editor. Sorry this one took slightly longer than we planned (eek!), but I hope you're as pleased as I am with the result! Huge thanks to Ellie Hughes, Rebecca Hilsdon and all at Michael Joseph and Penguin Random House for being my cheerleaders and doing so with many smiles along the way. Thanks again to my copyeditor Fiona Brown for working through yet another of my books with such care, and to the page proof team for making sure everything is as it should be.

To my team at YM&U, thanks for giving me the space in a busy diary to breathe, fall in love with these characters and properly get this book written.

My family – sorry I've not seen you much since things have started to lift. But guess what? The book is in. Hopefully we're still allowed to get together for bubbles, hugs and laughter. Giorgie, Dad and Debbie – I hope this book brought back many memories of our own Peruvian adventure.

My CoppaFeel! family – firstly to Ellie, Emma, Jo, Nat and Kris, thank you for letting me head your treks. You will never know how much of 'me' you've given back to me, or how much these adventures mean to me. To my fellow trekkers – gaaaaaaaaaah! It makes me emotional just thinking about the times we've had together. Thank you for the raw, open, honest chats. For showing me your vulnerabilities and allowing me to show you mine. You all will have a place in my heart forever more.

Bob, Debbie, Lou and Susana – I always get asked how I manage to do what I do. The truth is there's no way I could do it without you all helping me in the individual ways that you do. Above all, I'm so grateful for your friendship and support.

Buzz, Buddy and Max, it turns out it's not that easy to write when you guys are in the house. I cannot switch off from all the things I need to be and do as your mummy. In many ways this is a good thing. You will always be my number one, top top top, main priority. Sometimes, though, I just need a little quiet to help my brain work, or simply so my brain can have a moment to do and think of nothing at all.

Tom, I love you and the family we have created. Let's never drift. Let's keep returning to each other time and time again.

And to you, the reader. Thank you for joining me, Vicky, Zaza and Mike on this adventure. I hope it makes you think about pushing yourself out of your comfort zone or, at the very least, reminds you that you're so worthy of love. Just the way you are.

An extra note from me . . .

If any of the topics covered in this book have hit home for you, please know that help is out there. Here are a few charities and organizations that might be useful but your GP should also be able to point you in the direction of local support groups. Never be afraid to lean on others when you need to. Trust me when I say, you would do the same for them – and, in time, you will.

Love as always,
Giovanna
xx

PANDAS Foundation
pandasfoundation.org.uk
0808 1961 776

Samaritans
www.samaritans.org
116 123

Mind
www.mind.org.uk
0300 123 3393

AtaLoss.org
www.ataloss.org

BRIGHTEN UP YOUR
BOOKSHELF WITH MORE
BOOKS FROM

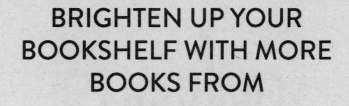

When the love of your life says
you're not The One . . . what next?

THE NUMBER ONE BESTSELLING AUTHOR

SOME KIND OF
WONDERFUL

Giovanna
Fletcher

Happiness can be found where you least expect it

'A MUST-READ. Funny, heartwarming'
Closer

'Giovanna Fletcher is at the top of her game'
Heat

Sophie May has a secret . . .
but will she be able to keep it?

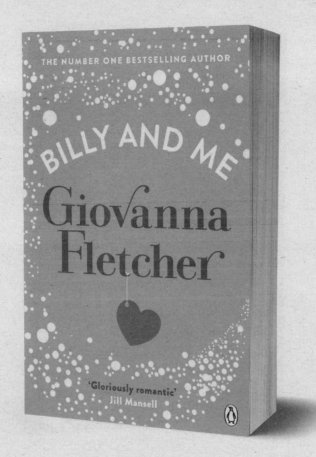

'Gloriously romantic'
Jill Mansell

'Warm and romantic, this will brighten up your day'
Closer

Sophie's got used to being the girlfriend of Billy Buskin the biggest movie star in the world. Sort of . . .

THE NUMBER ONE BESTSELLING AUTHOR

ALWAYS WITH LOVE

Giovanna Fletcher

'Giovanna steals our hearts again'
New! Magazine

'Simply gorgeous. Sit back and let yourself be swept up into the life of Sophie and Billy'
★★★★★ Reader Review

'I cried tears of joy and happiness . . . Beautifully written'
★★★★★ Reader Review

Maddy has a choice to make,
but will she choose wisely?

'A gorgeously tender, funny and big-hearted novel
with wonderful characters you'll fall in love with'
Miranda Dickinson

No one ever really finds the person of their dreams . . . do they?

'Saucy, fun and full of heart! This book ticked every one of our must-have boxes'
Heat

'I was totally and utterly captivated'
Paige Toon

He just wanted a decent book to read ...

Not too much to ask, is it? It was in 1935 when Allen Lane, Managing Director of Bodley Head Publishers, stood on a platform at Exeter railway station looking for something good to read on his journey back to London. His choice was limited to popular magazines and poor-quality paperbacks – the same choice faced every day by the vast majority of readers, few of whom could afford hardbacks. Lane's disappointment and subsequent anger at the range of books generally available led him to found a company – and change the world.

'We believed in the existence in this country of a vast reading public for intelligent books at a low price, and staked everything on it'
Sir Allen Lane, 1902–1970, founder of Penguin Books

The quality paperback had arrived – and not just in bookshops. Lane was adamant that his Penguins should appear in chain stores and tobacconists, and should cost no more than a packet of cigarettes.

Reading habits (and cigarette prices) have changed since 1935, but Penguin still believes in publishing the best books for everybody to enjoy. We still believe that good design costs no more than bad design, and we still believe that quality books published passionately and responsibly make the world a better place.

So wherever you see the little bird – whether it's on a piece of prize-winning literary fiction or a celebrity autobiography, political tour de force or historical masterpiece, a serial-killer thriller, reference book, world classic or a piece of pure escapism – you can bet that it represents the very best that the genre has to offer.

Whatever you like to read – trust Penguin.